FAMILY TREE

THE MURRY-O'KEEFES, *KAIROS* *

A Wrinkle in Time, A Wind in the Door, A Swiftly Tilting Planet, Many Waters

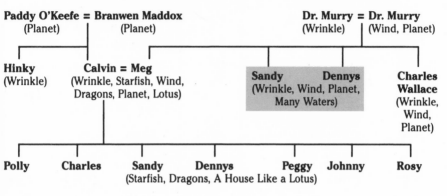

Paddy O'Keefe = Branwen Maddox
(Planet)   (Planet)

Dr. Murry = Dr. Murry
(Wrinkle)   (Wind, Planet)

Hinky
(Wrinkle)

Calvin = Meg
(Wrinkle, Starfish, Wind,
Dragons, Planet, Lotus)

Sandy   Dennys
(Wrinkle, Wind, Planet,
Many Waters)

Charles
Wallace
(Wrinkle,
Wind,
Planet)

Polly   Charles   Sandy   Dennys   Peggy   Johnny   Rosy
(Starfish, Dragons, A House Like a Lotus)

THE AUSTINS, *CHRONOS* * *

Meet the Austins, The Moon by Night, The Twenty-four Days before Christmas,
The Young Unicorns, A Ring of Endless Light, The Anti-Muffins

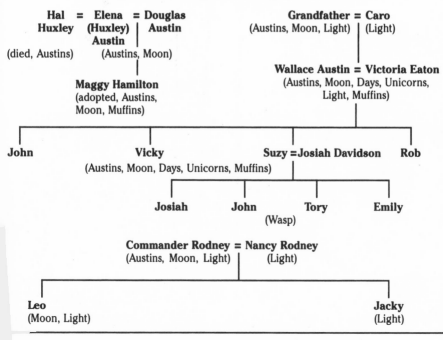

Hal = Elena = Douglas
Huxley (Huxley) Austin
        Austin

(died, Austins) (Austins, Moon)

Grandfather = Caro
(Austins, Moon, Light) (Light)

Maggy Hamilton
(adopted, Austins,
Moon, Muffins)

Wallace Austin = Victoria Eaton
(Austins, Moon, Days, Unicorns,
Light, Muffins)

John   Vicky   Suzy =Josiah Davidson   Rob
        (Austins, Moon, Days, Unicorns, Muffins)

Josiah   John   Tory   Emily
        (Wasp)

Commander Rodney = Nancy Rodney
(Austins, Moon, Light) (Light)

Leo   Jacky
(Moon, Light)   (Light)

Many Waters

MANY WATERS

Madeleine L'Engle

Farrar · Straus · Giroux

New York

For Stephen Roxburgh

Contents

Many Waters

1 ~ Virtual particles
and virtual unicorns

A sudden snow shower put an end to hockey practice.

"We can't even see the puck," Sandy Murry shouted across the wind. "Let's go home." He skated over to the side of the frozen pond, sitting on an already snow-covered rock to take off his skates.

There were calls of agreement from the other skaters. Dennys, Sandy's twin brother, followed him, snow gathering in his lashes, so that he had to blink in order to see the rock. "Why do we have to live in the highest, coldest, windiest spot in the state?"

Hoots of laughter and shouted goodbyes came from the other boys. "Where else would you want to live?" Dennys was asked.

Snow was sliding icily down the inside of his collar. "Baki. Fiji. Someplace warm."

One of the boys knotted his skate laces and slung his skates around his neck. "Would you really? With all those tourists?"

"Yeah, and jet-setters crowding the beach."

"And beautiful people."

"And litterbugs."

One by one the other boys drifted off, leaving the twins. "I thought you liked winter," Sandy said.

"By mid-March, I'm getting tired of it."

"But you wouldn't really want to go to some tourists' paradise, would you?"

"Oh, probably not. Maybe I would have, in the olden days, before the population explosion. I'm famished. Race you home."

By the time they reached their house, an old white farmhouse about a mile from the village, the snow was beginning to let up, though the wind was still strong. They went in through the garage, past their mother's lab. Pulling off their windbreakers, they threw them at hooks, and burst into the kitchen.

"Where's everybody?" Sandy called.

Dennys pointed to a piece of paper held by magnets to the refrigerator door. They both went up to it, to read:

DEAR TWINS, AM OFF TO TOWN WITH MEG AND CHARLES WALLACE FOR OUR DENTAL CHECKUPS. YOUR TURN IS NEXT WEEK. DON'T THINK YOU CAN GET OUT OF IT. YOU'VE BOTH GROWN SO MUCH THIS YEAR THAT IT IS ESSENTIAL YOU HAVE YOUR TEETH CHECKED.

LOVE, MOTHER

Sandy bared his teeth ferociously. "We've never had a cavity."

Dennys made a similar grimace. "But we *have* grown. We're just under six feet."

"Bet if we were measured today we'd be over."

Dennys opened the door to the refrigerator. There was half a chicken in an earthenware dish, with a sign:

VERBOTEN. THIS IS FOR DINNER.

Sandy pulled out the meat keeper. "Ham all right?"

"Sure. With cheese."

"And mustard."

"And sliced olives."

"And ketchup."

"And pickles."

"No tomatoes here. Bet you Meg made herself a BLT."

"There's lots of liverwurst. Mother likes that."

"Yuck."

"It's okay with cream cheese and onion."

They put their various ingredients on the kitchen counter and cut thick slices of bread fresh from the oven. Dennys peered in to sniff apples slowly baking. Sandy looked over to the kitchen table, where Meg had spread out her books and papers. "She's taken more than her fair share of the table."

"She's in college," Dennys defended. "We don't have as much homework as she does."

"Yeah, and I'd hate that long commute every day."

"She likes to drive. And at least she gets home early." Dennys plunked his own books down on the big table.

Sandy stood looking at one of Meg's open notebooks. "Hey, listen to this. Do you suppose we'll have this kind of junk when we're in college? *It seems quite evident that there was definite prebiotic existence of protein ancestors of polymers, and that therefore the primary beings were not a–amino acids.* I suppose she knows what she's writing about. I haven't the foggiest."

Dennys flipped back a page. "Look at her title. *The Million Doller question: the chicken or the egg, amino acids or their polymers.* She may be a mathematical genius, but she still can't spell."

"You mean, you know what she's writing about?" Sandy demanded.

"I have a pretty good idea. It's the kind of thing Mother and Dad argue about at dinner—polymers, virtual particles, quasars, all that stuff."

Sandy looked at his twin. "You mean, you *listen?*"

"Sure. Why not? You never know when a little useless knowledge is going to come in handy. Hey, what's this book? It's about bubonic plague. I'm the one who wants to be a doctor."

Sandy glanced over. "It's history, not medicine, stupe."

"Hey, why are lawyers never bitten by snakes?" Dennys asked.

"I don't know. And don't care."

"Well, you're the one who wants to be the lawyer. Come on. Why do lawyers never get bitten by snakes?"

"I give up. Why do lawyers never get bitten by snakes?"

"Professional courtesy."

Sandy groaned. "Very funny. Ha. Ha."

Dennys slathered mustard over a thick slice of ham. "When I think about the amount of schooling still ahead of us, I almost lose my appetite."

"Almost."

"Well, not quite."

Sandy opened the refrigerator door, looking for something else to pile on his sandwich. "We seem to eat more than the rest of the family put together. Charles Wallace eats like a bird. Well, judging by the amount we spend on bird feed, birds are terrible gluttons. But you know what I mean."

"At least he's settling down in school, and the other kids aren't picking on him the way they used to."

"He still doesn't look more than six, but half the time I think he knows more than we do. We're certainly the ordinary, run-of-the-mill ones in the family."

"The family can do with some ordinary, run-of-the-mill people. And we're not exactly dumb. If I'm going to be a doctor and you're going to be a lawyer, we've got to be bright enough for all that education. I'm thirsty."

Sandy opened the cupboard above the kitchen door. Only a year before, they had been too short to reach it without climbing on a stool. "Where's the Dutch cocoa? That's what I want." Sandy moved various boxes of lentils, barley, kidney beans, cans of tuna and salmon.

"Bet Mother's got it out in the lab. Let's go look." Dennys sliced more ham.

Sandy put a large dill pickle in his mouth. "Let's finish making the sandwiches first."

"Food first. Fine."

With sandwiches an inch or more thick in their hands, and full mouths, they went back out to the pantry and turned into the lab. In the early years of the century, when the house had been part of a working dairy farm, the lab had been used to keep milk, butter, eggs, and there was still a large churn in one corner, which now served to hold a lamp. The work counter with the stone sink functioned as well for holding lab equipment as it had for milk and eggs. There was now a formidable-looking microscope, some strange equipment only their mother understood, and an old-fashioned Bunsen burner, over which, on a homemade tripod, a black kettle was simmering.

Sandy sniffed appreciatively. "Stew."

"I think we're supposed to call it *boeuf bourguignon*." Dennys reached up to the shelf over the sink and pulled down a square red tin. "Here's the cocoa. Mother and Dad like it at bedtime."

"When's Dad coming home?" Dennys wanted to know.

"Tomorrow night, I think Mother said."

Sandy, his mouth full, held his hands out to the wood stove. "If we had our driver's licenses, we could go to the airport to meet him."

"We're good drivers already," Dennys agreed.

Sandy stuffed another large bite of sandwich into his mouth, and left the warmth of the stove to wander to the far corner of the lab, where there was a not-quite-ordinary-looking computer. "How long has Dad had this gizmo here?"

"He put it in last week. Mother wasn't particularly pleased."

"Well, it *is* supposed to be her lab," Sandy said.

"What's he programming?" Dennys asked.

"He's usually pretty good about explaining. Even though I don't understand most of it. Tessering and red-shifting and space/time continuum and stuff." Sandy stared at the keyboard, which had eight rather than the usual four ranks of keys. "Half of these symbols are Greek. I mean, literally Greek."

Dennys, ramming the last of his sandwich into his

mouth, peered over his twin's shoulder. "Well, I more or less get the usual science signs. That looks like Hebrew, there, and that's Cyrillic. I haven't the faintest idea what these keys are for."

Sandy looked down at the lab floor, which consisted of large slabs of stone. There was a thick rug by the sink, and another in front of the shabby leather chair and reading lamp. "I don't know how Mother stands this place in winter."

"She dresses like an Eskimo." Dennys shivered, then put out one finger and tapped on the standard keys of the computer: "TAKE ME SOMEPLACE WARM."

"Hey, I don't think we ought to mess with that," Sandy warned.

"What do you expect? A genie to pop up, like the one in Aladdin and the magic lamp? This is just a computer, for heaven's sake. It can't do anything it isn't programmed to do."

"Okay, then." Sandy held his fingers over the keyboard. "A lot of people think computers are alive—I mean, really, sort of like Aladdin's genie." He tapped out on the standard keys: "SOMEPLACE WARM AND SPARSELY POPULATED."

Dennys shouldered him aside, adding: "LOW HUMIDITY."

Sandy turned away from the odd computer. "Let's make the cocoa."

"Sure." Dennys picked up the red tin, which he had set down on the counter. "Since Mother's using the Bunsen burner, we'd better go back to the kitchen to make the cocoa."

"Okay. It's warmer there, anyhow."

"I could do with another sandwich. If they've gone all the way into town, supper'll probably be late."

They left the lab, closing the door behind them. "Hey." Sandy pointed. "We didn't see this." There was a small note taped to the door: EXPERIMENT IN PROGRESS. PLEASE KEEP OUT.

"Uh-oh. Hope we didn't upset anything."

"We'd better tell Mother when she gets back."

"Why didn't we *see* that note?"

"We were busy stuffing our faces."

Dennys crossed the hall and opened the kitchen door and was met with a blast of heat. *"Hey!"* He tried to step back, but Sandy was on his heels.

"Fire!" Sandy yelled. "Get the fire extinguisher!"

"Too late! We'd better get out and—" Dennys heard the kitchen door slam behind them. "We've got to get out—"

Sandy yelled, "I can't find the fire extinguisher!"

"I can't find the walls—" Dennys groped through a pervasive mist, his hands touching nothing.

Came a great sonic boom.

Then absolute silence.

Slowly the mist began to clear away, to dissipate.

"Hey!" Sandy's changing voice cracked and soared. "What's going on?"

Dennys's equally cracking voice followed. "Where on earth . . . What's happened . . ."

"What was that explosion?"

"Hey!"

They looked around to see nothing familiar. No kitchen door. No kitchen. No fireplace with its fragrant logs. No table, with its pot of brightly blooming geraniums. No ceiling strung with rows of red peppers and white garlic. No floor with the colorful, braided rugs. They were standing on sand, burning white sand. Above them, the sun was in a sky so hot that it was no longer blue but had a bronze cast. There was nothing but sand and sky from horizon to horizon.

"Is the house all right?" Sandy's voice shook.

"I don't think we went into the house at all . . ."

"You don't think it was on fire?"

"No. I think we opened the door and we were here."

"What about the mist?"

"And the sonic boom?"

"And what about Dad's computer?"

"Uh-oh. What're we going to *do*?" Dennys's voice started out in the bass, soared, and cracked to a piercing treble.

"Don't panic," Sandy warned, but his voice trembled.

Both boys looked around wildly. The brazen sunlight beat down on them. After the cold of snow and ice, the sudden heat was shocking. Small particles of mica in the sand caught the light and blazed up at them. "Hey." Dennys's voice cracked again. "What're we going to *do*?"

Sandy tried to speak calmly. "We're the ones who do things, remember?"

"We just did something." Dennys was bitter. "We just blew ourselves here, wherever here is."

Sandy agreed. "Stupid. We were stupid, mucking around with an experiment-in-progress."

"Only we didn't know it was in progress."

"We should have stopped to think."

Dennys looked around at sky and sand, both shimmering with heat. "What do you suppose Dad was up to? If we knew that—"

"Space travel. Tessering. Getting past the speed of light. You know that." Anxiety made Dennys sharp.

The sun beat down on Sandy's head, so that he reached up and wiped sweat from around his eyes. "I wish we'd never thought of that Dutch cocoa."

Dennys pulled off his heavy cable-knit sweater. Licked his dry lips. Moaned. "Lemonade."

Sandy, too, stripped off his sweater. "We got what we asked for, didn't we? Heat. Low humidity. Sparse population."

Dennys looked around, squinting against the glare. "Sparse wasn't meant to mean *no*body."

Sandy unbuttoned his plaid flannel shirt. "I thought we asked for a beach."

"Not on Dad's gizmo we didn't. Just sparse population. Do you suppose we've blown ourselves onto a dead planet? One where the sun is going into its red-giant phase before it blows up?"

Despite the intense heat, Sandy shivered, glanced at the sun, then quickly away. "I think the sun in its red-giant phase would be bigger. This sun doesn't look any larger than our own sun in movies set in deserts."

"Do you suppose it is our own sun?" Dennys asked hopefully.

Sandy shrugged. "We could be anywhere. Anywhere in the universe. If we were going to play with that doggone keyboard, we should have been more specific. I wish we'd just settled for Baki or Fiji, beautiful people or no."

"I'd just as soon see a beautiful person. Right now. I wish we hadn't done whatever it is we've done." Dennys pulled off his cotton turtleneck, stripping down to his white briefs and tank top.

Sandy stood on one leg to start pulling off his warmly lined pants, glanced again at the fierce sun, then quickly closed his eyes. "They'll miss us when they get back from the dentist."

"But they won't know where to look. Mother has more sense than we have. She'd never mess around with anything of Dad's unless he was right there."

"Mother's not interested in astrophysics. She's into virtual particles and things like that."

"She'll still miss us."

"Dad'll be home tomorrow," Sandy said hopefully. He was now stripped to his underclothes.

Dennys picked up his things and made a tidy bundle. "Unless we find some shade, we're going to have to put our clothes back on in half an hour, or at least some of them, or we'll get a vicious sunburn."

"Shade." Sandy groaned, and scanned the horizon. "Den! Do I see a palm tree?"

Dennys held his hand to shade his eyes. "Where?"

"There. All the way over there."

"Yes. No. Yes."

"Let's head toward it."

"Good. At least it's something to *do*." Dennys trudged off. "If it's the same time of day it was when we left home—"

"It was winter at home." Sandy's eyes were almost closed against the glare. "The sun was already setting."

Dennys pointed to their shadows, as long and skinny as they were. "The sun's slightly behind us . . . We might be heading east, if it's our own kind of sun."

Sandy asked, "Are you scared? I am. We've really got ourselves into a mess."

Dennys made no reply. They trudged along. They had left on their shoes and socks, and Dennys suggested, "It might be easier walking barefooted."

Sandy bent down and touched the sand with the palm of his hand, then shook his head. "Feel it. It would burn our feet."

"Do you still see that palm tree?"

"I think so."

They moved across the sand in silence. After a few minutes it seemed firmer under their feet, and they saw that there was rock under the sand.

"That's better," Sandy said.

"Hey!"

The ground seemed to shudder under their feet. Dennys flailed his arms to try to keep his balance, but was flung to the ground. "Is this an earthquake or something?"

Sandy, too, was thrown down. Around them they could hear a noisy grating of rock, and a deep, thunderous roaring beneath them. Then there was silence, abrupt and complete. The rock steadied under them. The earthquake, or whatever it was, had lasted less than a minute, but it had been of sufficient force to push up a large section of rock, making a small cliff about six feet high. It was striated and raw-looking, but it provided a shadow that stretched across the sand.

Both boys climbed to their feet and headed into the

welcome shade. Sandy touched the sheared-off rock, and it felt cool. "Maybe we could sit here for a minute . . ."

The sun was still fiercely hot, but the slab of rock they sat on was cool. The relief of the shade was so great that for a few minutes they sat in silence. Their bodies were slippery with sweat; it trickled into their eyes. They sat without moving, trying to take every advantage of the shade.

"I don't know what's going to happen next, but whatever it is, I'm not likely to be surprised," Sandy said at last. "Are you sure it was Dad's experiment we weren't supposed to interrupt? Couldn't it have been Mother's?"

"Mother's doing something with sub-atomic particles again," Dennys said. "Last night at dinner, she spent most of the time talking about virtual particles."

"It sounded crazy to me," Sandy said. "Particles which have a tendency to life."

"That's right." Dennys nodded. "Virtual particles. Almost-particles. What you said. Particles which tend to be."

Sandy shook his head. "Most of Mother's sub-atomic experiments are so, oh, so sort of infinitesimal, it hasn't mattered if we've come into the lab."

"But maybe if she's looking for a virtual particle—" Dennys sounded hopeful.

"No. It sounds to me more like something of Dad's. It was just sort of wishful thinking when I asked if it could be something of Mother's. Why didn't we see that notice on the door?"

"Yeah. Why?"

"*And* I wish our parents did ordinary things," Sandy complained. "If Dad was a plumber or an electrician, and if Mother was somebody's secretary, it would be a lot easier for us."

"And we wouldn't have to be such great athletes and good guys at school," Dennys agreed. "And—" He broke off as the earth started to tremble again. It was a brief tremor, with no heaving of stones, but both boys sprang to their feet.

"Hey!" Sandy jumped, almost knocking Dennys over.

From behind the rock cliff came a very small person, perhaps four feet tall. Not a child. He was firmly muscled, darkly tanned, and there was a down of hair across his upper lip and on his chin. He wore a loincloth, with a small pouch at the waist. As he saw them, he reached for the pouch in a swift, alarmed gesture.

"Hey, wait." Sandy held up his open hands, palm forward.

Dennys repeated the gesture. "We won't hurt you."

"Who are you?" Sandy asked.

"Where are we?" Dennys added.

The small man looked at them in mingled curiosity and fear. "Giants!" he cried. He had a man's voice, a young man's voice, deeper than Sandy's or Dennys's.

Sandy shook his head. "We're not giants."

"We're boys," Dennys augmented. "Who are you?"

The young man touched himself lightly on the forehead. "Japheth."

"That's your name?" Sandy asked.

He touched his forehead again. "Japheth."

Perhaps this was the custom of the country, wherever in the universe it was. Sandy touched his own forehead. "Alexander. Sandy."

Dennys made the same gesture. "Dennys."

"Giants," the young man stated.

"No," Sandy corrected. "Boys."

The young man rubbed his head where a purplish egg was forming. "Stone hit me. Must be seeing double."

"Japheth?" Sandy asked.

The young man nodded. "Are you two? Or one?" He rubbed his eyes perplexedly.

"Two," Sandy said. "We're twins. I'm Sandy. He's Dennys."

"Twins?" Japheth asked, his fingers once more reaching for the pouch at his side, which appeared to be filled with tiny arrows, about two inches long.

Dennys opened his hands wide. "Twins are when"—he had started to give a scientific explanation, stopped himself—"when a mother has a litter of two babies instead of one." His voice was soothing.

"You're animals, then?"

Sandy shook his head. "We're boys." He was ready to ask "What are you?" when he noticed a tiny bow near the pouch of arrows.

"No. No." The young man looked at them doubtfully. "Only giants are as tall as you. And the seraphim and nephilim. But you have no wings."

What was this about wings? Dennys asked, "Please, J— Jay—where are we? Where is this place?"

"The desert, about an hour from my oasis. I came out, dowsing for water." He bent down and picked up a wand of pliable wood. "Gopher wood is the best for dowsing, and I had my grandfather's—" He stopped in midsentence. "Higgaion! Hig! Where are you?" he called, as the twins might have called for their dog at home. "Hig!" He looked, wide-eyed, at the twins. "If anything has happened to him, my grandfather will—there are so few of them left—" He called again urgently, "Higgaion!"

From behind the outcropping of rock came something grey and sinuous which the twins at first thought was a snake. But it was followed by a head with small, bright, black eyes, and great fans of ears, and a chunky body covered with shaggy grey hair, and a thin little rope of a tail.

"Higgaion!" The young man was joyful. "Why didn't you come when I called you?"

With its supple trunk, the little animal, the size of a small dog or a large cat, indicated the twins.

The young man patted its head. He was so small that he did not have to bend down. "Thank El you're all right." He gestured toward the twins. "They seem friendly. They say they aren't giants, and while they are as tall as seraphim or nephilim, they don't seem to be of their kind."

Cautiously, the little animal approached Sandy, who dropped to one knee, holding out his hand for the creature to sniff. Then, tentatively, he began to scratch the hairy chest, as he would have scratched their dog at home. When the little animal relaxed under his touch, he asked Japheth, "What's seraphim?"

"And nephilim," Dennys added. If they could find out what these people were who were as tall as they, it might give them some kind of a clue as to where they had landed.

"Oh, very tall," Japheth said. "Like you, but different. Great wings. Much long hair. And their bodies—like you, not hairy. The seraphim are golden and the nephilim are white, whiter than sand. Your skin—it is different. Pale, and smooth, and as though you never saw sun."

"At home, it's still winter," Sandy explained. "We get very tan in the summer when we work outdoors."

"Your little animal," Dennys questioned, "looks sort of like an elephant, but what is it?"

"It's a mammoth." Japheth slapped the creature affectionately.

Sandy withdrew his hand from petting Higgaion. "But mammoths are supposed to be huge!"

Dennys saw in his mind's eye a picture of a mammoth in a nature book at home, very like Japheth's animal. Japheth himself was a miniature version of a strong and handsome young man, not a great deal older than themselves, perhaps as old as their sister's friend Calvin, who was in graduate school. Perhaps in this place, wherever it was, everything was in miniature.

"There aren't many mammoths left," Japheth explained. "I'm a good dowser, but mammoths are very fine for scenting water, and Higgaion is the best of all." He patted the little animal's head. "So I borrowed him from Grandfather Lamech, and together we found a good source of water, but I'm afraid it's too far from the oasis to be much use."

"Thank you for explaining," Sandy said, then turned to Dennys. "Do you think we're dreaming?"

"No. We came home from hockey practice. We made sandwiches. We went into the lab to find the Dutch cocoa. We messed around with Dad's experiment-in-progress. We were stupid beyond belief. But it isn't a dream."

"I'm glad to hear you say that," Japheth said. "I was beginning to wonder, myself. I thought I might be dreaming, because of the stone hitting my head in the earthquake."

"It was an earthquake?" Sandy asked.

Japheth nodded. "They come quite often. The seraphim tell us that things aren't settled yet."

"So maybe this is a young planet." Dennys sounded hopeful.

Japheth asked, "Where have you come from, and where are you going?"

"Take me to your leader," Sandy murmured.

Dennys nudged him. "Shut up."

Sandy said, "We're from planet earth, late twentieth century. We got here by accident, and we don't know where we're going."

"We'd like to go home," Dennys added, "but we don't know how."

"Where is home?" Japheth asked.

Sandy sighed. "A long way away, I'm afraid."

Japheth looked at them. "You are flushed. And wet." He himself did not seem to feel the intense heat.

Dennys said, "We're perspiring. Profusely. I'm afraid we'll get sunstroke if we don't find shade soon."

Japheth nodded. "Grandfather Lamech's tent is closest. My wife and I"—he flushed with pleasure as he said *my wife*—"live halfway across the oasis, by my father's tent. And I have to return Higgaion to Grandfather, anyhow. And he's very hospitable. I'll take you to him, if you like."

"Thank you," Sandy said.

"We'd like to come with you," Dennys added.

"At this point, we don't have much choice," Sandy murmured.

Dennys nudged him, then took his turtleneck from the bundle of clothes and pulled it back on, his head emerging from the rolled cotton neck, which had mussed up his light brown hair so that a tuft stuck out like a parakeet's. "We'd better cover ourselves. I think I'm sunburned already."

"Let's go, then," Japheth said. "I'd like to be home before dark."

"Hey—" Sandy said suddenly. "At least we speak the same language. Everything's been so wild and weird I hadn't realized it till—"

Japheth looked at him in a puzzled manner. "You sound very strange to me. But I *can* understand you, if I listen with my under-hearing. You talk a little like the seraphim and the nephilim. You can understand me?"

The twins looked at each other. Sandy said, "I hadn't really thought about it till now. If I think about it, you do sound, well, different, but I can understand you. Right, Den?"

"Right," Dennys agreed. "Except it was easier when we weren't thinking about it."

"Come on," Japheth urged. "Let's go." He looked at Sandy. "You'd better cover yourself, too."

Sandy followed Dennys's example and pulled on his turtleneck.

Dennys unrolled his flannel shirt and draped it over his head. "Sort of like a burnoose to keep us from getting sunstroke."

"Good idea." Sandy did the same.

"If," Dennys added morosely, "it isn't already too late."
Then he said, "Hey, Japh—" stumbled over the name.
"Hey, Jay, what's that?"

On the horizon to the far left, moving toward them,
appeared a creature which shimmered in and out of their
vision, silvery in color, as large as a goat or a pony, with
light flickering out from its forehead.

Sandy also shortened Japheth's name. "What's that,
Jay?" The mammoth pushed its head under Sandy's hand,
and he began to scratch between the great fan-like ears.

Japheth looked toward the barely visible creature, smiling in recognition. "Oh, that's a unicorn. They're very
odd. Sometimes they are, and sometimes they aren't. If we
want one, we call and it'll usually appear."

"Did you call on one?" Sandy asked.

"Higgaion may have thought about one, but he didn't
really call it. That's why it isn't all the way solid. Unicorns
are even better about scenting for water than mammoths,
except that you can't always count on them. But probably
Higgaion thought one might be able to confirm where we
thought there was a spring." He smiled ruefully. "Grandfather always knows what Hig is thinking, and I make
guesses."

The twins stopped and looked at each other, but the
mammoth had left Sandy and was trotting after Japheth,
who was walking toward the oasis again, so they followed.
In the intensity of the desert heat, their limbs felt heavy
and uncooperative. When they looked to where the unicorn had been, it was no longer there, though there was
left in its place a mirage-like shimmering.

Sandy panted. "I don't believe this."

Dennys, jogging beside him, agreed. "We've never had very willing suspensions of disbelief. We're the pragmatists of the family."

"I *still* don't believe it," Sandy said. "If I blink often enough, we'll be back in the kitchen at home."

Dennys took one of the flapping sleeves of his shirt and wiped his eyes. "What I believe right now is that I'm hot. Hot. Hot."

Japheth turned his head and looked back. "Giants! Come on. Stop talking."

With their long legs, it was easy enough for the twins to catch up with Japheth. "We're not giants," Dennys reiterated. "My name is Dennys."

"Dennysim."

Dennys touched his forehead, as Japheth had done. "One Dennys. Me."

Sandy, too, touched his forehead. "I'm Sandy."

"Sand." Japheth looked around. "We have plenty of Sand."

"No, Jay," Sandy corrected. "It's short for Alexander. Sandy."

Japheth shook his head. "You call me Jay. I call you Sand. Sand is something I understand."

"Talking of strange names"—Dennys looked at the mammoth, who was again butting at Sandy, to be petted— "Hig—"

"Hig-gai-on." Japheth sounded it out.

"Are all mammoths his size? Or are there some really big ones?"

Japheth looked puzzled. "Those that are left are like Higgaion."

Sandy looked at his brother. "Didn't horses start out very little, back in pre-history?"

But Dennys was looking at the horizon. "Look. Now you can see that there are lots of palm trees."

Although they could now see that there were many trees, the oasis was still far away. Despite their much longer legs, the boys began to lag behind Japheth and the mammoth, who were moving across the sand at an easy run.

"I'm not sure I can make it," Dennys said, grunting.

Sandy's steps, too, lagged. "I thought we were the great athletes," he said, panting.

"We've never been exposed to heat like this before."

Japheth, evidently realizing that they were no longer behind him, turned around and jogged back toward them, seemingly cool and unwinded. "What's the matter? You're both all red. The same red. You truly are two people?"

"We're twins." Sandy's voice was an exhausted croak.

Dennys panted. "I think—we're getting—heat—heat prostration."

Japheth looked at them anxiously. "Sun-sickness can be dangerous." He reached up and touched Dennys's cheek. Shook his head. "You're cold and clammy. Bad sign." He put his hand against his forehead. Appeared to be thinking deeply. Then: "What about a unicorn?"

"What about it?" Sandy asked. He felt tired and irritable.

"If we could get a couple of unicorns to become real and solid for us, they could carry you to the oasis."

The twins looked at each other, each seeing a red, sweating mirror version of himself. "We've never gone in for mythical beasts," Dennys said.

Sandy added, "Meg says unicorns have been ruined by overpopularity."

Japheth frowned. "I don't understand what you're saying."

Dennys, too, frowned. Thinking. Then: "Jay's unicorns sound more like Mother's virtual particles than like mythical beasts."

Sandy was exasperated. "Virtual particles aren't mythical. They're theoretical."

Dennys shot back, "If Mother can believe in her way-out theories, we ought to be able to believe in virtual unicorns."

"What kind of unicorns?" Japheth looked puzzled. "Is it because you're some strange kind of giant that there's all this confusion?"

"Unicorns have never been a matter of particular importance before." Sandy wiped his hands across his face and was surprised to find that the beads of sweat were indeed cold.

"They're important now." Dennys groaned. "Mother believes in virtual particles, so there's no reason there can't be virtual unicorns."

"Hig—" Japheth urged.

The mammoth turned and faced the horizon. A faint shimmering glimmered on the sand in front of him. Slowly it took the shape of a unicorn, transparent but recognizable. Beside it, another unicorn began to shimmer.

"Please, unicorns," Dennys begged. "Be real."

Slowly the transparency of both creatures began to solid-ify, until there were two unicorns standing on the sand, with silvery-grey flanks, silver manes and beards. Silver hooves, and horns of brilliant light. They looked at the twins and docilely folded their legs under to lie down.

"Oh!" Japheth exclaimed. "It's a good thing you're both so young. For the moment, I'd forgotten that unicorns will not let themselves be touched by anyone who is not a virgin."

The twins glanced at each other. "Well, we don't even have our driver's licenses yet," Dennys said.

"Get up on them before they decide they aren't needed," Japheth ordered.

The twins climbed each onto the back of one of the silver creatures, both feeling that this was a dream from which they could not wake up. But, without the unicorns, they would never make it to the oasis.

The unicorns flew across the desert, their hooves barely touching the surface. Occasionally, where the sand had been blown clear and there was rock, a silver hoof struck with a clang like a bell, and sparks flew upward. Small desert creatures watched them fly by. Sandy noticed, but did not mention, some scattered bones bleached by sun and wind.

"Hold on!" Japheth cried in warning. "Don't fall off!"

But there was a sense, in riding the unicorns, of un-reality. If this was no stranger than their mother's world of particle physics, it was at least equally as strange.

"Hold on!" Japheth shouted again.

But Dennys felt himself sliding off the smooth flanks. He tried to grasp the mane, but it sifted through his fingers like sand. Was the unicorn becoming less real, or was the still-blazing sun affecting him?

"Dennys! Don't fall off!" Sandy shouted.

But Dennys felt himself slipping. He did not know whether it was himself or the unicorn who kept flickering in and out of being.

Then he felt something solid, Sandy on his unicorn pressing against him. Sandy's strong arms shoving him back onto the unicorn, the virtual particle suddenly real, not just something in the lab. His head hurt.

Japheth and the mammoth were running beside them, amazingly swift for such small creatures. "Hurry," Japheth urged the unicorns. "Hurry."

Sandy, his flannel shirt still draped over his head, was hardly aware that he was supporting his brother. His arms felt as fluid as water. He was breathing in great searing gulps which burned his throat. His head began to swell, to be filled with hot air like a balloon, so that he was afraid he was going to float off into the sky.

The mammoth passed Japheth and the unicorns, leading the way to the oasis, so that his stocky legs were no more than a blur of motion, like hummingbirds' wings. Occasionally he would raise his trunk and make a trumpeting noise, urging the unicorns along. Japheth ran alongside, beginning to breathe, open-mouthed, with effort.

But they were not fast enough for Dennys, who was slipping into unconsciousness, and as the world blackened before his eyes, his unicorn's horn became dim and the silver creature began to dissolve as Dennys lost sight and hearing and thought. And Dennys flickered in and out of being with his mount.

Sandy, barely holding on to consciousness, was not aware that the arm he had held Dennys with was now holding nothing. He felt himself drop to the ground. He did not land on searing sand but on soft green. His burning body was shaded and cooled by the great fans of a palm tree.

His unicorn had made it to the oasis.

2 ❧ *Pelican in the wilderness*

Sandy slid slowly into consciousness, eyes tightly closed. No alarm clock jangling, so it must be Saturday. He listened to hear if Dennys was stirring in the upper bunk. Felt something cool and wet sprayed across his body. It felt good. He did not want to wake up. On Saturday they had heavy chores. They washed the floor of their mother's lab, of the bathrooms. If it was snowing again, there would be snow to shovel.

"Sand—"

He did not recognize the odd, slightly foreign voice. He did not recognize the smell that surrounded him, pungent and gamy. Again his body was sprayed with cool wetness.

"Sand?"

Slowly, he opened his eyes. In the light which came from directly above him, he saw two brown faces peering anxiously into his. One face was young, barely covered with deep amber down. The other face was crisscrossed with countless wrinkles, a face with ancient, leathered skin and a long beard of curling white.

Unwilling to believe that he was not waking from a dream, he reached up to touch Dennys's mattress above him. Nothing. He opened his eyes more widely.

He was in a tent, a sizable tent made of goatskins, judging by the smell. Light came in from the roof hole, a rosy, sunset light. A funny little animal crossed the tent to him and sprayed his body with water, and he realized that he was hot with sunburn. The animal was bringing water from a large clay pot and cooling him with it.

"Sand?" the young man asked again. "Are you awake?"

"Jay?" He struggled to sit up, and his burned skin was scratched by the skins on which he was lying.

"Sand, are you all right?" Japheth's voice trembled with anxiety.

"I'm okay. Just sunburned."

The old man put his hand against Sandy's forehead. "You have much fever. The sun-sickness is hard on those unaccustomed to the desert. Are you from beyond the mountains?"

Sandy looked at the ancient man, who was even smaller than Japheth but had the same brightly blue eyes, startling against the sun-darkened skin. Sandy touched his forehead as Japheth had done. "I'm Sandy."

"Sand. Yes. Japheth has told me." The old man touched his forehead, tipped with softly curling white hair. "Lamech. Grandfather Lamech. Japheth carried you to my tent."

Sandy looked around in alarm. "But Dennys—where's Dennys?" He was now fully awake, aware that he was not in the bunk bed at home but in this strange desert place which might be on any planet in any solar system in any galaxy anywhere in the universe. He shuddered. "Dennys?"

"He went out with the unicorn."

"What!"

"Sand," Japheth explained patiently, "Dennys must have fainted. I told you about unicorns. Sometimes they are, sometimes they aren't. When Den fainted, the unicorn went out, and took Den with him."

"But we've got to find him, bring him back!" Sandy tried to struggle to his feet.

Grandfather Lamech pushed him back down onto the skins with amazing strength for so small a person. "Hush, Sand. Do not worry. Your brother will be all right."

"But—"

"Unicorns are very responsible," Lamech explained.

"But—"

"It is true that they are unreliable in that we cannot rely on them to be, but they are very responsible."

"You're crazy," Sandy said.

"Hush, Sand," Grandfather Lamech repeated. "We do not know where the unicorns go when they go out, but when somebody calls the unicorn again and it appears, Den will appear, too."

"You're sure?"

"Yes. I am sure," the old man said, and for a moment Sandy relaxed at the authority in his voice.

Then: "Well, call a unicorn, call him now!"

The old man and Japheth looked at Higgaion. Higgaion raised his trunk toward the roof hole of the tent. The rosy glow had faded, and the old man and Japheth and Higgaion were barely visible shadows in the tent. There was a sudden flash, and Sandy could see the shimmering silver body of a unicorn. But no Dennys.

"Dennys!" he cried.

And heard Japheth echo, "Den!"

Higgaion appeared to be consulting with the unicorn. Then he looked toward Japheth and the old man. Trumpeted.

There was another flash of light, and then a faint glimmering and the unicorn was gone.

Grandfather Lamech said, "It would appear that someone has already called the unicorn on which the Den was riding."

Sandy jumped to his feet, but was so weak that he sank back onto the skins. "But he could be anywhere, anywhere!" he cried wildly.

"Hush," the old man repeated. "He is on the oasis. We will find him."

"How?" Sandy's voice was a frightened small boy's squeak.

Japheth said, "I will look for him. When I find him, I will bring him to you."

"Oh, Jay—I want to come with you."

"No." Grandfather Lamech was firm. "You have the sun-sickness. You must stay here until you are well." He looked up at the roof hole. The fading sunset was gone, and the moon, not full, but beaming bright, shone down on them. The old man touched Sandy's arm, his thigh. "Tomorrow you will be all blisters."

Sandy's head felt strangely buzzing and he knew that it

was from fever and that Grandfather Lamech was right. "But Dennys—"

"I will find him and bring him to you," Japheth promised.

"Oh, Jay, thank you."

The young man turned to his grandfather. "One of the women—my wife, or one of my sisters—will bring you a night-light, Grandfather."

The old man looked at the moonlight which brightened the tent. "Thank you, my dear grandson. My grand-children are kind to me, so kind . . ." His voice faltered. "My son . . ."

Japheth sounded embarrassed. "You know I can't do anything with Father. I don't even tell him when I've come to your tent."

"Better that way." The old man was sorrowful. "Better that way. But one day—"

"Of course, Grandfather. One day. I'll be back with the Den as soon as I can." He pushed out of the tent, and the flap slapped closed behind him.

Higgaion dribbled cool water from the jar onto the cloth on Sandy's burning forehead.

"Giant"—the little old man leaned over him—"where do you come from?"

"I'm not a giant," Sandy said. "Really. I'm just a boy. Dennys and I are still growing, but we're not giants, we're just ordinary tall."

The old grandfather shook his head. "In our country you are giants. Can you tell me where you come from?"

"Home." Sandy felt hot and feverish. Home might be

galaxies away. "New England. The United States. Planet earth."

The wrinkles in the old man's forehead crisscrossed each other as he frowned. "You don't come from around here. Nor from Nod. The people there are no taller than we are." He put his hand on Sandy's forehead. The hand felt cool, and dry as an autumn leaf crumbling to dust. "Your fever will go down, but you must stay here, in my tent, out of the sun, until the burning is healed. I will ask one of the seraphim to come tend to you. Seraphim do not burn in the sun. They are better healers than I." Sandy relaxed into Grandfather Lamech's kindness.

The mammoth started toward the water jar, then dropped to its haunches, whimpering in terror, as something screeched past the tent like an out-of-control jet plane. But on this planet, wherever it was, there were no planes.

The old man leaped to his feet with amazing agility and grabbed a wooden staff.

The hideous screech, not bird, not human, came again, closer, and then the tent flap was pushed aside and a large face peered in. It was the largest face Sandy had ever seen, a man's face with filthy hair and a matted beard, tangled eyebrows over small, suspicious eyes, and a bulbous nose. From the mat of hair came two horns, curved downward, with sharp points like boar's teeth. The mouth opened and shouted, *"Hungry!"*

The rest of the creature pushed into the tent. The head did not belong to a man's body but to a lion's, and as it came all the way into the tent, Sandy saw that the lion did not have a lion's tail but a scorpion's. Sandy was terrified.

The old man beat at it futilely with his staff. The man / lion / scorpion knocked the staff out of his hand and sent him flying across the tent. Grandfather Lamech fell onto a pile of skins. The mammoth lay flat on the skins by Sandy, trembling.

"Hungry!" The roar made the skins of the tent tremble.

Instinctively, Sandy thrust the mammoth behind him and, exerting the last remnant of his strength, rose, tottering, to his full height and took a step toward the monster.

"Giant!" the man's head screeched. "Giant!" And scorpion's tail, lion's body, and man's head backed out of the tent, so that the flap snapped back into place.

The old man pulled himself out of the corner where he had been flung. "Ridiculous manticore," he grumbled, "wanting to eat my mammoth."

Higgaion got unsteadily to his feet, raised his trunk, and trumpeted, but it was more of a whiffle than a call of triumph. He rubbed up against Sandy.

The old man retrieved his staff. "Thank you. You saved my mammoth from being eaten."

"I didn't do anything." Sandy's legs crumpled under him as he fell back onto the skins. "It's the first time I've ever scared anybody, just by being tall and sunburned."

"A gentle giant," the old man said.

Sandy felt too weak to contradict him. "Anyhow, the manticore is a mythical beast."

Grandfather Lamech shook his head. "I don't know what you mean."

"Things like manticores are mythical," Sandy stated.
"They aren't supposed to be real."

Grandfather Lamech's smile crinkled. "You will have
to ask the seraphim to explain. In this time many things
are real, you see." He looked around. "Where's the scarab
beetle?"

The mammoth, too, looked around, but they both
stopped, and the old man's face lit up as a soft scratching
was heard on the outside of the tent flap. It was obviously
some kind of signal, because he called out gladly, "Come
in, Granddaughter." Then he turned courteously to Sandy.
"Yalith, my youngest granddaughter."

The tent flap opened enough to let a girl through, a
girl about the size of the old man, barely four feet tall. She
carried a shallow stone bowl which contained oil and a
softly burning wick. By its light, which was brighter than
the moonlight, which had moved beyond the roof hole,
Sandy could see that the girl, who wore only a loincloth,
like Japheth and Grandfather Lamech, was gently curved,
with small rosy breasts. Her skin was the color of a ripe
apricot. Her softly curling hair was a deep bronze, which
glimmered in the lamplight and fell against her shoulders.
She looked, Sandy thought, about his age, and suddenly
his burning skin was not as painful as it had been, and he
felt energy returning to his limbs. He got to his knees and
stood to greet her, bowing clumsily.

She saw him and almost dropped the stone lamp. "A
giant!"

The mammoth reached up with his trunk to Sandy, and
Grandfather Lamech said, "He says that he is not a giant,

dear Yalith. Japheth carried him here, and they tell me that there is another one just like him, but he went out with a unicorn. Japheth is looking for him. This one"—he beamed at Sandy—"appears to be human, and he just saved Higgaion from the manticore."

Yalith shuddered. "I heard it screeching and going off with a rat." She put her stone lamp on a wooden keg. "I've brought your night-light, Grandfather Lamech."

"Thank you, my dear." There was a deep tenderness in the old man's voice.

Sandy bowed again. "Hello. My name's Sandy Murry." He could not keep a foolish grin off his face.

She looked at him dubiously, backing away slightly. "You do not speak like one of us. Are you sure you're not a giant?"

"I'm a boy. I'm sorry I look so awful. I have a fierce sunburn."

Now she looked at him without flinching. "Oh, yes, you do. How do we help you?"

Higgaion dipped his trunk into the water pot again and showered Sandy with it.

Grandfather Lamech said, "Higgaion is keeping his skin wet. But I think we ought to get one of the seraphim to look at him."

"Yes. That would be good. Where did you say you were from, giant—Sand?"

"The United States," Sandy said, though he knew it would mean nothing to this beautiful, strange girl.

The girl smiled at Sandy, and the warmth of her smile enveloped him.

"The United States is—are—a place," he tried to explain. "You might say that my brother and I are representatives." —Even if inadvertent ones.

"And you have a brother, who is out with a unicorn?"

Her question made it sound as though Dennys and the unicorn had gone off cavorting someplace together.

"My brother Dennys. We're twins. Identical twins. We do look a lot alike to people who don't know us well. Your brother Japheth is trying to find him."

"Well, he will find him, then. Do you need anything more, Grandfather Lamech?"

"No, my dear Yalith."

"I'd better go home, then. My brothers' wives are all there, and our mother likes to have me around to help keep everybody from fighting."

She smiled, turning from the old man to Sandy, who was dizzy with fever, but also with Yalith. He gazed at her as she said good night to them. For the first time in his life, Sandy had a flash of gratitude that Dennys was not with him.

Then anxiety surfaced. "Dennys—"

"Japheth will find him," the old man said. "Meanwhile —Higgaion, see if you can find our scarab friend."

Higgaion trumpeted softly and left the tent.

After Yalith and Higgaion had gone, Sandy was assailed by a wave of feverish sleep. It was dark now, with no moonlight coming through the tent's roof hole, and the oil lamp burned low. He closed his eyes, curled on his side to sleep, and felt an emptiness.

Dennys. He was just as happy that Dennys had not seen

Yalith. Nevertheless, he had never before gone to sleep without Dennys. At home he could just reach up and punch the mattress above his to get his twin's attention. At Scout camp they had always been in the same cabin. Despite their parents' efforts to allow the twins to develop as individuals, never dressing them alike, the fact remained that they were twins. He did not know what it was like to go to sleep without Dennys.

Higgaion came in and went to Grandfather Lamech, plucking something from his ear with his trunk and holding it out to the old man. Grandfather Lamech took it on his palm, a scarab beetle, glinting bronze in the lamplight. The old man stroked it gently with a trembling forefinger, and closed his palm.

Then came a vivid flash of light, similar to that of the unicorn's horn, and a tall presence stood in the tent, smiling at the old man, then looking quietly at Sandy. The personage had skin the same glowing apricot color as Yalith's. Hair the color of wheat with the sun on it, brightly gold, long, and tied back, falling so that it almost concealed tightly furled wings, the light-filled gold of the hair. The eyes were an incredibly bright blue, like the sea with sunlight touching the waves.

Lamech greeted him respectfully. "Adnarel, we thank you." Then he said to Sandy, "The seraph will be able to help you. Seraphim know much about healing."

So this was a seraph. Tall, even taller than the twins. But the only resemblance was in height. Otherwise, it was totally different, beautiful, but alien. The seraph turned to Lamech. "What have we here?"

Lamech bowed, seeming more than ever like a small

brown nut in comparison with the great winged one. If all the ordinary people in this strange place were as little as Japheth and Lamech and Yalith, it was small wonder that Sandy and Dennys were confused with giants. Lamech said, "We have with us a stranger—"

Adnarel touched Sandy's shoulder, pressing him back down on the skins as he started to struggle to his feet.

Lamech continued, "He is, as you can see, almost as tall as you are, but not as—not as completely formed."

"He is very young," Adnarel the seraph said, "barely hatched, as it were. But you are correct. He is not one of us. Nor of the nephilim."

"Nor of us," Lamech said. "But we think he is not to be feared."

Adnarel reached out to touch Sandy gently on the back, the long fingers delicately exploring the shoulder blades. "No wings, not even rudimentary ones."

Higgaion approached the seraph, butting him to get his attention, then indicated the water pitcher.

Adnarel reached down to scratch between the mammoth's ears. "Call the pelican," he ordered.

Higgaion left the tent. Lamech looked up, up, to meet Adnarel's startling blue eyes. "Are we doing the right thing, keeping him cool and wet to bring down the fever and heal the burning?"

Adnarel nodded, as the tent flap opened and Higgaion returned, followed by a pelican, large and white and surprising. It waddled over to the clay water pitcher, opened its great beak, and filled the pitcher.

Lamech asked anxiously, "The pelican will see to it that

we have plenty of water? It will take many trips to the well, too many for me now that I am old and—"

"Fear not. Alarid will see to it," Adnarel reassured.

"A pelican in the desert?" Sandy asked, feeling that the great bird was part of a fevered dream.

"A pelican in the wilderness," Adnarel agreed. He dropped to one knee and put his hand against Sandy's reddened cheeks. Through the fingers flowed a healing warmth, a warmth which had nothing to do with the stifling heat in the tent. Sandy had almost grown accustomed to the strong, gamy smell of the skins, but the seraph seemed to bring a lightness and a freshness to the air.

"Where, young one, are you from?" Adnarel asked.

Sandy sighed. "Planet earth, where I hope I still am?"

The seraph smiled again, not answering the question. He touched Sandy's forehead gently, and the touch helped him to clarify his thoughts, which seemed to lose their focus. "And from where on planet earth do you come?"

"From the United States. The Northeast. New England."

"How did you get here?"

"I'm not sure, uh, sir." There was something about Adnarel's presence which brought out the old-fashioned forms of respect. "Our father is working with a theory about the fifth dimension and the tesseract . . ."

"Ah." Adnarel nodded. "Did he send you?"

"No, uh, no, we—"

"We?"

"Dennys, my twin brother, and I. It was our fault. I mean, we have never before done anything so incredibly stupid as to mess with anything of Dad's when an experiment was in progress, except we didn't realize that an experiment was in progress."

"Where is Dennys?"

"Oh, please—" Sandy implored.

Grandfather Lamech explained, "The brother, the Dennys, went out with a unicorn, and has evidently been called back elsewhere. Japheth is looking for him."

The seraph listened gravely, nodding at what Sandy felt was an insufficient and unclear explanation. "Fear not," Adnarel said to Sandy. "Your brother will be returned. Meanwhile, Grandfather Lamech and Higgaion are doing the best thing for you, in keeping your skin moistened." From a pocket deep in his gown he took out what looked like a handful of herbs and dropped them into the water jar. "This will help the healing." He smiled. "It is good that you have at least some knowledge of the Old Language."

"But I don't—" Sandy started.

"You have been able to understand, and talk with, first Japheth, and now Grandfather Lamech, have you not?"

"Well. Yes. I guess so."

"Perhaps the gift has been awakened because you have not had time to think." The seraph's smile illumined the tent. Adnarel turned from Sandy to Lamech. "When the cool of night comes, wrap him in this." And the seraph took off his own creamy robe. His wings were visible now, as golden and shining as his long hair. He gave an effect of sunniness in the dark tent, lit only by the oil lamp. "The animal skins are too rough for his burned flesh. I will come by in the morning to see how he is doing. Meanwhile, I will check on Japheth and see if he has found the brother."

As Adnarel talked, Sandy felt his eyes close. Japheth was looking for Dennys. Adnarel was going to help him. Surely, if the seraph was involved, then everything would be all right.

His thoughts drifted off into soft darkness.

3 ✌ Japheth's sister Yalith

When Yalith left her grandfather's tent, she hurried toward home, near the center of the oasis. At her side she had a small pouch of darts, similar to Japheth's, but instead of the miniature bow she carried a small blowpipe. The arrows were tipped with a solution which would temporarily stun but not kill a predator, even one as large as the manticore. The manticores were strong and bad-tempered, but not intelligent or brave. She feared the manticores less than she feared some of the young men in the town, and she kept a dart in her hand in case she needed it.

After leaving the grazing grounds around Lamech's tent, she walked through one of his groves that led her onto the desert of white sand lapping against brown grasses. Wherever there were not enough wells to provide for irrigation, the desert took over. But she preferred walking across the desert to the dusty, dirty paths of the oasis. Stars were bright against the velvet black of sky. At her feet, a late beetle hustled to burrow itself under the sand until morning. To her right, high in the trees of Lamech's groves, the baboons were chittering sleepily.

She looked toward the horizon, and on an outcropping of rock similar to the one the earthquake had made when Sandy and Dennys met Japheth and the mammoth Higgaion, she saw the shadow of a supine form. She looked to make sure it was a lion, then called softly, "Aariel!"

The creature rose slowly, languidly, and then leapt down from the rock and loped toward her, and she saw that she had been deceived in the starlight, for it was not a lion but one of the great desert lizards, called dragons by most people, although its wings were atrophied and it could not fly.

She stood frozen with anxiety on the starlit sand, her hand holding one of the tiny arrows. As the lizard neared her, it rose straight upward to a height of at least six feet, and suddenly arms were outstretched above the head; the tail forked into two legs, and a man came running toward her, a man of extraordinary beauty, with alabaster-white skin and wings of brilliant purple. His long hair was black with purple glints, and his eyes were the color of amethysts.

"You called me, lovely one?" He bent down toward her tenderly, a questioning smile on his lips, which were deeply rosy in his white face.

"No, no," she stammered. "Not you. I thought—I thought you were Aariel."

"No. I am Eblis, not Aariel. And you called, and here I am," his voice soothed, "at your service. Is there anything you want?"

"Oh, no, thank you, no."

"No baubles for your ears, your lovely little neck?"

"Oh, no, thank you, no," she repeated. Her sisters would think her stupid for refusing his offer. The nephilim were generous. This nephil could give her everything he had offered, and more.

"And all of a sudden you have changed," he said. "You were a child, and now you are not a child any longer."

Instinctively, she folded her hands across her breasts, stammering. "B-but, I am a child. I'm not nearly a hundred years old yet . . ."

He reached out one long, pale hand and softly pushed her starlit hair back from her forehead. "Do not be afraid of growing up. There are many pleasures ahead for you to taste, and I would help you to enjoy them all."

"You?" She looked, startled, at the glorious creature by her, light shimmering like water from the purple wings.

"I, sweet little one, I, Eblis, of the nephilim."

No nephil had paid attention to her before. She was too young. Then she saw, in her mind's eye, the strange young giant in her grandfather's tent. She was no longer a child. She did not react to the young giant as a child.

"There are many changes to come," Eblis said, "and you will need help."

Her eyes widened. "Changes? What kind of changes?"

"People are living too long. El is going to cut the life span back. How old is your father?"

"He must be, oh, close to six hundred years. Middle-aged." She looked at her fingers. Ten. That was really as far as she could count accurately.

"And your Grandfather Lamech?"

"Let's see. He was very young when he had my father, not quite two hundred years old. He, too, has lived for very long. His father, Methuselah, my great-grandfather,

lived for nine hundred and sixty-nine years. And his father
was Enoch, who walked with El, and lived three hundred
and sixty and five years, and then El took him—" Involved
in the great chronologies of her fathers, she was not prepared for him to unfurl his great wings and gather her in,
enveloping her in great swirls of purple touched with
brilliance as with stars. She gasped in surprise.

He laughed softly. "Oh, little one, little innocent one,
how much you have to learn, about men's ways, and about
El's ways, which are not men's ways. Will you let me teach
you?"

To be taught by a nephil was an honor she had never
expected. She was not sure why she was hesitant. She
breathed in the strange odor of his wings, smelling of stone,
of the cold, dark winds which came during the few brief
weeks of winter.

Enveloped in Eblis's wings, she did not hear the rhythmic thud as a great lion galloped toward them across the
desert, roaring as it neared them. Then both Yalith and
Eblis turned and saw the lion rising to its hind legs, as the
lizard had done, leaping up into the sky, a great, tawny
body with creamy wings, gilt-tipped, unfurling and stretching to a vast span. The great amber eyes blazed.

Eblis removed his wings from around Yalith, hunched
them behind his back. "Why this untoward interruption,
Aariel?"

"I ask you to leave Yalith alone."

"What's it to you? The daughters of men mean nothing
to the seraphim." Eblis smiled down at Yalith, stroking his
long fingers delicately across her burnished hair.

"No?" Aariel's voice was low.

"No, seraph. A nephil may go to a daughter of man. A nephil understands pleasure." He touched a fingertip to Yalith's lips. "I would teach you, sweeting. I think you would like what I can give you. I will leave you now to Aariel's tender ministries. But I will see you again." He turned away from them, toward the desert, and his nephil form dropped into that of the great dragon/lizard. He loped away into the shadows.

Yalith said, "Aariel, I don't understand. I thought I saw you on the rock. I was sure it was you, and I called, and then it wasn't you, it was Eblis."

"The nephilim are masters of mimicry. He wanted you to think it was I. I beg you, little one, be cautious."

Her eyes were troubled. "He was very kind to me."

Aariel put his hand under her chin and looked into her eyes, clear and still childlike. "Who would not be kind to you? Are you on your way somewhere?"

"Home. I took Grandfather Lamech his night-light. But, oh, Aariel, there is a strange young giant in Grandfather Lamech's tent. Japheth carried him there. He has a terrible sunburn. He can't be from anywhere around here. He says he is not a giant, and I have never seen anyone like him. He is as tall as you are, and his body is not hairy, it is smooth like yours, like the nephilim, and his skin, where it wasn't burned red, was pale. Not white, like the skin of the nephilim, but pale and tender, like a baby's."

"You seem to have observed him carefully," Aariel said.

"There's never been anyone like him on the oasis before." She flushed, turned slightly away.

Aariel asked, "What is being done for his burn? Does he have fever?"

"Yes. Higgaion is keeping him sprayed with cool water, and they are going to ask a seraph what to do for him."

"Adnarel?"

"Yes. The scarab beetle."

"Good."

"He is not one of you, this young giant, and he is not one of the nephilim. Their skin burns white and whiter in the sun, like white ash when the fire has burned fiercely in the winter weeks."

The creamy wings trembled, the golden tips shimmering in the starlight. "If his skin burns, he is not of the nephilim."

"Nor of you."

"Does he have wings?"

"No. In that, he is like a human. He seemed very young, though he is as long as you, and thin."

"Did you observe his eyes?"

She did not notice the twinkle in his own. "Grey. Nice eyes, Aariel. Steady. Not burning, like—not giving out light, like yours. More like human eyes, mine, and my parents' and brothers' and sisters'."

Aariel touched her gently on the shoulder. "Go on home, child. Do not fear to cross the oasis. I will see that you are not harmed."

"You and Eblis. Thank you." Like a child, she held her face up for a kiss, and Aariel leaned down and pressed his lips gently against hers. "You will not be a child much longer."

"I know . . ."

He touched her lips again, lightly, and a moment later a large lion was running lightly across the desert.

Yalith turned onto a sandy path through a field of barley. At the end of the path was a stone road cutting through white buildings of sun-baked clay, low buildings, built to withstand the frequent earth tremors. Some of these low buildings contained small shops for baked goods, for stone lamps, for oil; there were shops with hanging meat, shops with bows and arrows, shops with spears of gopher wood. Some entryways were curtained with strands of bright beads, which tinkled in the evening breeze.

Out of one of these came a nephil, his arm around a young woman who was gazing up at him adoringly, leaning against him so that her rosy breasts touched his pale flesh. Her glossy black hair fell down her back, past her hips; and the eyes with which she regarded him were the deep blue of lapis lazuli.

Yalith stopped in her tracks. The girl was Mahlah, Yalith's sister, the only girl besides Yalith to be in the home tent. Their two older sisters were married and lived in another part of the oasis with their husbands. Mahlah had been away from the home tent a great deal lately. Now Yalith knew where she had been.

Mahlah saw her younger sister and smiled.

The nephil smiled, too, graciously acknowledging Yalith.

Before they came out of the shadows, Yalith thought he was Eblis, with a sense of shock and betrayal. But in the full starlight she could see that his wings were much lighter, a delicate lavender. She could not tell what color his long hair was, but it, too, was lighter, and seemed to have an orange glow. He had a sinuous, snake-like curve to his neck, and hooded eyes.

He smiled again, tenderly. "Mahlah will stay with me this night. You will let your mother know."

Yalith blurted out, "Oh, but she will worry. We are not allowed to stay out at night . . ."

Mahlah laughed joyously. "Ugiel has chosen me! I am his betrothed!"

Yalith gasped. "But does Mother know?"

"Not yet. You tell her, little sister."

"But shouldn't you tell her yourself? You and—"

"Ugiel."

"But shouldn't you—"

Mahlah's laugh pealed again, like little bells. "The old ways are changing, little sister. This night I meet Ugiel's brethren."

The nephil stretched a soft wing about Mahlah. "Yes, little sister. The old ways are changing. Go and tell your mother."

Yalith turned, and they watched her go, fingers waving at her in farewell. At the end of the street she heard footsteps and turned to see a young man following her. She reached for a dart and put it in her blowpipe, but he disappeared around the corner of a building.

The low white buildings gave way to tents, each tent surrounded by the land of the dweller, at first the small plots of the shopkeepers, then groves and fields, sometimes many acres. Along the path she saw sheep, goats, camels grazing. Grapes were ripe on the vines.

Her father's tent was a large one, flanked by several

smaller tents. She hurried into the main tent, calling out
to her mother.

It was the smell that brought Dennys back to consciousness. His nostrils twitched. His stomach heaved. There
was a smell of cooking, smoky, rancid. A smell worse than
the rotten-cheese smell of silage which clung to the farm-
hands near home. A smell far stronger than that of the
manure spread on the fields in the spring; that was a fresh,
growing smell. This was old manure, rotting. A smell that
made the urinals in the lavatories at school seem sweet.
And over it all, but not covering it, a cloying smell of perfume and sweat, body sweat which had never been near a
shower.

He opened his eyes.

He was in an enclosed space, lit by the moonlight pour-
ing in through a hole in what seemed to be some kind of
curved roof, and by the equally brilliant light which
poured from a unicorn's horn. The silver creature looked
around, sniffing, pawing the dirty earthen floor. At its feet,
a mammoth cringed.

Dennys almost cried out, "Higgaion!" But this mammoth was not the one who had accompanied Japheth. This
mammoth had matted fur on its flanks, and it was so thin
that the skeleton showed through. Its eyes were dulled,
and it seemed to be apologizing to the unicorn.

Staring at the unicorn, still unaware of Dennys, were
several small people. But, just as the mammoth was unlike
Higgaion, so these people were unlike Japheth. They
smelled. The men's bodies were hairy, giving them a

simian look. Their goatskin loincloths were not clean.
There were two full-bearded men, and two women, naked
except for the loincloths. Both the women had red hair,
and the younger woman's hair was so vivid it almost
seemed like flame, and some care had been taken with it.
The older woman was wrinkled and discontented-looking.

The unicorn's light flashed against the younger woman's
green eyes, making them sparkle like emeralds. "You see!"
she cried triumphantly. "I knew our mammoth could call
us a unicorn!"

The light in the horn dimmed.

The younger of the two men, who had matted brown
hair and a red beard unkempt and spotted with food,
snarled at the girl. "And now, dear sister Tiglah, that we
have a unicorn in the tent, what do you want of it?"

The girl approached the unicorn, her hand held out as
though to pet it. The horn blazed with blinding brilliance,
and then the tent was dark so suddenly that it took several
seconds for Dennys's eyes to adjust to the moonlight coming through the hole in the roof.

The men roared with laughter. "Ho, Tiglah, you
thought you could fool us, didn't you?"

Even the older woman was laughing. Then she saw
Dennys, who was struggling to his knees. "Great auk, what
have we here?"

The redheaded girl gasped. "A giant!"

The older, bowlegged man approached Dennys. He held
a spear, and Dennys, gagging from the stench in the tent,
felt an overriding surge of fear. The man nudged him with
the spear, so that he fell back onto a pile of filthy skins.

The man flipped him over, using the spear, which scratched but did not cut him. He felt the tip of the spear as it was drawn lightly along his shoulder blades.

"Is this one yours, Tiglah?" the younger man asked. "I thought you were seeing a nephil."

Tiglah looked curiously at Dennys. "He's no nephil."

The older woman stared. "If he's a giant, he's a baby giant. He can't hurt us."

"What will we do with him?" Tiglah asked.

The brown, hairy man withdrew his spear. "Throw him out." His voice held no particular malice. Dennys was just a thing, to be disposed of. He felt two pairs of hands lifting him, as the younger man helped his father. The mammoth whimpered, and the older woman kicked at him. Certainly, Dennys thought, anything would be better than this horrible-smelling place full of horrible little people.

There was a brief whiff of fresh air. A glimpse of a night sky crusted with stars. A smoky redness on the horizon, like the light from some enormous industrial city. Then he felt himself being flung, thrown, like offal. He felt himself rolling down a steep incline. He gagged. Vomited. He had been thrown into what was evidently a garbage dump. It was even worse than wherever he had been before.

He managed to pull himself up onto his knees. He was in some kind of pit. There was an overwhelming stench of feces, of rotting flesh. He did not know what else was in the pit with him, and he did not want to know. Frantically he scrambled up the side, climbing, slipping on bones, on ooze, on decaying filth, sliding back, climbing, sliding, slipping, scrabbling, until at last he pulled himself out and up onto his feet and stood there tottering, filthy and terrified.

There was no sign of Sandy. No sign of the unicorn. Or of Japheth and Higgaion. He had no idea where he was. He looked around. He was standing on a dirt path which bordered the pit. Beside it was his rolled-up bundle of clothes. On the other side of the path were a number of tents. He had seen pictures of bedouin tents in his social-studies books at school. These were similar, though they seemed smaller and more closely clustered. It was probably from one of these tents that he had been thrown. Beyond the tents were palm trees, and he staggered toward these.

He needed to shower. Did he ever need to shower! He carried with him the smell of the pit. He ran, barely keeping himself upright, to the grove of palms. Beyond these he could see white. White sand. The desert. If he could only reach the desert, he could roll in the moon-washed sand and get clean.

"Sandy!" he called, but there was no Sandy. "Jay! Jay!" But no small, kind young man appeared. "Higgaion!" He shuddered. If he never saw any human being again, he would not go back to the tent where he had been poked at with a spear, and from which he had been thrown, like garbage.

Racing, he was suddenly out of the grove of palms and sliding in sand. He fell down, rolled and rolled, then picked up handsful of sand and rubbed it over himself, wiping off the slime and filth of the pit. He pulled off his turtleneck and flung it away. Rolled again in sand. His underclothes were filthy from the pit and he tore them off, flinging them after the turtleneck. He did not even realize that he was scraping off his own sunburned skin, so eager was he to get clean. The sand was cool under the daisy field of stars, and he took off his sneakers and socks, flinging them after his clothes. They would never be clean again. He rubbed more sand on his feet, his ankles, his legs, not even realizing that he was sobbing like a small child.

After a while, from sheer exhaustion, he calmed down. Began to assess his situation. He was badly sunburned. He had made it worse by scouring himself with sand. He was shivering, but it was not from cold; it was from fever.

He sat there, naked as Adam, on the white desert, his back to the oasis. The not yet full moon was sliding down toward the horizon. Above him, there were more stars than he had ever seen before. Ahead of him was that strange reddish glow, and then he saw that it came from a mountain, the tallest in a range of mountains on the far horizon. Of course. If he and Sandy had somehow or other blown themselves onto a young planet in some galaxy or other, naturally volcanoes would still be active.

How active? He hoped he wouldn't find out. At home the hills were low; old hills, worn down by wind and rain, by the passing of the glaciers, by eons of time. Home. He began to sob again.

With a great effort, he calmed himself. He and Sandy were the practical ones of the family, the ones who found solutions to problems. They could do minor repairs when the plumbing misbehaved. They could rewire an old lamp and make it work again. Their mother's reading lamp in the lab was one they had bought at a church bazaar and made over for her. Their large vegetable garden in the summer was their pride and joy, and they sold enough of their produce to augment their allowances considerably. They could do anything. Anything.

Even believe in unicorns. He thought of the unicorn, the unicorn he had come to think of as a virtual unicorn, and who had, somehow or other, brought him to that tent of horrible, primitive little people who had thrown him into the pit. The sad, undernourished mammoth evidently had called the unicorn, and Dennys had been called back into being, too. But the unicorn had gone out in a blaze of light. A unicorn, even a virtual one, evidently could not stand the smell.

All right. If he thought that a unicorn couldn't stand the ugliness of the smell, it must mean that he believed in unicorns. Virtually.

Of course there were no unicorns. But neither was it possible that he and Sandy, tapping into their father's partly programmed experiment, could have been flung to wherever in the universe they were, on a backward planet of primitive life forms. Again he looked around. The stars were so clear that he seemed to hear a chiming of crystal. From the mountain came a wisp of smoke, a small tongue of fire.

"Oh, virtual unicorn!" he cried. "I want to believe in you, and if you don't come, I will die." He felt something cool and soft nudging his bare body, and there was the scraggly little mammoth, touching him tentatively with the pink tip of its long grey trunk. And then a burst of silver blazed in front of him, and was reduced to a shimmer. A unicorn knelt before him on the sand. Dennys did not have the strength to mount the unicorn and sit astride. He gave the mammoth a look of mute gratitude, then draped himself over the unicorn's back. He closed his eyes. He was burning with fever. He would burn the unicorn. He felt that they were exploding like the volcano.

Mahlah, Yalith's sister, betrothed to Ugiel the nephil, lay on a small rock ledge, ten minutes' walk into the desert. Her heart beat rapidly with excitement. Ugiel had brought her to the rock, covered her with kisses, and then told her to wait until he returned with his brethren to seal their betrothal.

She heard the beating of wings and looked up, catching her breath. Above her a pelican, white against the night sky, flew in circles which grew smaller as it descended. It touched the ground and raised its great wings until they seemed to brush the stars, and there was no longer a pelican in front of Mahlah but a seraph, with wings and hair streaming silver in the desert wind, and eyes as bright as stars.

Mahlah scrambled to her feet, letting her long black hair swirl about her. "Alarid—"

The seraph took her hand, looking down into her eyes. "Are we really losing you?"

She withdrew her hands, dropping her gaze, laughing a small, self-conscious laugh. "Losing me? What do you mean?"

"Is it true that you and Ugiel—"

"Yes, it is true," she said proudly. "Be happy for me, Alarid. Ugiel is still your brother, is he not?"

Alarid dropped to one knee, so that he no longer towered over her. "Yes, we are still brothers, though we have chosen very different ways."

"And you're sure yours is the better way?" There was scorn in Mahlah's voice.

Alarid shook his head sadly. "We do not judge. The seraphim have chosen to stay close to the Presence."

"But you're too close to be able to see it! The nephilim have distance and objectivity." He looked at her, and her glance wavered for a moment. "Yes. Ugiel told me that."

Alarid rose slowly to his full height. With one silver wing he drew her briefly to him, and she smelled starlight. Then he let her go. "You will not forget us?"

"How could I forget you!" she exclaimed. "You have been my friend since Yalith took me out to greet the dawn and I met you and Aariel."

"You have not greeted the dawn lately."

"Oh—I am learning about the night."

Alarid bent down and kissed the top of her dark head. Then he walked slowly across the desert. Tears fell silently onto the sand.

Mahlah looked down. When she raised her head, she saw a pelican flying up, up, to be lost among the stars.

Yalith hurried into her family tent. "Mahlah is betrothed to one of the nephilim!"

No one heeded her. Her parents, brothers, and sisters-in-law were lying around on goatskins, eating, and drinking wine her father had made from the early grapes. Several stone lamps lit the tent with a warm glow; too warm, Yalith thought. Almost no breeze came through the open tent flap, or the roof hole. The moon was descending, and only stars were visible. She looked around for Japheth, her favorite brother, but did not see him. Probably he was still out looking for the brother of the young giant in her grandfather's tent.

Her mother was stirring something in a wooden bowl, intent on what she was doing. A mammoth, well fed, with lustrous long hair on its flanks, lay sleeping at her feet.

Someone had been sick, probably Ham, who had a weak stomach, and the smell of Ham's sickness mingled with the smell of wine, of meat from the stewpot, of the skins of the tent. Yalith was accustomed to all these odors, and noticed only that Ham was lying back on a pile of skins, looking pale. Ham was, in any event, the lightest-skinned in the family, and the smallest, having been, according to Matred, born a full moon early. Anah, his red-haired wife, knelt by him, offering him wine. Languidly he pushed it away, then pulled Anah down to him, kissing her full, sensual mouth.

Yalith went up to Matred, her mother. Repeated: "Mahlah is betrothed."

Matred looked up briefly. "She's not old enough."

"Oh, Mother, of course she is. And she is."

"Old enough?" Matred was preoccupied with what she was doing.

"Betrothed."

"Who is it this time?"

"It's not one of us. It's one of the nephilim."

Matred shivered, but went on stirring, without focus. "Mahlah has changed. She is no longer my merry little girl who was satisfied to see a butterfly, or a drop of dew on a spider's web. She is no longer satisfied to be with us in the home tent." A tear dropped into the bowl.

Yalith patted her mother's arm. "She's grown up, Mother."

"So have you. But you don't go chasing about the oasis at night. You don't run after nephilim."

"Maybe the nephil ran after her?"

"She's pretty enough. But it is not right for me to hear something like this at secondhand. That is not how things are done. That is not how my daughter behaves."

"I'm sorry," Yalith said uncomfortably. "I was walking home from Grandfather Lamech's, and I saw them, Mahlah and a nephil. His name is Ugiel. He asked me to tell you, so that you would not be worried."

"Worried!" Matred exclaimed. "Just don't tell your father, that's all. What's to prevent this Ugh—"

"Ugiel."

"This nephil from coming himself, with Mahlah, to tell me and your father, according to the custom."

Yalith frowned worriedly. "He said that times are changing." Eblis had said that, too. She felt a jolt of insecurity in the pit of her stomach. She did not tell her mother about Eblis.

Matred put down her wooden spoon with a bang. "There

are many who think it an honor to be noticed by a nephil and accept their ways. Anah"—Matred looked across at her son Ham's wife, redheaded, still luscious, but beginning to be overblown—"Anah tells me that her younger sister, Tiglah, is being singled out by a nephil for marriage. Anah is thrilled."

"But you're not."

"Tiglah is not my daughter. Mahlah is." Matred turned away. "Child, I am not star-dazzled by the nephilim. They are very different from us."

"They are beautiful—"

"Beautiful, yes. But they will make changes, and not all changes are good."

—I don't want things to change, Yalith thought. And then, in her mind's eye, she saw again the young giant who had bowed to her in Grandfather Lamech's tent, and who was unlike anybody she had ever seen.

Matred continued: "Change is, I suppose, inevitable, and sometimes it brings good things." She looked across the tent to her oldest son, Shem, who was sitting with his wife, Elisheba, eating some of the grapes from the vineyard which were not pressed for wine but kept for the table. Shem was pulling one grape at a time from the bunch, and throwing it to Elisheba. She would catch each grape in her open mouth and they would both laugh with pleasure at this simple, sensual game. It seemed amazingly young and romantic for this stocky, solid couple. "Elisheba is a great help to me. And then, Japheth's wife—"

Yalith looked to where a young woman with softly curling black hair against creamy skin was scouring a wooden

bowl with sand. The young woman looked up and waved
in greeting.

Matred said, "She comes to us from another oasis, and
with a strange name."

"O-holi-bamah." Yalith sounded it out.

"Look at her," Matred commanded.

Yalith looked again at her sister-in-law. Oholibamah was
fairer of complexion than Yalith or the other women, even
fairer than Ham. Her hair and brows were blacker than
the night sky, a rippling, purply black. When Oholibamah
stood, she was nearly a head taller than the other women.
And beautiful. She always seemed lit by moonlight, Yalith
thought. "What about her?" she asked her mother.

"Look at her, child. Look at her."

Yalith was shocked. "You mean you think she—"

Matred shrugged slightly. "She is the youngest daughter
of a very old man." She held up the fingers of both hands.
"More than ten years younger than her brothers and sisters. I love Oholibamah as though she were my own. And
if Oholibamah was indeed sired by a nephil, then great
good has been brought into our lives."

Yalith looked at Oholibamah as though seeing her for
the first time. After Yalith and Mahlah, Oholibamah was
the youngest woman in the tent, younger by several years
than Elisheba, Shem's wife, or Anah, Ham's wife. All three
of Yalith's brothers had married at unusually young ages,
and all three had grumbled at having to take on domestic
duties so soon. Shem had protested, "But we are too young
to marry. I'm the oldest, and I've barely reached my first
hundred years."

His father had replied, "There is a certain urgency, my son."

"Why? And how will you find wives for us when we are so young?"

"You are fine-looking men," the patriarch assured him.

Ham had joined in. "But why the rush, Father? What is this urgency you speak of?"

The patriarch pulled at his long beard, which was beginning to show white. "Yesterday, when I was working in the vineyard, the Voice spoke to me. El told me that I must find wives for you."

"But why?" Ham protested. "We're young, and we need time."

"There are changes, great changes coming," the patriarch said.

"Is the volcano going to erupt?" Shem asked.

"If the volcano erupts," Ham said, "wives won't do us any good."

Their father told them only that the word of El had come to him in the vineyard, and that El had given no explanation.

Elisheba and Anah were easily found for Shem and Ham. The patriarch had a reputation as an honest man. He had the largest and best vineyards on the oasis, and fine flocks of goats and sheep. The fame of his wine had spread to many other oases round about. Matred was a woman of unquestionable virtue and beauty, and her girth attested to her skills as a cook. It was a privilege to marry into her tent.

Japheth was young enough so that no one stepped forward. His face was still smooth and beardless. His body hair was no more than soft down. His eyes were friendly and guileless. But he was on the threshold of manhood. His father went off on his camel one day, and came back with Oholibamah.

Japheth had been at the well, getting water for the animals, when he saw a young girl on a white camel, a young girl of fair complexion, with dark hair tumbling richly against her ivory shoulders. His eyes met Oholibamah's eyes, dark as the night sky between stars, and his knees became fluid. She slid off the white camel's back and came toward him, slender hands outstretched. Their love was a bright flower, youthful, and radiantly beautiful.

Oholibamah. O-holy-bamah. A name as strange as her moonlit beauty. But soon it flowed easily from their lips.

Oholibamah was Yalith's first real friend. They were not far apart in age, both of them barely out of childhood and into womanhood. They were alike, too, in their unlikeness to the others. They saw and rejoiced in what most people of the oasis never noticed. Both liked to leave the tent at first dawn to watch and wait for the sun to rise over the desert, delighting in the calling of the stars just before daylight. It was during one of her dawn walks that Yalith had met the great lion who was the seraph Aariel, and on another walk, when she had persuaded Mahlah to join her, that she had introduced Aariel and Alarid the pelican to her sister. But once Oholibamah came, Mahlah preferred to sleep in the morning.

So Yalith and her youngest sister-in-law would slip out quietly. When the great red disk of day pulled above the white sand, and the stars dimmed and their songs faded out, scarab beetles who had slept under the sand during the hours of the dark came scuttling up into the light. At the edge of the oasis, the baboons leapt from the trees, clapping their hands and shrieking for joy at the rising of the sun. Behind them on the oasis the cocks crowed, and in the desert the lions roared their early-morning roar before retreating to their caves to sleep during the heat of the day. Yalith and Oholibamah shared a silent and joyful companionship.

Now, in the warm and noisy tent, Oholibamah beckoned to Yalith. "Have you eaten?"

"No." Yalith shook her head. "I meant to eat with Grandfather, but I forgot all about food because there was a strange young—"

Ham interrupted her, calling out from the pile of skins on which he was reclining. "I have a headache, Oholi. I need you."

Oholibamah said sharply, "Let Anah rub your head. She is your wife."

"Her fingers do not have the touch that yours do." And, indeed, Oholibamah had a reputation for having healing in her fingers.

She was still sharp. "If you don't want a headache, don't eat and drink too much." She turned away and went to the cook pot, ladled some stew into a wooden bowl, and handed it to Yalith. The mammoth left Matred and came and nudged Yalith's knee.

"No, Selah," Yalith scolded. "You know I won't give you anything more to eat. You're getting fat." She deftly picked pieces of meat and vegetable from the bowl and ate them, then raised it to her lips to drink the broth. It tasted wonderful, and she realized that she was very hungry.

Beside her, Oholibamah sighed.

"What's the matter?" Yalith asked.

The mammoth moved to the older girl, who scratched its grey head. "I was walking through the town this morning. We needed some provisions. One of the nephilim came out of one of the bathhouses, smelling of oil and spices, and stood in my path." She paused.

"And?" Yalith prodded.

"He said that I was one of them, one of their daughters."

Yalith glanced at her mother, then back at Oholibamah. Thought of Eblis and his glorious purple wings. "Would that be so terrible?"

"It is absurd. I love my parents. I love my father."

Yalith had never seen Oholibamah's parents. And how would she herself feel if someone suggested that her father was not, in fact, her father? But now that Matred had put the thought in her mind, it was easy to believe that Oholibamah had been sired by a nephil. She had gifts of healing. Ham was right about that. Her voice when she sang was beautiful as a bird's. She saw things no one else saw.

But then, Yalith reminded herself, she, too, was different, the seventh child of her parents, and she knew quite well who her parents were, and that they had been disappointed when they had had a fourth daughter instead of a fourth son.

"Did you hear me saying that Mahlah is betrothed to a nephil?" she asked Oholibamah.

"Yes, I heard. Mahlah likes pretty things. The wives of

the nephilim live in houses of stone and clay, not in tents. I'm sure Mahlah feels proud to have been chosen."

"What do you think about it?" Yalith asked.

"I'm not sure. I'm not sure what I think about the nephilim. Especially if—" She broke off.

"And the seraphim?" Yalith asked.

"I'm not sure what I think about them, either." Oholibamah pressed her fingers against her ears as Ham started to shout.

For a small man, he had a powerful voice. "Selah, come here! If Oholibamah won't help me, then I need a unicorn!"

Anah said crossly, "You know a unicorn can't come near you."

"It doesn't have to come near," Ham grunted. "They can cast their light from any distance. It's only the light I need."

Anah muttered, "You need more than that."

"Yalith! You can call a unicorn. Or Selah! Call me a unicorn!"

A sudden flash of light made them all blink. It was as though lightning had somehow managed to get inside the heavy hides of the tent, perhaps flashing down through the roof hole.

"Get away!" Ham cried. "Who are you!"

He was not referring to the unicorn, which stood glimmering in the tent. On the skins right by Ham lay a very young man, with raw, sunburned skin, and eyes glazed with fever.

Matred peered down at the boy. "How did he get here? Ham, is he a friend of yours?"

Ham looked totally bewildered. "I've never seen him before."

"What is he?" Shem demanded.

The patriarch, who had been chewing on a mutton bone, looked at the boy. "Another kind of giant," he said disgustedly.

Oholibamah said, "Whoever he is, give him air. Don't crowd around. Look, he has sun fever. Oh my, he looks terrible."

Elisheba, Shem's wife, peered at the boy. "If he's a giant, he's a very young one."

Yalith managed to push between Matred and Oholibamah so that she could see. She shrieked, "It's my young giant!"

"What's that, daughter?" Matred asked. "You've seen him before?"

"In Grandfather's tent, when I took him his night-light."

The patriarch scowled. "If my father, Lamech, doesn't want a giant in his tent, why should I have him in mine?"

"Oh, please, Father," Yalith begged.

"You've really seen him before?" Oholibamah asked.

"When I brought Grandfather Lamech his night-light," Yalith repeated, "there was this young, sunburned giant in his tent." She looked at the fevered young man. "I'm not sure this is . . . Where's Japheth?"

The tent flap was pushed aside, and Japheth came in. "Why, here I am, looking for a unicorn and—"

Selah raised her trunk and trumpeted.

"Why!" Japheth exclaimed. "I've been looking all over the oasis and there's one right here! And—so is the Den, the one I've been looking for!" He dropped to his knees. "Great auk. Is he alive?"

Oholibamah ordered, "Move back, all of you." She put her hand against Dennys's bare chest. "He's alive, but he's burning with fever."

Anah moved back slightly, pushing her red hair away from her face with a dirty hand. "Is he a seraph or a nephil?"

Yalith shook her head. "He doesn't have wings. Oh, Japheth, I'm glad you're back. He is the other one, isn't he, the one you were looking for?"

"Yes," Japheth said. "But he looks burned nearly to death."

Oholibamah pressed her hand against the reddened forehead, wincing at the heat of it, turning to look for the unicorn, who had almost dimmed out of being. "Unicorn, can you help?"

The unicorn's outline sharpened, and it bent toward the flushed boy, and light flowed from its forehead, cooling the burning skin.

Ham pushed up from his pelts and blundered toward the unicorn. "Me. I need help. I feel sick. Help *me*." His fair hair was stringy with sweat. The even lighter hair on his chest held drops of moisture.

Again there was a flash of light, and when they could see again, the unicorn had disappeared.

"Idiot." Anah's green eyes sparked. "You know you can't get near a unicorn."

"Meanwhile," the patriarch said, "how are we going to get rid of this half-baked giant?"

"My dear," Matred protested, "surely we should show him some hospitality."

"My good father, Lamech, evidently threw him out of *his* tent," her husband retorted.

"No, Father!" Yalith protested. "You don't understand! There are *two* giants, and Grandfather has the other one in his tent and is taking care of him."

"I don't know what you're talking about," her father said. "How can there be two of these peculiar giants?"

"Oh, Father, if only you'd go to *see* Grandfather Lamech!"

"I will have nothing to do with coddling the old man. Or his strange giants. We have enough troubles without sick giants being added to them."

Yalith knelt beside Oholibamah and looked at the boy, who lay breathing shallowly, eyelids twitching slightly. Yalith reached out a tentative finger and touched the boy's flushed cheek. "You're not Sand? You're his brother?"

The reddened eyelids opened slightly. "Dennys. Dennys." Then the boy flung his arm over his face, as though to ward off a blow. His limbs began to shake convulsively.

"What's happened?" Japheth demanded. "Somebody's hurt him. And he doesn't recognize me."

"He's afraid!" Elisheba's voice was shocked.

Shem protested, "Surely Grandfather Lamech couldn't have hit him!"

"Never," Japheth defended swiftly.

"Not Grandfather!" Yalith spoke at the same time.

"El! His skin is rubbed raw!" Oholibamah exclaimed.

"Someone between Grandfather Lamech's tent and here has hurt him."

Matred bent close, asking softly, "Who could have done this? Even to a deformed giant?"

Japheth asked, "Dennys?"

"Dennys," the boy moaned.

"Where have you been? Did someone call you and the unicorn back into being? Who was it?"

Oholibamah touched her husband's hand. "Selah called a unicorn, and suddenly this wounded giant was here."

"But he's been somewhere else on the oasis." Japheth took his wife's hand and pressed it against his cheek. "And he has been abused. He's barely conscious. This is terrible."

Anah peered over Yalith's shoulder. "Are you sure he's human?"

Japheth frowned. "They said they are twins, but I think twins is human."

The patriarch murmured, "What with the wingèd creatures around, sleeping with the daughters of men, it is hard to know anymore who is human and who is not." He looked at Oholibamah, but not unkindly.

Oholibamah touched Dennys's forehead again, and he opened his eyes and flinched. "Shh. I will not hurt you." She looked at Yalith and Japheth. "The unicorn's horn has taken away some of his fever, but he is still very hot. Was it this bad when you saw him, Japheth?"

Japheth shook his head. "He was sun-sick, worse than the Sand, but not like this."

The patriarch asked, "You say there are two of these giants?"

"Two. Exactly alike. I left the one called Sand in Grandfather Lamech's tent"—he looked rather defensively at his father—"to go look for this one. And then, to my surprise, when I'd given up for the night, he was here, right in our own home tent."

Ham suggested, "We've never seen two look-alikes. We should send someone to Grandfather Lamech's tent to make sure there's another one."

"You doubt me?" Japheth demanded.

"Just want to make sure," Ham said.

Less hotly, Japheth said, "I found it difficult to believe at first, myself."

Cutting across their conversation, Oholibamah said, "We should bathe him with water, to try to keep him cool and moist."

"Water!" Matred exclaimed. "Even the mammoths are having difficulty scenting for water. But there is plenty of wine."

"Not my wine!" the patriarch roared. "Woman! You have no idea how hard I work in the vineyard."

"I do," Japheth commented mildly. "I work with you."

Oholibamah frowned slightly. "I don't think wine will do."

Japheth said, "Higgaion sprayed water from Grandfather Lamech's water pot on the Sand, and I think it helped." He looked toward Selah, who again was at Matred's feet.

Anah glanced out of the corner of her green eyes at pasty Ham, then at Dennys's recumbent form. "If his skin didn't look like raw meat, he'd be quite gorgeous."

Elisheba, Shem's wife, stocky and sensible-looking, with

thickly curling black hair and dark, placid eyes, snorted. "Keep away from him, Anah. You saw that the unicorn went right to him. For all his giant's size, he's barely more than a baby. And he's trembling. He's frightened."

Matred said fiercely, "Whatever, he shall not be ill-treated again."

Yalith looked gratefully at her mother.

Her father snorted. "Women. I'm always being bullied by women and their good works. Matred feeds any lazy beggar who comes to the tent, and Elisheba helps her keep the soup pot full."

"People do not choose to be poor and hungry," Matred said calmly. "We have enough, and to spare. Husband, I will not have this young giant abused."

"Do what you want with him," the patriarch said. "It makes no difference to me, as long as I'm not bothered about it."

Oholibamah looked at her husband. "We shouldn't leave him here. It's too hot and crowded. He was near death when the unicorn's light touched him, and I think he's still very ill."

"Listen to Oholi," Ham said. "She knows what she's talking about."

For Yalith, no matter what Japheth had said, Dennys was the same young man she had seen in her grandfather's tent. She had been afraid of him when she had first seen him, and now, this time, it was the young giant who seemed terrified. "Where can we take him?"

"He's just a child," Oholibamah suggested. "What about the women's tent?"

In Yalith's eyes, Sandy/Dennys was not a child.

Elisheba asked, "How near to the time of the moon is it for any of us?"

Matred, who was the one to keep track of such things, drew her brows together in thought, and touched her fingers, counting. "Not for a while. Soon he will be well enough to sleep here in the big tent. Or he will be dead."

Yalith shuddered. "Don't say that. He is our guest. We don't let our guests die."

"My dear," Matred said. "He is badly burned. His skin is raw, as though someone has been scraping him, like a carrot."

"Perhaps we should call on one of the seraphim?" Japheth suggested.

His mother nodded. Looked at Yalith. "Your friend Aariel would come, would he not?"

"I think so, yes." If she had to call Aariel, Yalith would make very certain that it was Aariel, not Eblis, though she was not sure why she felt that making sick calls was not part of the business of the nephilim.

"Elisheba," Matred continued, "if you will look into the chest by my sleeping skins, you will find some soft linen for him to lie on. The animal skins are too rough."

Anah simpered, "Mother always knows best, eh, Ham?" and moved away.

"I will crush some figs and make juice for him to drink." Matred always felt better when there was something to do.

Oholibamah pressed her palm against Dennys's forehead again. "He is so hot." She frowned, as he flinched and moaned, eyes tightly closed.

The patriarch said, "If he's going to die on us, get him out of the tent, quickly."

Yalith protested, "Father!"

Japheth reached comfortingly for her hand.

The patriarch said, "You will have to learn, daughter, that you cannot nurse every broken-winged bird or wounded salamander back to health."

"I can try!"

"Perhaps you make them suffer more that way," her father suggested, "than if you let them die?"

"Oh, Father—"

"Now." Matred bustled back. "Enough talk. Japheth will help us carry our strange little giant to the women's tent. Quick, now!"

4 ~ Grandfather Lamech
and Grandfather Enoch

When Dennys opened his eyes and found himself surrounded by little brown people, he was terrified. How had he got back into that terrible tent? Surely the unicorn wouldn't have returned him to the people who had tossed him out into the dung heap. Where was the unicorn?

Brilliant light flared against his closed eyelids, then darkness. He began to shiver, uncontrollably, and he felt a hand against his forehead. Cool. Gentle. It might almost have been his mother's hand. When he had had flu, only his mother's touch could cool him. "Mother," he moaned. Then, like a small child, "Mommy . . ."

A small woman leaned over him, looked at him with twinkly eyes surrounded by a crisscrossing of wrinkles. She did not look as though she would throw him into a garbage pit.

She moved away, and then two pairs of younger eyes were looking at him. One pair was a deep amber, with golden flecks, and belonged to a girl with hair as amber as the eyes. Beautiful eyes. Pure. The other girl's eyes were black, but a black which held light, and wisdom. Wherever he was, it could not be the tent from which he had been thrown by the men while the girl with flaming-red hair looked on.

Men. He looked around fearfully. There were men there. Spears were stacked against the side of the tent. One of the men held a wineskin. They did not seem to be threatening.

Then one of the small men came over to him, and smiled down at him, and he felt a great wave of relief. It was Japheth.

"Jay—" he whispered through parched lips.

"Den!" Japheth exclaimed gladly. "Oholi, he's coming back to consciousness!"

"Jay—" Dennys's teeth were chattering.

"Who's hurt you?" Japheth asked. "Can you tell us?"

Dennys closed his eyes again.

"Don't bother him with questions now," Oholibamah said.

"Don't be afraid, Den," Japheth encouraged. "We're not going to let anybody hurt you." Japheth bent down to him. "I'm going to carry you to some place where it's cool and quiet. Don't be afraid." Japheth picked Dennys up as carefully as possible and slung him over his shoulder.

Japheth was the tallest man in the tent; even so, he was so much smaller than Dennys that the boy's feet dragged on the ground, and he curled his fingers to keep them from scraping, too. No wonder in this place he and Sandy were thought of as giants. Dennys had a feverish vision of a trip his class had taken to a museum, where everybody had been amazed at the exhibition of knights' armor. How small those knights must have been! The people on this planet where he and Sandy had been flung were even smaller than the medieval knights.

His thoughts misted off, as tenuous as the virtual unicorns. The remembrance of the field trip to the museum was no more of a dream than his being carried by Japheth, who was amazingly strong for so small a man, a short young shepherd carrying a lamb. A very small shepherd. Dennys's toes scraped over a rock, and he cried out. If he could wake up, if he could shake off the heat of this feverish dream, he and Sandy would be in their bunk bed at home.

He opened his eyes, and the stars were brilliant, and he took a gulp of fresh air. Then his head brushed against a tent flap, and he felt himself being lowered onto something soft but so delicate that he could feel the rough skins underneath. He licked his cracked lips and realized that he had a raging thirst. "Water, Jay," he managed to croak, but could not summon the energy to add, *please.*

The black-eyed girl bent over him and held a wineskin to his lips, and he tasted something bitter and sweet at the same time. It stung his throat as he swallowed, but at least it was wet.

The black-eyed girl withdrew the skin. "We shouldn't give him too much wine."

"I forgot the fig juice," the plump, nut-like woman exclaimed. "I'll be right back."

Dennys heard the pad of bare feet, and the thud of a leather tent flap falling.

"He recognizes me now." Japheth's voice was troubled.

"I don't think he's afraid of us anymore," the younger girl said, the one with amber eyes.

"Water—" Dennys begged.

The amber-eyed girl said, wistfully, "Grandfather Lamech's wells still have water to spare."

The other girl agreed. "I wouldn't mind going to get a pitcherful, but I wish Grandfather Lamech did not live at the bottom of the oasis."

Japheth put his arm lovingly about the girl. "I'll take one of the camels and go. I don't want either of you crossing the oasis at this time of night. Every moon, there are more bandits and thieves."

"Oh, but be careful," the younger girl begged.

"Take my camel, love," the black-haired woman offered. "She's the swiftest, and you'll be safe on her."

"Thank you, Oholibamah, my wife." Japheth leaned to her and kissed her on the lips. Dennys, watching through the confusion of headache and fever, thought that it was a nice kiss. It was the kind of kiss he had seen his father give his mother. A real kiss. If he lived through this, he would like to kiss someone like that.

He heard Japheth leave, and closed his eyes, sliding into a fevered sleep. Like his virtual unicorn, he seemed to flicker in and out of being. He retreated deep within himself in order to retreat from the flaming pain of his scraped skin. He did not know how long he had been unconscious before he became aware of the two women speaking softly.

"Why won't my father reconcile with Grandfather Lamech?" the lighter voice asked. "I had to beg him for the oil for Grandfather's night-light."

The older girl, the one Japheth had kissed, with an odd name, Oholi something, had a voice like velvet. "Your father was hurt when Grandfather Lamech insisted on staying in his own tent."

"But as long as Grandfather can care for himself—"

"It's complicated," the dark voice said. "People don't revere old people the way they used to. They don't want to listen to their stories."

"I love Grandfather's stories!"

"I, too, Yalith."

Yalith, that was the name of the amber-eyed one. Yalith and Oholi. Dennys was vaguely aware of something cool touching his skin, something that numbed the pain.

The one called Oholi continued. "I always enjoy it when it's my turn to take him the night-light. And at least your mother feels as we do. She'll always manage to get the oil for us to take to him."

"When did it change?" Yalith asked. "People need to sit at the feet of the old people and listen. But now—I heard Anah say that her grandfather was put out in the desert to die, and his bones were picked clean by vultures."

"Oh, El, what are we coming to!"

At the trouble in the dark voice, Dennys opened his eyes.

"He is still so hot, so hot," Oholi said. "I wish we knew who had hurt him."

"But what could we do?" Yalith asked. "What in El's name could we do? People are ugly to one another today. Were we this cruel before the nephilim and the seraphim came?"

"I don't know."

"And who came first?"

"I don't know," the dark-eyed one repeated. "There is much we don't know. Where did this young wounded giant come from, for instance?"

"The other one," Yalith said, "the one in Grandfather Lamech's tent, said that they came from some kind of Nighted Place."

"United States," Dennys corrected automatically. Then Yalith's words registered. "Where is my brother?"

"Oh, good, he's coming to!" Yalith cried. Then said, kindly, to Dennys, "He's in my Grandfather Lamech's tent, being cared for by Grandfather and Higgaion. He's sun-struck, too, but not nearly as badly as you are."

The words began to buzz into meaninglessness as Dennys slid back into unconsciousness. He knew that the combination of too much sun, of being thrown into the pit, of scraping himself with sand, had made him ill. Very ill, indeed. This was far worse than when he had flu and a temperature of over 105°. Then he had antibiotics to fight the fever. Heaven knew what had been in that garbage pit. Heaven knew what horrible infection might follow. He thought that he was probably dying from overexposure to the sun, and he didn't much mind, except that he wished he was at home, on his own planet, rather than here, wherever in the universe here was, with these strange small people. He wished he was young enough to call out and wake his mother, so that she would come in to him and she would wake him from the nightmare and take off the knight's helmet that was pinching his skull and giving him a terrible headache.

He drifted into darkness.

For the first few days in Grandfather Lamech's tent, Sandy was miserable. His reddened skin bubbled into blisters. Where he didn't sting, he itched. But as his fever abated he began to look for Yalith in the evening. She did not come, and he felt only a weary indifference to the older women who brought the light, often staying to chat with the old man so that they would have an excuse to stare at Sandy.

He knew now that Dennys was safe in a tent near Japheth's, and that he was being well cared for. He knew that he and Dennys were objects of intense curiosity to the women who came each evening.

"I've never seen anything like it!" the oldest one, called Matred, exclaimed. "Except that our giant is burned so much more badly, I would not believe that they are two."

Anah and Elisheba took their turns taking the night-light to Grandfather Lamech, whispering over Sandy and his likeness to their own twin, still burning with fever in the women's tent. But they shyly held back from talking with Sandy, speaking softly so that he could not hear what they were saying.

Adnarel came each day, at least long enough to drip fresh herbs or powders into the water with which Higgaion continued to bathe the burned skin. The pelican kept the water jar filled, and when Grandfather Lamech thanked the great bird, he treated it as more than a pelican, causing Sandy to wonder. The old man spent hours cooking concoctions to tempt Sandy's appetite, and the ones that tasted best were the ones which reminded him of his mother's Bunsen-burner stews. Sandy wanted to ask the old man about the women who came in the evening and, most importantly, to ask him why Yalith was not one of them, but he was embarrassed and held his peace. And slept, and slept, healing.

On the first night when it was apparent that Sandy's fever had left him and he was weak but recuperating, Lamech suggested that they go out of the tent and sit under the stars. "Their light cannot harm your healing skin. Your skin is so fair, so fair. No wonder you had the sun fever." He held out his hand and Sandy took it, letting the old man pull him to his feet. His legs felt weak and unused. Lamech pushed through the tent flap, holding it aside for Sandy, who had to bend over to go through. Not far from the tent was a large and ancient fig tree, too old to bear fruit any longer. One root had pulled up from the ground and formed a low seat, before it dipped down into the earth again. Lamech sat on it, and beckoned to Sandy to sit beside him.

"Look." Lamech pointed to the sky.

Sandy had already been staggered by the glory of the night sky on his nocturnal visits to the grove which served as outhouse. He had tried to question the old man as to where he was, what planet, what galaxy. But Lamech had been bewildered. Sun, moon, and stars revolved around the oasis and the desert, put there by El for their benefit. So Sandy still had no idea where he and Dennys had ended up with their foolishness.

Now he simply looked up at the sky in awe. At home, even in winter when the air was clearest, even deep in the countryside where they lived, the stars were not like these desert stars. It seemed that he could almost see the arms of spiral galaxies moving in their great circular dance. Between the radiance of the stars, the blackness of the firmament was deeper and darker than velvet.

Except at the far horizon. "Hey," Sandy asked. "Why is it so light over there? Is there a big city, or something?"

"It is the mountain," Lamech said.

Sandy squinted and could just make out a range of mountains against the sky, with one peak higher than the others, a long way off, much farther off than the palm tree which had led them to Japheth and Higgaion and the oasis. "A volcano?" he asked.

Lamech nodded.

"Does it erupt often?"

Lamech shrugged. "Perhaps once in every man's lifetime. It is far away. When it goes off, we do not get the fire, but we get a rain of black dust that kills our crops."

The light tingeing the horizon was indeed so far away that it did not even dim the magnificence of the stars. Sandy asked, "Is it always this clear?"

"Except during a sandstorm. Do you have sandstorms on the other side of the mountain?" Lamech had set it in his mind that the twins came from beyond the mountains. That was as far away as he understood.

"No. We're nowhere near a desert. Everything is green where we live, except in winter, when the trees lose their leaves and the ground has a good cover of snow."

"Snow?"

Sandy reached down and picked up a handful of the clean white sand. "It is even whiter than this, and it is softer, and it—in winter it falls from the sky and covers the ground, and it's called poor man's fertilizer, and we need it to make sure we'll have good crops in summer. Dennys and I have a big vegetable garden."

The old man's face brightened. "When you are better and can go out in the daylight, I will show you my garden. What do you grow in yours?"

"Oh, tomatoes and sweet corn and broccoli and brussels sprouts and carrots and onions and beans, and almost anything you want to eat. We eat what we can, and what we can't, we can." Then he realized that the old joke would mean nothing to Lamech. He amended, "We can some of our produce, or freeze it."

"Can? Freeze?"

"Well, uh, putting by food that we've grown in the summer so that we'll have it to eat in the winter."

"Do you grow rice?" Lamech asked.

"No."

"You don't have good enough wells for it?"

"We have wells," Sandy said, "but I don't think we have the right kind of growing conditions for rice." He was going to have to look up rice cultivation when they got home.

"Lentils?" Lamech pursued.

"No."

"Dates?"

"It's too cold where we live for palm trees."

"I've never been on the other side of the mountains. It must be a very strange place."

Sandy did not know how to correct him. "Well, where we live, it's very different."

The old man murmured. "You are the beginning of change. We are living in end times. It can be very lonely."

Sandy, looking at the stars, did not hear. "Grandfather Lamech, is my brother really getting better?"

"Yes. That is what I am told."

"Who tells you?"

"The women, when they bring the night-light."

"Do the men never come? I haven't seen your son."

"It is only the women who care." Lamech's voice was bitter.

"Japheth—"

"Ah, Japheth. Japheth comes when he can, my youngest grandson, my dear boy." He sighed, wearily. "When my son, my only son, was born, I predicted that he would bring us relief from our work, from the hard labor that has come upon us because of the curse upon the ground."

Sandy felt an uncomfortable prickling. "What curse?"

"When our forebears had to leave the Garden, they were told, *Accursed shall the ground be on your account. It will grow thorns and thistles for you. You shall gain your bread by the sweat of your brow.*" He sighed again, then all his many wrinkles wreathed upward in a smile. "It is as I predicted. My son has brought us relief. The vines flourish. The herds and flocks increase. But he has grown proud in his prosperity. I am lonely in my old age. I am glad that you have come."

The mammoth came out of the tent and came to them, putting his head on Lamech's knee. "The women keep telling me that I am welcome in my son's tent. But I will stay here, where my son was born, where his mother died. That is no reason for my son to refuse to come see me, because I choose to remain in my own tent. He is stiff-necked. What will he do in his turn when his sons want his tent?"

"Does he want your tent?"

"I have the deepest and best wells on the oasis. I have always given him all the water he needs for his vineyards, but he complains about having to fetch it. Too bad. I will stay in my own tent."

"Maybe," Sandy suggested, "your son is stubborn because his father is stubborn?"

The old man smiled reluctantly. "It could be so."

"If he doesn't come to see you, why don't you go see him?"

"It is too far for an old man to walk. I have given my camels and all my animals to my son. I keep only my groves and garden." Lamech reached out and patted Sandy's knee with his gnarled hand. "I hope you won't be wanting to leave right away, now that you are getting well. It is pleasurable having someone to share my tent."

Higgaion nudged the old man.

Lamech laughed. "You're a mammoth, my dear Higgaion. And while I have deep devotion for you, I am feeling the need of a human companion, especially during my last days."

"Your last days?" Sandy asked. "What do you mean?"

"I am not as old as my father, Methuselah, but I am older than *his* father, Enoch. Now, there was a strange man, my grandfather. He walked with El and then he was not. And he was younger than I. El has told me to number my days."

Sandy felt distinctly uncomfortable. "How many numbers?"

Lamech laughed. "Dear young giant, you know that numbers are merely many or few. The voice of El said few. Few can mean one turn of the moon, or several."

"Hey, wait a minute," Sandy said. "Grandfather Lamech, are you telling me that someone said you're going to die?"

Lamech nodded. "El."

"El what?"

"El. These are troubled times. Men's hearts are turning to evil. It is good that I will be able to go quietly. My years are seven hundred and seventy and seven—"

"Hey! Wait!" Sandy said. "Nobody lives that long. Where I come from."

Lamech pursed his lips. "We have not used our long years well."

Suddenly the starlight seemed cold. Sandy shivered. Lamech's fingers again touched his knee. "Don't worry. I won't leave you until you are all well, and reunited with your brother, and are both able to take care of yourselves and return home."

"Home," Sandy said wistfully, looking up at the stars. "I don't even know where home is, from here. I'm not sure how we got here, and I'm a lot less sure about how we're going to get home."

Higgaion raised his trunk to touch his ear, and Sandy noticed that the scarab beetle was there, bright as an earring. Sandy understood that the glorious seraph Adnarel sometimes took the form of a scarab beetle—but of course that was impossible. Now he looked at the bronze glitter, suddenly wondering.

Lamech mused, "Japheth asked me where I would go when I die." He smiled. Even in the starlight, the skin of his skull showed through the thin wisps of hair. "I thought my Grandfather Enoch might come back, or send some kind of message. I hope my son will put aside his stubbornness long enough to come and plant me in the ground."

Higgaion nudged him again, and the old man laughed. "Who knows? Perhaps I will come up again in the spring, like the desert flowers. Perhaps not. Very little is known about such things. After living for so many hundreds of years, I look forward to a rest."

The mammoth moved over to Sandy, standing on his stocky hind legs and putting his big forepaws on Sandy's knees, like a dog. Sandy picked him up, holding him tightly for comfort, and the pink tip of the trunk delicately patted his cheek. "Grandfather Lamech, I think I'd better go back to the tent. I'm cold."

Lamech looked first at Sandy, then at the mammoth. "Yes. This is enough for a first excursion."

Sandy went gratefully to his sleeping skins, and Higgaion lay down at Sandy's feet. Sandy tried not to scratch. The pink skin under the paper-like flakes was tender. He closed his eyes. He wanted to see Yalith. He wanted to talk to Dennys. How were they going to be able to get home from this strange desert land into which they had been cast and which was heaven knew where in all the countless solar systems in all the countless galaxies?

5 ❦ The nephilim

Dennys was sleeping fitfully when he heard the tent flap move. He opened his eyes and could see only the small light of a stone lamp coming toward him. He called out in alarm. "Who is it?" Yalith or Oholibamah would not have needed the light.

He felt a gentle pressure, something soft touching his arm, and realized that it was a mammoth. He vaguely remembered seeing a mammoth when he had been in the big tent.

A bearded man squatted beside him. "We thought you might like Selah, our mammoth, for company, now that you are getting better."

"Thank you," Dennys said. "Who are you?"

"Yalith's father, Noah."

It was not always easy for Dennys to remember where he was. When his fever rose, he thought he was at home, and dreaming. When the fever dropped, he understood dimly that somehow or other he and Sandy had precipitated themselves into a primitive desert world inhabited by small brown people. He remembered Yalith, the beautiful, tiny person with amber hair and eyes who tended him gently. He remembered the slightly older person, and at least part of her name, Oholi, who poured first water and then unguents and oils onto his skin, and who seemed to know what to do to make him feel better. He remembered Japheth, Oholi's husband, who, like a shepherd, had carried Dennys to this tent, which he thought of as a strange kind of hospital.

He had not seen Yalith's father since he had been taken, half dead, from the big smelly tent to this smaller, quieter one. The piece of linen he had been given to lie on helped protect his raw, healing skin. Even so, it hurt to move. He shifted position carefully. "My brother Sandy, how is he?"

"Almost all well, I am told." Noah's deep voice was kind. The name had a familiar ring in this unfamiliar world, but Dennys could not place it in his fever-muddled mind. The man continued, "The women tell me he has made new skin. You, too, will be well soon."

Dennys sighed. That was still hard to believe, with the remains of his skin coming off in painful patches, leaving oozing misery until dark scabs formed. "When can I see my brother?"

"As soon as you are well. Not long."

"Where is he?"

"As you have been told. In my father Lamech's tent."

"I keep forgetting."

"That is from the sun fever."

"Yes. Brain fever, I think it used to be called in India."

"India?"

"Oh. Well. That's a place on our planet where the British—people with skin like mine—used to go to, oh, muck around with white men's burdens and stuff, and built an enormous empire. Anyhow, they couldn't take the sun. And their empire's gone. Thank you for taking such good care of me. How did you know the right things to do for burns?"

"It was mostly common sense," the man said. "Oholibamah can tell with her fingers how much fever you have, and we try to cool you accordingly. And she consulted with the seraphim about the use of herbs."

"Who are the seraphim?" Dennys asked.

The stocky brown man smiled. "You are better. This is the first time you have asked questions."

"You have been to see me before?"

"Several times."

Selah snuggled up against him, and he put his arm around her, and his skin was healed enough so that her fur did not scratch and hurt. "And seraphim?"

"They are sons of El. We do not know where they came from, or why they are here."

"Are they angels?"

"You have angels where you come from?"

"No," Dennys said. "But we don't have mammoths or virtual unicorns, either. I am not as much of a skeptic as I used to be."

"Skeptic?"

"Someone who doesn't believe in anything that can't be seen and touched and proved one hundred percent. Someone who has to have laboratory proof."

"Lab what?"

"Oh. Well. I guess you can't prove virtual particles any more easily than you can prove virtual unicorns."

"What kind of unicorns?"

"Oh. Just what I call them."

The man interrupted. "Are you feverish again?"

"No." Dennys touched the back of his hand to his cheek, which felt quite cool. "Sorry. Your name is—what?"

"Noah. How many times do I have to tell you?"

Noah. Noah and the flood. So they were on their own earth after all, and not in some far-flung galaxy. Somehow or other, he and Sandy had been flung through time into the pre-flood desert. That was a lot better than being in some unknown corner of the universe. Or was it? "I wish I had a Bible," he said.

"A— Perhaps you need a drink of something cool?"

"I'm all right. I'm sorry." There would not have been a Bible in Noah's time. Probably not even a written language. Not yet. Neither Dennys nor Sandy had given much of their concentration to Sunday school. They didn't go in for stories.

No? He remembered their mother reading to them every night until too much homework got in the way. What did she read? Stories. Greek and Roman myths. Indian tales, Chinese tales, African tales. Fairy tales. Bible stories.

Who was Noah? Noah and the flood. Noah built an ark and took his wife, and their sons and their sons' wives, and many animals, onto the ark. What about Yalith? He couldn't remember anything about Yalith. Or Oholi— Oholibamah. Japheth. Maybe that had a familiar ring.

Shem. Yes. Maybe. But not Elisheba. Elisheba was all right. She had rubbed ointment all over him one day, matter-of-factly, when something had taken Yalith and Oholi away, not flinching at the suppurating sores, the crusting scabs. She had talked through, at, and around him the day she had attended him in the hospital tent, and he remembered her muttering something about it being a shame to leave the old grandfather all alone in his tent with only a mammoth to take care of him.

Selah snuggled against Dennys's shoulder. He continued to try to think. There was Shem. And there was Ham. He barely remembered a small, pale man and a redheaded woman in the big tent that first night. "Is Higgaion all right?" he asked suddenly.

"Higgaion?" Noah sounded surprised. "He's helping take care of your brother."

"Are there many mammoths around?" Dennys asked.

"Very few. Many have been eaten by manticores, and most of the rest have fled to where they feel safer." Noah shook his head. "It is a hard time for mammoths. Hard times are coming for us all. El has told me that."

Dennis frowned. This pre-flood world was weird. Mammoths. Manticores. Virtual unicorns. Seraphim and—

"Who are the nephilim?" he asked.

Noah pulled at his beard. "Who knows? They are tall, and they have wings, though we seldom see them fly. They tell us that they come from El, and that they wish us well. We do not know. There is a rumor that they are like falling stars, that they may be falling stars, flung out of heaven."

"Seraphim, too?"

"We do not know. We do not know how it is that their skin is young and not yet shriveled from the sun, though they are ageless, it would seem—older, even, than my Grandfather Methuselah."

—Old as Methuselah. It had a familiar ring. Vaguely.

Dennys shifted on Matred's linen cloth. The remnant of his bundle of clothes had been found, and taken by Japheth and Oholibamah, to be aired and put away. In this hot land he would not need flannel shirts or cable-knit sweaters. He had been given a soft kid loincloth, and Yalith had told him that Sandy had been given one, too.

In this tent where he was recovering, the stench was less disturbing than in the big tent. Yalith had bathed him with water scented with herbs and flowers. Oholibamah had rubbed him with fragrant ointment. Both young women were reticent about where they came by the perfumes, and Dennys thought he had heard Yalith saying something about Anah and Mahlah. Anah: Ham's redheaded wife, he reminded himself. Mahlah was Yalith's sister, who, it appeared, seldom came home. Who were all these people he did not remember as being part of the story? He needed Sandy. Sandy might be able to suggest some way for them to get home before the flood. How much had this El told Noah?

Noah said, "El has told me that these are end times for us all. Perhaps we will have a great earthquake."

"An earthquake?"

Noah shrugged. "The mind of El is a great mystery."

"Is he good, this El?"

"Good and kind. Slow to anger, quick to turn again and forgive."

"But you still think he's going to nuke everybody?"

"What's that?"

"You think he's going to send some big disaster and wipe everybody out?"

Noah shook his head. "It is true, as El says, that people's hearts are turned to wickedness."

"Yalith's isn't," Dennys said. "Oholibamah's and Japheth's aren't. I'd be dead if it wasn't for them."

"And for my wife, Matred," Noah added. "I might not have let you stay in my tents had it not been for Matred." He looked thoughtfully at Dennys. "Sometimes I have wondered why I let the women insist on keeping you. But I think you mean us no harm."

"I don't. We don't. Listen, what about my brother? When can I see Sandy?"

"As you have been told, he is in my father's tent." Noah's voice indicated that the subject was now closed.

"Have you seen him? Sandy?" Dennys asked.

"I do not go to my father's tent."

"Why not?"

"He is a stiff-necked old man, insisting on staying alone in his own tent, with his wells, the best in the oasis."

"But why don't you go see him?" Dennys was baffled.

"He is old. It is nearly time for him to die. He can no longer tend to his crops."

"But don't you help him?"

"I have all I can do, taking care of my herds and my vineyards."

"But he's your father!"

"He should not be so stubborn."

"Listen, he's taking care of Sandy all by himself. He

doesn't have Yalith or Oholibamah to do the nursing. Only the mammoth."

"One of the women takes him a light every night."

"But he's your father," Dennys protested. "Wouldn't he appreciate it if you took him the night-light?"

Before Noah's growl became audible, the tent flap shifted and a pelican waddled in, followed by Yalith. A pelican seemed a strange creature to appear in this desert place. The bird approached Dennys, then opened its enormous bill, and from it flowed a stream of cool, fresh water, filling the large bowl from which the women bathed him.

Dennys asked, "Hey, you've been here before, haven't you?"

Yalith spoke delightedly. "He is truly better! He's remembering things."

The water felt healing as Yalith dipped a cloth in it and cooled his skin. She knelt beside him and with the wet cloth touched some of the loosened scabs. "They will soon be off."

Dennys regarded the pelican. "Where did the water come from?"

"From Grandfather Lamech's. And the pelican has been kind enough to bring it to us, flying across the oasis."

The pelican nodded gravely to Dennys.

"Do you have a name?"

The pelican blinked.

Yalith said, "When he is a pelican, we usually call him pelican."

"When he is a pelican! What else is he?"

"Don't confuse the young giant," Noah said.

"I can't be much more confused than I am," Dennys

expostulated. It was a relief to know that he was still on his own planet; even so, he felt lost, and far from anything familiar.

The pelican stretched its angled wings toward the roof hole, raised its beak, seemed to thin out and stretch upward, and suddenly a tall and radiant personage was looking down at Dennys.

"What—" he gasped.

"A seraph," Yalith said.

The glowing skin of the seraph was the color of Yalith's, and there were great silvery wings, and hair the color of the wings. Was it a man? A woman? Did it matter? Yet, with Yalith and Oholibamah, and even more with Anah, Dennys was very well aware that he was male and they were female.

The seraph raised its wings, then dropped them loosely. "Fear not. I am Alarid, and I have been helping with your healing. At last you are getting better. No. Don't try to stand. You are still too weak." Strong arms enfolded Dennys, and he was taken out of the tent and lowered onto a soft bed of moss. In the starlight, the moss shimmered like water.

"There," the seraph said. "So. I am Alarid. And you are the Den."

"Dennys."

"Den is simpler."

"And your name is Alarid? And what about Oholibamah?"

Alarid smiled gravely. "I take your point, Dennys. Forgive me. Now, I have conferred with my companion, Adnarel, who has been helping to take care of the Sand."

"Sandy. Alexander."

"Alexander? Is there not an Alexander who wants to conquer the world?"

"Not in our time," Dennys said. "Way back in history. Not as far back as now. But back."

"Ah," Alarid said. "I tend to see time in pleats. Now, Dennys, there seems to be considerable confusion over who and what you are, and why you are here."

In his weakness, Dennys could not hold back the tears which sprang to his eyes. "We are fifteen-year-old boys who come from a long time away."

"You come from a far time, and yet you speak the Old Language?"

"The what?"

"The Old Language, the language of creation, of the time when the stars were made, and the heavens and the waters and all creatures. It was the language which was spoken in the Garden—"

"What garden?"

"The Garden of Eden, before the story was bent. It is the language which is still, and will be, spoken by all the stars which carry the light."

"Then," Dennys said flatly, "I don't know why I speak it."

"And speak it with ease," Alarid said.

"Does Sandy speak it, too?" Dennys asked.

Alarid nodded. "You were both speaking it when you met Japheth and Higgaion in the desert, were you not?"

"We certainly didn't realize it," Dennys said. "We thought we were speaking our own language."

Alarid smiled. "It *is* your own language, so perhaps it

is best that you didn't realize it. Do others of your time and place speak the Old Language?"

"I don't know. Sandy and I aren't any good at languages."

"How can you say that," Alarid demanded, "when you have the gift of the original tongue?"

"Hey. I don't know. Sandy and I are the squares of the family. Our older sister and our little brother are the special ones. We're just the ordinary—"

Alarid interrupted him. "Because that is how you are, or because that is how you choose to be?"

Dennys looked at the seraph, his eyes widening. "What happened to the Old Language?"

"It was broken at Babel."

"Babel?"

"The tower of human pride and arrogance. It has not happened yet, in this time you are in now. You do not know the story?"

Dennys blinked. "I think I remember something. People built a big tower, and for some reason they all began to speak in different languages, and couldn't understand each other anymore. It was in, oh, pre-history, and it's a story to, sort of, explain why there are so many different languages in the world."

"But underneath them all," Alarid said, "is the original language, the old tongue, still in communion with the ancient harmonies. It is a privilege to meet one who still has the under-hearing."

"Hey," Dennys said. "Listen. I guess because we got here so unexpectedly and everything was so strange, and

we didn't have time to think, and when we met Japheth
it just seemed natural to speak to him—"

"It is a special gift," Alarid told him.

"We're not special, neither Sandy nor I. We're just the
sort of ordinary kid who gets along without making waves."

"Where in the future," Alarid asked him abruptly, "do
you come from?"

"A long, long way," Dennys said. "We live at the end of
the twentieth century."

Alarid closed his eyes. "A time of many wars."

"Yes."

"And the heart of the atom has been revealed."

"Yes."

"You have soiled your waters and your air."

"Yes."

"Because you speak the Old Language there must be
some reason for you to be here. But for the future to touch
the past can be dangerous. It could cause a paradox. How
did you get here?"

"I'm not sure." Dennys frowned, then added, "Our
father is a physicist who specializes in space travel, in the
tesseract."

"Ah, yes. But space travel is supposed to deal with space,
not time."

Dennys said, "But you can't separate space and time. I
mean, space/time is a continuum, and . . ."

Yalith and Noah came out of the tent, and Yalith put
her hand lightly against Alarid's. "Look, he is very pale.
You are tiring him."

"Be careful of our young giant," Noah warned.

Alarid regarded Dennys. "You are right. This is enough for tonight." The seraph's eyes were compassionate, and their silver-green seemed to darken. "I am glad that you are better, and that you are coming back to yourself. Please, be very careful what you say, what you do. Be careful that you do not change anything."

"Listen," Dennys said. "All I want is to go home. To my own time. I'm just grateful to be on my own planet, and I'm not a bit interested in rewriting the Bible." Did Alarid know that there was going to be a Bible? That there was going to be a flood? He looked at the seraph, whose face, serene and severe at the same time, did not change expression. Dennys was willing to accept that Alarid and the pelican who brought the water were somehow one and the same, but he was not willing to accept that his presence in this time and place might have an effect on anyone except himself. And, of course, Sandy.

"Sleep well, Dennys," Alarid said. "Yalith and Oholibamah will continue to take good care of you."

—Yalith, Dennys thought. For Yalith he might be willing to change history.

Sandy could not sleep. Not only was the tent hot, but Higgaion was snoring. Grandfather Lamech was not. Grandfather Lamech was tossing. Turning. Grunting. Sighing.

At last, Sandy could not stand it any longer. He crawled over to Grandfather Lamech's sleeping skins. "Grandfather, are you awake?"

"Um."

"What's the matter?"

The old man grunted.

Sandy spoke to him as he would have to Dennys. "Come on. I know something's bothering you. What is it?"

"El spoke to me."

Sandy tried to peer at him through the dark. Did this mean that the old man was about to die? Right then? That night?

But the old man said, "Great troubles are coming after I die. Terrible things are going to happen."

"What kind of terrible things?"

Lamech moved restlessly. "El did not say. Only that men's hearts are evil and hard, and it repents El that he has made human creatures."

"So what's he going to do about it?"

"I don't know," Lamech said. "But I fear for my son and his family. El plans to spare no one. I fear for Yalith. I fear for you, Sand, so far from your home."

"Oh, I can take care of myself," Sandy said automatically. But his words sounded hollow.

Yalith and Oholibamah came to Dennys in the deep dark just before dawn.

"You need to get out of the tent into some air," Oholibamah told him. "You need to exercise. You will not recover until you walk about under the sky."

"Starlight is healing." Yalith's voice was as gentle, he thought, as a small brook. But there were no brooks in this arid land.

He followed them out of the tent. Each took one of his

hands, and their hands were small as children's. They walked past the grove which served as outhouse, which was as far from the tents as he had ventured. Beyond them, the large tent was a dark shadow, with the smaller tents clustered about it.

His bare feet were still tender, and he walked gingerly. The girls guided him to the smoothest ways, until the sharp dry grasses and pebbles gave way to sand, and they were in the desert. The sand felt cool to the burning soles of his feet.

They paused at a low slab of white rock, which cast a silvery shadow on the sand. "Japheth and I agreed that this is as far as you should go," Oholibamah said. "Let's sit here and rest for a while. We'll take you back to the tent before dawn."

He sat between them on the rock, leaning back on his elbows so that he could look up at the sky. "I've never seen so many stars."

"You don't have stars where you come from?" Yalith asked.

"Oh, yes, we have stars. But our atmosphere is not as clear as yours, and not nearly as many stars are visible."

Yalith clasped Dennys's arm tightly. "It is frightening when the stars are hidden by the swirling sand. Their song is distorted, and I can't hear what they say."

"What the stars say?" Dennys asked.

"Listen," Yalith suggested. "Alarid says you are able to understand."

At first, Dennys heard only the desert silence. Then, in the distance, he heard the roar of a lion. Behind them, on the oasis, the birds chirred sleepily, not yet ready for their dawn concert. A few baboons called back and forth. He listened, listened, focusing on one bright pattern of stars. Closed his eyes. Listened. Seemed to hear a delicate, crystal chiming. Words. *Hush. Heal. Rest. Make peace. Fear not.* He laughed in excitement. Opened his eyes to twinkling diamonds.

Yalith laughed, too. "What did they say?"

"They told me—I think—to get well, and—and to make peace. And not to be afraid. At least, I think I heard them, and I don't think it was just my imagination." Suddenly he was glad that Sandy was not there. Sandy was pragmatic. Sandy would likely think Dennys was hallucinating from sunstroke. At school, if Dennys got lost in a daydream, Sandy always managed to cover for him.

"Yes, that is what the stars told you." Yalith turned toward him with a delighted smile, very visible in the starlight. "You see!" she said to Oholibamah. "It is not everybody who can listen to the night. If the stars told you to make peace, Den, perhaps you will be the one to make peace between my father and my grandfather."

"A big perhaps," Oholibamah said.

"But maybe, maybe he can." She turned back to Dennys. "What else do you hear?"

Dennys listened again. Heard the wind rattling the palm leaves like sheafs of paper. There seemed to be words in the wind, but he could not make any sense out of them. "I can't understand anything clearly—"

Yalith withdrew her fingers and clasped her hands together. Shook her head. Opened her eyes. "The wind seems to be talking of a time when she will blow very hard, over the water. That's strange. The nearest water is many days away from here. I cannot understand what she is trying to say."

"The wind blows where she wills," Oholibamah said. "Sometimes she is gentle and cooling. Sometimes she is fierce and blows in our eyes and stings our skin like insects and we have to hide in the tents until she is at peace again. It is good, dear Den, that you have not come at a time when the wind blows hot against the sand. You will heal better now, at the time when she is more gentle, and the grapes and gardens grow."

They were silent then, listening to the dawn noises becoming louder, as birds and baboons began to get ready to greet the day. Tentatively, Dennys reached for Yalith's hand. She gave his fingers a little squeeze, then freed herself and jumped up. "It is time we took you back to the tent. This is more than enough for a first excursion. How do you feel?"

"Wonderful." Then, acknowledging: "A little tired." It would be good to lie down on the soft linen spread over the skins. To sleep a little. To have something cool to drink. He stifled a yawn.

"Come." Oholibamah held out her strong hands. To his surprise, he needed her help in getting up.

When Yalith and Oholibamah needed ointments and unguents for Dennys's burned skin, Anah, or Mahlah, if she happened to be home, would take them across the oasis to the close cluster of houses and shops to meet Tiglah, Anah's sister.

"I don't like it," Japheth said to his wife. "I don't like your going to such places."

She bent toward him to kiss him. "We don't go in. I wouldn't take Yalith into such a place even if Mahlah—"

Japheth gave a shout of anger and anguish. "What has happened to Mahlah!"

Oholibamah said, softly, "We all have choices to make, dear one, and we do not all choose the same way."

"Why can't I get what you need for you?"

"Oh, love, it is a house for women. You would not be welcome."

"I have seen men coming out. And nephilim."

"Japheth. My own. Please don't argue. We'll be all right. Anah is tough."

"And Mahlah?"

Oholibamah put her arms around her husband, pressed her cheek against his. Did not answer.

Mahlah went with Oholibamah and Yalith less and less frequently, because she was less and less often in the home tent. And when she was there, she came in late, after everybody else was asleep, then slept late herself, and managed to avoid confrontation with Matred.

Matred, herself, allowed Mahlah to avoid her. She was waiting for her daughter to come to her and her husband with Ugiel, according to custom, but Ugiel did not come, and Mahlah did not speak, and Matred said nothing to Noah of Mahlah's betrothal to a nephil. Until the betrothal was made formal, and recognized by Mahlah's family, there would be no talk of marriage.

Marriages were often casual affairs, no more than an agreement between the two sets of parents, with the bride's mother and father bringing her to the tent of the groom. Matred liked to have things done properly, not overdone, but well done. Yalith and Mahlah's two older sisters, Seerah and Hoglah, had been taken to their husbands' tents after Matred and Noah had prepared a feast, with plenty of Noah's good wine.

Elisheba, Shem's wife, had come quietly to Noah's compound and Shem's tent, accompanied by her widowed father, and bearing several gold rings, and her teraphim, the small figures of her household gods. Anah, Matred said, had had a vulgar wedding, with crowds of people, many uninvited. There were musicians, dancers, and far too much wine, inferior, at that—who would dare compete with Noah's wine?—for far too many days. Such excesses were not only unnecessary, they were unseemly.

Cleaning out the big tent with Yalith's help, Matred said, "I do not understand Mahlah."

Yalith shook out a sleeping skin. "Neither do I. I wish she would come speak to you and Father, instead of avoiding you."

Matred fiercely beat the dust out of one of the floor skins. "If your father knew what she's up to, he'd be furious. There's something on his mind, something he's not telling me about, or he'd have noticed her strange behavior. You think that this Ugh—"

"Ugiel."

"That nephil—you think he means to marry her?"

"I don't know." Yalith scrubbed out one of the stone lamps with sand. "Mahlah thinks so."

"Speak to her," Matred begged. "Try to make her see

reason. All she needs is to come to us with her nephil and tell us that they are betrothed, and we will make all the arrangements for a wedding feast."

"I'll try," Yalith said, "but I'm not sure she'll listen." Mahlah had always been closer to and more like the older sisters than Yalith, the youngest, the different one. "I'll try," she reassured her mother.

The next day she went with Oholibamah and Anah to get a fresh supply of the ointment that softened Dennys's scabs. Perhaps Mahlah would be with the redheaded Tiglah, and Yalith could talk with her then.

Anah walked slowly, with her usual undulating of hips. Yalith and Oholibamah walked on ahead.

"Tiglah frightens me," Yalith whispered to Oholibamah. "I know she's Anah's sister, and she is probably the most beautiful woman on the oasis, but—"

"Her beauty is for sale," Oholibamah stated flatly. "But there is no reason to be afraid of her."

They turned onto the narrow path which ran between low white stone buildings. "I don't like coming here," Yalith murmured.

"I don't like it, either," Oholibamah said, "but there is no other way to get the salves for the Den. The last of his scabs will be off in a few days. Then we can forget the ointment. The herbal water the pelican brings will be enough."

"Den is getting better," Yalith said. "That's one good thing."

"Only one?" Oholibamah laughed.

Yalith shuddered. "Everything seems to be changing.

Mahlah avoids our parents. And my father keeps hearing the Voice in the vineyards, and whatever it says is upsetting him, but he won't tell us what El says."

"What El says is good." Oholibamah smiled. "El said that Japheth was to marry. That is why I am here."

"You wouldn't rather have waited?"

"I love Japheth." Oholibamah's voice was tender. "I know we were both very young and unready for marriage. But we love each other. When the time comes, we will have children together."

Yalith sighed. "I would like to love someone the way you love Japheth."

"Be patient, little sister. Your time will come."

They had reached the white house with the brightly beaded curtains at the entry, the house where Tiglah got the ointments they needed, and they stopped to wait for Anah, who made it very clear that she was doing them a great favor in being the go-between. The beads glittered and jangled, and Tiglah came out, followed by Mahlah— Tiglah with her head of radiant red hair, Mahlah with her cascade of black hair, the two girls startling foils for each other.

"Where's Anah?" Tiglah asked.

"She's coming." Oholibamah looked back down the path to where Anah was slowly following them.

"Mahlah!" Yalith exclaimed. "I'm glad to see you. I need to talk to you."

Mahlah raised her hands and pushed back a thick fall of black hair. "That's funny. I want to talk to you, too. Shall we go inside?"

"No." Yalith drew back. "Please—"

"I could have your hair brushed," Mahlah coaxed, "the way Tiglah's and mine is, so it would look more beautiful."

"No," Yalith repeated.

Mahlah shrugged. "We can sit over here then, while Anah and Oholibamah go with Tiglah to get the ointment." She led Yalith a little way down the path to a low wall. Yalith, with sudden and unexpected shock, saw that Mahlah's usually flat belly was softly rounding.

"Mahlah," she urged. "Please, please, you and Ugiel please come to our parents and tell them that you're betrothed."

Mahlah's little hands proudly touched the small roundness. "And will be married soon."

"Then please come and tell them. Mother will need time to prepare a wedding feast."

"No, she won't," Mahlah said. "That is not how things are done with the nephilim. I will have a nephil wedding."

"But Mother—"

Again Mahlah's little hands stroked her stomach. "I'm sorry, really, I'm sorry. But she had it her own way with our sisters. She'll probably have it her own way with you. So she'll just have to let me do it my way."

"But why? Isn't the old way good enough for you?"

Mahlah laughed. "Customs change. We have to move with the times." There was a slight hiss to her speech which Yalith had never heard before. She sounded more like Ugiel than like Mahlah. The sisters sat side by side on the wall, the silence between them becoming more and more uncomfortable, until at last Yalith broke it.

"What did you want to see me about?"

"Can't you guess?"

"No."

"Eblis."

Yalith looked at her in surprise. "But why—"

"He likes you," Mahlah said. "He says he has offered to teach you."

"No—"

"Why not?"

"I'm taking care of the Den. That's why we're here, to get salve for him."

Again Mahlah sounded more like Ugiel than like Yalith's sister. "That's all very noble. But it needn't stop you from going out with Eblis. Don't you realize what an honor that is, to have Eblis interested in you?" She sounded strangely sibilant.

"I know he does me much honor." Yalith's voice was low.

"What's wrong, then?"

"I have to stay with the Den," Yalith whispered.

"I know you're taking good care of him. But Oholi is there, too, isn't she?"

"She—she is Japheth's wife. She has to be in her own tent. She tells me what to do, but—"

"Little sister," Mahlah said. "Don't be foolish."

Yalith looked down at her long, straight toes. Blurted out, "I don't care about Eblis as much as I do about the Den and the Sand."

"What!" Mahlah was scandalized.

"You heard me."

"But we don't know if they're even human!"

"We know that the nephilim are not," Yalith retorted.

"They're more than human," Mahlah said proudly.

"The two—what are they? twins?—they seem subhuman."

"No," Yalith protested. "They're human, I know they are."

"Giants human?"

"Yes."

"And you think if you start going out with giants, human or no, our parents wouldn't be upset?"

"Everybody loves them . . ."

"Yes? Anyhow, they're too young, much too young."

"I know that." Yalith hung her head even lower. "But I think that, where they come from, years are counted differently than here. And I would be willing to wait."

"For which one?" Mahlah demanded.

A slow flush spread across Yalith's cheeks. She still thought of the twins as one person divided into two places. "I saw the Sand first, in Grandfather Lamech's tent, and I have helped bring the Den back to life when he was nearly dead."

"That is not enough reason for this stupidity. Eblis can give you anything you want."

"Even if I want the twins?"

"Don't be a fool," Mahlah snapped, and jumped down from the wall as Anah and Oholibamah came toward them, Oholibamah carrying a small jar.

"Well, Mahlah." Anah looked at her pointedly. "Are you getting ready to move into your own tent?"

Mahlah smiled a secret smile and tossed her head so that the dark hair glinted in the light. "I will not have a tent. I will have a house, a house of white stones." She drew back as a snake uncoiled at her feet, spreading a jeweled hood. "Ugiel—" she gasped.

For a moment of mirage, the snake seemed to uncoil upward, to raise great lavender wings, to quiver with white skin and amethyst eyes. Then the mirage was gone, and the snake undulated across the path and disappeared into a clump of scrubby palmettos.

Yalith reached for Oholibamah's hand.

Anah gave Mahlah a malicious smile. "Is he playing tricks with you?"

Mahlah raised her head proudly. "Ugiel comes to me only when I am alone." She turned back to Yalith, asking in such a low voice that she excluded the others, "If it were not for the young giants, would you go with Eblis?"

"I don't know," Yalith said. "I don't know."

Mahlah spoke in a louder voice. "Tell our parents I'll be sure to let them know when I'm married."

"Couldn't you bring yourself to tell them, beforehand?" Yalith begged.

Mahlah shrugged. "We'll see. I have to go now." And she turned back to the low white house and shouldered her way through the tinkling curtain of beads.

"Let's go," Anah said. "I have other things to do." And instead of dawdling as she had done on the way in, she strode off impatiently.

Oholibamah spoke calmly. "It's really very good of Anah, and of Tiglah, too, to get the ointments for us."

"They aren't doing it for nothing," Yalith said. "I gave them all my share of the figs, and the crop was good this year. And you gave them all your almonds."

Oholibamah stated a known fact. "Anah and Tiglah don't know how to do something for nothing. That's how they are."

"But Mahlah wasn't like that," Yalith protested. "She's changed. I don't know her anymore."

She jumped as a rat scuttled across her toes. Again there was a flickering of height, of wings and brilliant eyes, and then there was only the sleek body of the rat. Yalith thought of the dragon/lizard Eblis, who could offer her more than she could dream. And then she thought of the twins, of Sandy bowing to her in her grandfather's tent, of Dennys sitting with her at night—Dennys, who was able to understand the language of the stars.

And she knew she would never go with Eblis.

She turned, to see tears in Oholibamah's eyes. "Oholi," she started in surprise.

Oholibamah reached up to wipe away her tears, smiled her quick smile. "This morning I saw my face reflected in the water jar. Oh, Yalith, little Yalith, I love my father, and now I don't know if he is my father, after all."

Yalith took her sister-in-law's hand. "If you love him, he is your father, no matter what."

Oholibamah nodded gratefully. "Thank you, little sister. I needed to hear that."

"You are my brother's wife," Yalith continued, "and my friend. And if—well, if the nephilim are related to the seraphim, which my father believes, then you are like the seraphim."

"Hurry up," Anah called, and beckoned to them imperiously.

"We're coming," Oholibamah said. And they hurried toward the central section of the oasis, where Noah's vineyards were, and his grazing grounds, and his tents. And where Dennys was waiting for them.

The moon set, its path whiter than the desert sands dwindling into shadow. The stars moved in their joyous dance across the sky. The horizon was dark with that deep darkness which comes just before the dawn.

A vulture flew down, seemingly out of nowhere, stretching its naked neck, settling its dark feathers.

—Vultures are underestimated. Without us, disease would wipe out all life. We clean up garbage, feces, dead bodies of man and beast. We are not appreciated.

No sound was heard and yet the words seemed scratched upon the air.

A scarab beetle burrowed up out of the sand and blinked at the vulture. —It is true. You help keep the world clean. I appreciate you.

And it disappeared beneath the sand.

A crocodile crawled across the desert, lumbering along clumsily, far from its native waters. It was followed by the dragon/lizard, who stretched his leather wings, showing off. A dark, hooded snake slithered past them both.

A small, brown, armored creature, not much bigger than the scarab beetle, skittered along beside the snake. —We are invulnerable. We have survived the fire of the volcanoes, the earthquakes that pushed the continents apart and raised the mountain ranges. We are immortal. We cover the planet.

A bat, brighter than gold, swooped low over the cockroach. —You are proud, and you can survive fire and ice, but I could eat you if I had to. I hope I never have to.

And the golden bat soared high, a bright flash against the dark.

A tiny mimicry of a crocodile, with a blunt nose, a skink scrabbled along beside the crocodile and the dragon/lizard. —I am small, and swift, and my flesh is not edible and causes damage to the brain. I am the way that I am. That is how I am made.

On the skink's back, a flea tried to dig through the armored flesh. —I, too, am the way that I am.

A shrill whine cut across the clear air. A mosquito droned. —I, too. I, too. I will feast on your blood.

A small, slimy worm wriggled across the sand, leaving a thin trail. A slug's viscous path followed. —I am not like the snail, needing a house. I am sufficient unto myself.

A red ant crawled along the dragon/lizard's wing, and held tight as it tried to shake the biting insect off. A rat, sleek and well filled, wriggled its nose and whiskers and looked at the vulture's naked neck. —I, too, eat the filth off the streets. I eat flesh. I prefer living flesh, but I will take what I can get. I, too, help keep the world clean.

No sound was heard. Like negative light, the words cracked the desert night.

The twelve oddly assorted creatures began to position themselves into a circle.

The nephilim.

Oholibamah lay in Japheth's arms on a large, flat stone a short walk into the desert. So intent were they in each other that they did not notice the lion pacing past them, the pelican flying high in the sky, the scarab beetle coming out of the sand.

"My beloved," Japheth whispered into the pearly shell of Oholibamah's ear. "My mother spoke to me about it long ago. If you have nephil blood, it explains some of your healing power."

"But I don't know—it isn't certain—"

Japheth covered her mouth with his. Then pulled back just enough to say, "You are my wife, and we are one, and that is all that matters."

And they were one. And it was good.

Yalith left the tent and went outside to wait for dawn. She had spent over an hour working at Dennys's scabs, carefully pulling off those which were loose enough. Most of the oozing sores had healed. More and more of Dennys's care was given over to her, as Oholibamah could trust her to do what the boy needed. Oholibamah, after all, had duties in her own tent.

Matred prepared meals for the boy, soups, and mashed fruits which were soft enough for him to swallow.

"But what do we do with him when he is well?" Noah asked his wife.

"He is our guest," Matred said. "We ask him what we can do to help him."

"He wants to go home," Yalith said.

"Yes, but where is home?" her mother asked.

Now Yalith crossed one of her father's vineyards, went to the small grove that the women used, and relieved herself, then walked on until she came to where the desert lapped whitely against the oasis. She picked up a handful of the fine sand and rubbed it against her palms, between her fingers, to clean them.

The moon had set, and the dawn stars were low on the horizon. She would take a long nap the next day during the heat of the sun. Often, the best sleeping was done then.

In the coolness just before morning she liked to go sit on one of the great exposed rocks and rest, and listen to the slow song of the setting stars. Lamech, her grandfather, had taught her how to listen to the stars. Only Yalith and Japheth, of Noah and Matred's children, could understand the celestial language.

Matred tended to think it a waste of time. "I have too much to do, keeping tent. How else would I keep the soup pot full for the poor who come to us for food? Who would keep the manticore from eating Selah if I didn't have boiling wine to throw in its ugly face? Who would see to it that the great auk's eggs aren't stolen? Who else dares to speak to the gorgons and griffins? And what with everybody's appetite, I never have a chance to get away from the hearth."

Yalith did her fair share of the work, and now she was doing most of Mahlah's, too, but she needed time to herself, to listen to what the stars might have to say. Her father heard a Voice in the vineyards, but it seemed to Yalith that in the quiet dawn there were voices all around her, waiting to speak, waiting for her to hear. When the birds woke and started their orchestra, the other voices would be quiet. She was filled with a vague sense of foreboding, but she had to come and listen.

When she was not listening for whatever it was that was going to be spoken, she found her mind sliding to thoughts of the twins. As she spent more time with Dennys, nursing him through the chills and fever of his delirium, she saw that the twins might look alike but they were definitely not one boy in two skins.

The twins were often the topic of conversation in the big tent in the evenings—how they were alike, and how they were different. It was generally accepted that they must be some strange breed of giant, from the other side of the mountains. Although they were immensely tall, they were also unbelievably young.

"Fifteen, he told me," Matred said one evening when it was she who had taken the lamp to Grandfather Lamech, and some of her special broth to Sandy. "Fifteen," she repeated to the others in the big tent. "At fifteen, our men are still children. The Sand and the Den are not babies. I simply do not understand."

"The Den is certainly not a baby," Yalith replied. "Now that he is getting better, he is full of questions. He wants to know what the herbs are that the pelican puts in the water, and what the salves are made of."

"The Sand," Elisheba said, "wants to know where the salves come from. They are certainly full of questions." She laughed her hearty laugh and told them that Sandy had wanted to know who ran the oasis. Was there a mayor? Or a selectman?

The words had no meaning. Elisheba had told Sandy that those who sought power were greedy, wanting gifts, and bribes, and willing to steal from the poor. "Shem hunts for us all, and I help with the winemaking," she said contentedly. "That is enough for us. We have plenty to eat, and to give to those in need. Matred is a good mother to us all, with her fine sons and daughters."

"Mahlah and Yalith are not married yet," Matred prodded.

"They are still young," Noah said.

"I thought the Voice told you—"

"Not about Mahlah and Yalith. They should have time to grow up."

"I think," Matred said pointedly, "that Mahlah is grown up."

Yalith sat on the cool, starlit stone, the echoes of the evening's conversation still in her ears. She wondered if Matred had noticed the swelling of Mahlah's belly— Mahlah, whose betrothal to the nephil was not yet acknowledged by her mother.

Yalith was so deep in thought that the stars had to hiss at her to get her attention.

6 ~ *Adnarel and the quantum leap*

Yalith looked up and saw a circle of strange animals. In the center of the circle stood Mahlah, looking pale and frightened. Her dark hair covered her breasts, her body. Yalith started to cry out, to leap up and go to her sister, but it seemed that a firm hand came across her mouth, held her down on the rock.

The cobra uncoiled, hood spreading, swaying as though to unheard music, then stretched up and up into the loveliness of lavender wings, and amethyst eyes that reflected the starlight. "I, Ugiel, call my brothers. Naamah!"

The vulture stretched its naked neck, until great black wings and coal-black eyes in a white face were revealed.

"Rofocale!"

A shrill drone, a mosquito whine, and then there stood on the desert a nephil with wings of flaming red and eyes like garnets.

"Eisheth!"

The crocodile opened its mouth, showing its terrible teeth. It appeared to swallow itself, and vomit forth a tall, green-winged, emerald-eyed nephil.

Yalith trembled as she saw the dragon/lizard.

"Eblis!"

He burst from his scales, beautiful; awe-inspiring.

"Estael!"

The cockroach scuttled a few inches and then burst open and dust rose, and dissipated to reveal another of the nephilim.

"Ezequen!" The skink.

"Negarsanel!" The flea.

"Rugziel!" The worm.

"Rumael!" The slug.

"Rumjal!" The red ant.

"Ertrael!" The rat.

One by one, the creatures transformed themselves into the nephilim with their white skin and brilliant, multicolored wings.

Ugiel raised his arms. "I, Ugiel, in the presence of my brother nephilim, take to wife Mahlah, penultimate daughter of Noah and Matred."

Mahlah slowly moved toward him, was folded in the great wings.

Yalith fought for breath. Her chest felt constricted, and she gasped for air.

Then she saw that there was another circle, outside the circle of the nephilim.

The pelican who daily brought water for her pitcher stretched himself into the tall, bright personage with silvery hair and wings. "Alarid!"

Light seemed to flash against the bronze shell of the scarab beetle, who rose up in a rush of golden wings and burnished skin. "Adnarel!"

A tawny lion with a great ruff of fur about its neck rose on its hind legs and stretched into its seraphic form. "Aariel!" The golden tips of his wings glimmered in the starlight.

A golden snake, as large as the cobra, but as bright as the cobra was dark, called out as it was transformed, "Abasdarhon!"

One by one, the seraphim called out their names as they changed form. A golden bat shot up into the air. "Abdiel!"

A ruffled white owl widened its round silver eyes, and the eyes were suddenly the silver eyes in a seraphim's face, and moon-blue wings seemed to touch the sky. "Akatriel!"

A white leopard, swift as the wind, called, "Abuzohar!"

A soft, furred mouse rose, crying, "Achsah!"

By the mouse a tiger moved, stood, stretched. "Adabiel!"

A white camel and a giraffe rose moments apart.

"Admael!"

"Adnachiel!"

Lastly, a white goose flew skyward, its wings changing to snow-white. "Aalbiel!"

There seemed a healing in the calling of their names.

Although the circle of seraphim was outside that of the nephilim, when they spread their great wings to the fullest span the wing tips touched.

Likewise, the nephilim raised their wings, turning so that they faced the seraphim, and the glory of their wings brushed.

"Brothers," Alarid said. "You are still our brothers."

Ugiel touched his lavender wings to Alarid's silver ones. "No. We have renounced you and all that you stand for.

This planet is ours. Its people are ours. We do not know why you stay."

Alarid replied firmly, "Because, no matter how loudly you renounce us, we are still brothers, and that can never be changed."

For a fragment of a second, Ugiel seemed more cobra than nephil. Yalith choked back a scream. Mahlah, small and frail, still stood in the center of the circle, protected only by her dark hair.

Eblis, shimmering in and out of his dragon/lizard form, touched wings with Aariel. "We have made our choice. We have forsworn heaven."

"Then the earth will never be yours." Aariel was once more a lion, and with a great roar he galloped away, vanishing into the far horizon.

The two circles broke up with a great flurry of brilliant wings. Yalith blinked, and when she opened her eyes, she saw only a tall, lavender-winged nephil, with his arm tenderly about Mahlah—Mahlah, who was no smaller than any other woman of the oasis, but who came barely to Ugiel's waist.

Yalith sat on the rock, as though frozen into motionlessness. Ugiel's wings spread, wrapped gracefully, protectingly, about Mahlah. Yalith thought she caught a whiff of stone. Then there was a flash, not bright like the unicorns', but a flash of darkness even darker than the night, and then the desert in front of her was empty. Mahlah and Ugiel were gone.

She cried out in fear.

"Little one," a gentle voice spoke behind her. "Why are you afraid?"

She turned to see Eblis, his purple wings lifted so that they seemed to mingle with the night sky.

"Mahlah—" she said. "I am afraid for Mahlah."

"Why fear, my precious? Ugiel will take care of her. As I will take care of you. There are rumors on the oasis of fearful things to come, the volcano erupting, the mountain falling, earthquakes such as have never been felt before, terrible heavings unlike the silly little tremors you hardly notice."

She nodded. "I think my father is afraid. But what can we do? If the volcano is going to erupt, there is no way we can stop it."

"No. Nor can you run from it. But I will protect you."

"How?"

"Nephilim have powers. If you will come with me, I will keep you safe."

"Come with you? Where?"

"I will make a home for you full of lovely things. You will no longer have to sleep on rough skins, still smelling of animals. I will give you food and wine such as you have never tasted. Come, my lovely little jewel, come with me."

"When—" She faltered.

"Now. Tonight."

She thought of the two circles, the seraphim and the nephilim. It was Eblis who was offering her protection, not Aariel. Mahlah had gone with Ugiel, not with Alarid. "What about my family?" she asked. "What about my twins?"

"Only you," Eblis said. "That is as far as my powers extend."

She looked up at the stars. Shook her head. "Twin Den still needs me."

"Love is patient," Eblis said. "I will wait. But I think that in the end you will come to me." His hand soothed her soft, burnished hair, and there was pleasure in his touch.

She blinked, looked at the brilliant pattern of stars, and it seemed that she could see Sandy bowing to her in her grandfather's tent, could see Dennys holding her hand as the pain of his burns made him cry out.

Eblis touched her hair again. "I will wait."

Japheth came to visit Dennys, examined him carefully, touching the remaining scabs, gently pulling off a flaking strip of paper-thin skin. "You are better."

"Much better." Dennys smiled at him, and the smile no longer seemed to crack the burned skin of his face. "I go out at night with Yalith and Oholibamah, and we listen to the stars."

"It is good that you can hear the stars." Japheth sat beside Dennys on a pile of skins, putting his hands, stained purple from winemaking, on his brown knees.

Dennys looked troubled. "They keep telling me to make peace. At least, I think that is what I hear the stars saying to me."

Japheth nodded. "Oholi told me. Peace between my father and grandfather. Have you talked to my father about his quarrel with Grandfather Lamech?"

"Yes, once when he came to visit me. But I didn't really understand what their quarrel is about."

"Water," Japheth said flatly. "That is what most quarrels on the oasis are about. Grandfather has the best and deepest wells on the oasis, and he's letting his own gardens and groves go to seed in his old age."

"But he lets you take all the water you need from his wells, doesn't he?"

Japheth sighed, then laughed. "Oh, Den, the quarrel is so old and stupid I think that both my father and grandfather have forgotten what it is about. They are both stiff-necked and stubborn."

"Your grandfather—what is he like? I mean, if he's so old, is he able to take proper care of Sandy?"

"Oh, I'm sure he is. Grandfather Lamech is as hospitable as our mother, and kind, and gentle. It was he who taught Yalith and me to listen to the stars, and to understand the wind, and to love El." He sighed again. "Oh, Den, I'm sorry to involve you in our family quarrel."

Dennys sighed, too. He did not reply. He looked up at the brazen sky, behind which were the stars. And they had already involved him.

He shivered.

Grandfather Lamech and Higgaion began taking Sandy out in the daylight, not into the direct and brutal sunlight, but in the shade of a thick grove. Like Dennys, Sandy wore only a loinskin. His underclothes were folded with the rest of his things, in case they were ever needed again. The loinskin, unlike his own clothes, could be scrubbed clean with sand, and eventually discarded and replaced. He liked the freedom of the loinskin, liked the way his own skin had healed and was slowly turning a rosy tan.

Adnarel came by Grandfather Lamech's tent almost every day, and as Sandy grew stronger and more willing to accept that he was not going to wake up in his own bed at home, he grew more aware of his surroundings and of the tender care given him by the tiny ancient man.

"Hey, Grandfather Lamech," he said one morning after breakfast, "now that I'm better, it's time I stopped free-loading."

The old man looked at him questioningly. "What's that?"

"What can I do to help?" Sandy asked. "I've never done any cooking, but isn't there stuff outdoors I could do to be useful? At home, Dennys and I chop wood and mow the lawn and we have this huge vegetable garden."

At the mention of the garden, Lamech's eyes brightened. "I have a vegetable garden, and lately I have much neglected it. Higgaion helps with the watering, but I am too old for the long hours of work, and now there are great weeds choking the plants."

"Let me at it!" Sandy cried. "Dennys and I are terrific gardeners."

Grandfather Lamech's face creased into a broad smile. "Not so fast, my son. The time for work in the garden is in the earliest morning, and just as the sun is setting in the evening."

"Oh."

The old man laughed. "Truly, you do not want to go out in the garden during the day, or you will be felled by the sun all over again. But as soon as the sun drops behind the palms I will show you the garden. I thank you, dear my Sand. You have been sent to me by El—this I believe."

"Hey, it's the least I can do," Sandy protested.

In the late afternoon, when the sun's rays were slanted, Lamech and Higgaion led him past a small grove to the garden, which was indeed in need of helping hands. Great weeds of varieties Sandy had never before seen grew higher than many of the vegetables. This was going to be a full-time job. The weeds had deep roots, he discovered as he tried to pull one up. He found a sharp stone and would have started digging had Lamech not stopped him.

"You are not quite ready for such hard work, and it is still hot. Tomorrow morning you can try coming out for an hour."

"All right. It'll make me feel at home, working in a garden again." Sandy knew that he did not have to win Grandfather Lamech's approval, but he had a deep sense of happiness that he could do something for the old man who had been so kind to him. Despite the profusion of weeds, the garden was lush with more vegetables than he had ever seen before. —Too bad there was no way to can or freeze them.

"We sun-dry some of these." Lamech pointed to a long row of red ovals on tall, leafy stalks, and another of something purple that looked like eggplant but was twice the height of the plants at home. If these people of the desert were smaller than anyone Sandy had ever seen, their plants were larger. "That way," the old man continued, "we can eat them in the winter in soups and stews. I have groves of fruit trees, too, that need pruning and harvesting. Japheth and Oholibamah come when they can, to help me out, but they have more than enough to do in my son's vineyards. It must have been ordered in the stars that you should come just as I have to accept that I can no longer manage on my own." His face was joyful.

Sandy felt bathed in the old man's joy. There was certainly going to be no time for boredom. And if there was plenty to do, there would be less time in which to worry about getting home.

One morning Adnarel said, "The Den is much improved."

Sandy nodded. "Good. But why do you call us the Sand and the Den, as though Sands and Dens were some kind of rare species?"

Adnarel's bright laugh pealed. "We picked it up from Japheth. And to Japheth the Sand and the Den are indeed rare species, of a kind never before seen on the oasis, or indeed on any oasis roundabout. It is good that your head is covered." Adnarel nodded approvingly at the woven straw hat Matred had brought over one night with the night-light. "Lamech tells me you are doing valiant work in the garden."

Sandy pulled the hat firmly down on his head. "The weeds are something else. We have weeds at home, but not like these. But I'm getting rid of them, little by little. Hey. Does your name, Adnarel, mean anything?"

"That I am in the service of the Maker of the Universe."

"Why are you sometimes Adnarel, the way you are now, and sometimes you seem to be a scarab beetle?" Sandy started to scratch his shoulder where skin still flaked, stopped himself.

"I am not sure you will understand," Adnarel said. "The scarab beetle is my earthly host."

"What on earth do you need an earthly host for?"

Adnarel sighed. "I said you might not understand."

"Hey." Sandy was indignant. "Dennys and I may not be the geniuses of the family, but we're nobody's idiots."

"True," Adnarel agreed. "And I suspect that you also understand that energy and matter are interchangeable."

"Well, sure. Our parents are scientists."

"On the other hand, you live in a time and place where those like myself are either forgotten or denied. It was not easy to get you to believe in a unicorn until the need was desperate."

Unthinkingly, Sandy scratched his forearm, and shreds of skin blew across the ground. "When you're in the scarab beetle, can you understand everything we say?"

"Certainly."

"Then why do you bother to come out?"

"When I am in the scarab beetle, I must accept its limitations."

Sandy grunted. "I think better when I have Dennys around to bounce ideas off. When am I going to be able to see him again?"

"As soon as he is able to be moved. Grandfather Lamech has offered his hospitality. It is less noisy and crowded here than in the big tent."

Sandy sighed. "People have been very kind to us. You, too."

Adnarel smiled a smile so grave that it was not far from a frown. "We do not yet know why you are here. There must be a purpose to your presence. But we do not know what it is." His eyes seemed to shoot golden sparks at Sandy. "Do you?"

"I wish I did," Sandy said. "It all seems to have been some kind of silly accident."

"I doubt that," Adnarel said.

Noah came again to visit Dennys. "I am told that you are nearly well."

"Yes. Thank you."

"Oholibamah says that you will soon be ready to be moved."

Dennys felt a surge of panic. "Moved? Where?"

"To my father Lamech's tent. To be reunited with your brother."

The panic subsided. "I would like that. Is it far?"

"Half the oasis."

The tent flap had been pegged open, and through it and through the roof hole Dennys could hear the stars. Could hear their chiming at him. "Will you take me?"

Noah pulled at his beard. "I do not go to my father's tent."

"I don't understand."

"It is his place to come to me."

"Why? Aren't you the son?"

"He is old. He cannot care for his land as it should be cared for."

"I'm sorry, Father Noah, but I still don't see why you won't help him."

"I told you." Noah's voice was gruff. "I work long hours in the vineyard. There is not time for coddling the old man."

"Is speaking to your father coddling, or whatever you call it? Sandy and I get mad at our father. He pays more attention to our sister and our little brother than he does to us, because they're the geniuses and we're only—but even when we're mad at him, he's still our father."

"So?"

"When we get home, we're going to have a lot of explaining to do to our father. He will probably be very angry with us."

"Why?"

"Well, we sort of got in the middle of something he was working on."

"I don't know what you're talking about," Noah said.

"Neither do I, exactly," Dennys admitted. "The thing is, we're going to have to talk to our father when we get home. It would be a stupid thing if we tried to avoid him."

"So why are you telling me this?"

"Well—I really do think you should talk with your father."

"Umph."

"I don't mean to be rude or anything, but it sounds to

me as though all this argument about wells and stuff has
gone on for so long it doesn't make sense anymore. And
he's an old man, and you're much younger, and you should
be strong enough to back down."

"Backing down is being strong?"

"It takes a lot of courage to say 'I'm sorry.' That's what
Sandy and I are going to have to say to our father when we
get home."

"Then why say it?" Noah growled.

"Because things won't be right between us till we do."

"You're too young to be telling me what to do." Noah
was testy. "You would not even be alive now if we hadn't
taken you in."

"That's true, and I am more grateful than words can
say." The stars chimed at him again. "Father Noah, please
go see your father, and make peace with him before he
dies."

Noah grunted. Rose. Walked out of the tent.

Dennys looked at the patch of velvet sky he could see
through the open flap. The stars were brilliant. And silent.

Tiglah, the red-haired, rubbed the juice of some red
berries on her lips, over her cheekbones. Took a stick of
wood which she had shredded at one end to make a brush,
and used it on her abundant curls. She had taken the worst
of the tangles out with her fingers, and the brush was only
to add sheen.

—I am beautiful, truly beautiful, she thought. —My
hair is as red as my nephil's wings. We are beautiful together.

A mosquito shrilled near her ear, lit on her neck, and bit.

"Ouch!" she protested. "Why did you do that?"

The mosquito was gone, and a nephil, with wings like flame, stood before her. "Because you are indeed truly beautiful. You are so beautiful I could eat you up."

She burst into tears. "Rofocale, don't bite me!"

The nephil laughed. "It was just a tiny bite. Tell me, little Tiglah, have you seen again the young giant your father and brother threw out of your tent?"

"No. I think the women from Noah's tent are nursing him."

"Your sister?"

Tiglah laughed. "I wouldn't want to depend on Anah if I needed nursing. The younger ones. Oholibamah and Yalith. Anah is helpful when they need ointments, and—"

"How did he get into your tent in the first place?"

She pouted. "How would I know? I called for a unicorn, and suddenly this pale young giant was there, too. I was sorry they threw him out. I'd like to have had a chance to talk with him."

"Tiglah, my beauty, you'll do anything I ask, won't you?"

"As long as you don't ask me to do anything I don't want to do."

"I want you to get to know this young giant. Find out where he comes from, why he is here. Will you do that for me?"

"With pleasure."

"Not too much pleasure," Rofocale chided. "I want him

to be attracted to you. I do not want you to be attracted to him. You are mine. Are you not?"

She raised her lips to his. His lips were as red as hers, although no berry juice had been rubbed on them.

"Mine," Rofocale purred. "Mine, mine, mine."

In the cool of the evening, Sandy sat on the low bench made by the root of the old fig tree. Higgaion was curled up at his feet, making little bubbles as he slept and dreamed.

A man with a full brown beard flecked with white, and with springing brown hair, strode toward him, turning in from the public path and toward Grandfather Lamech's tent. He went up to boy and mammoth. Stared. "You are the Sand."

"I am Sandy. Yes."

"They told me that you look like one boy in two bodies. Now I believe them."

"Who are you?" Sandy asked curiously.

"I am Noah. Your brother is in one of my tents, and my wife and daughters are taking good care of him."

"Thank you," Sandy said. "We're very grateful."

Noah continued to stare at him. "If I did not know that the Den is in one of my tents, I would think that you were he. How can this be?"

"We're twins," Sandy explained wearily.

"Twins. We have known nothing of twins before." He paused and looked at Sandy, then at the tent. "Is my father in his tent?"

Sandy nodded. "He's resting." Then he added, "But I

know he'd be happy to see you." He wished he felt as certain as he sounded. Grandfather Lamech struck him as being a very stubborn person, with his natural stubbornness augmented by age.

Without speaking further, Noah went into the tent.

Noah!

Suddenly the name registered. Sandy had not heard Noah called by name. Lamech referred to him, when he spoke of him, as 'my son.' The women who came with the night-light called him Father.

Noah.

The galaxies seemed to swirl. Sandy had been convinced that he and Dennys had blown themselves somewhere far from home, at least out of their own solar system, and probably out of their own galaxy. If this Noah was the Noah of the story of Noah and the flood, they were still on their own planet. They had blown themselves in time, rather than in space. And to get home from time might be far more difficult than getting home from space, no matter how distant.

But it seemed to fit. Desert people. Nomads, with tents. Cattle. Camels. People used to be smaller than end-of-twentieth-century people. Way back in pre-flood days it was logical that they would be a great deal smaller. Higgaion was small for a mammoth.

He put his head in his hands, suddenly dizzy.

Dennys sat with Japheth and Oholibamah, and with Yalith, on one of the desert rocks. The sky was still flushed with light. The first stars were trembling into being.

Japheth looked at Dennys in the last light. "You talked with my father."

"Yes."

"Oh, I'm so glad!" Yalith cried.

"Father has gone off somewhere," Japheth said. "In the direction of Grandfather Lamech's tent."

Oholibamah looked up at the sky. "He will be happier now. All of us will be happier. Where there is an unreconciled quarrel, everybody suffers."

Dennys looked troubled. "I'm not sure he really listened to me."

"But you heard the stars," Oholibamah said, "and you were obedient to their command."

Japheth added, "That is all anybody can do. Now it is in El's hands."

Briefly, Dennys closed his eyes. —I hope Sandy doesn't think I'm crazy. I hope *I* don't think I'm crazy. Obeying stars, yet.

"I feel like running," Oholibamah said, and jumped down and ran fleetly across the desert, Japheth following her.

"Come!" Yalith called, and leapt from the rock. Dennys, with his long legs, caught up with them easily, and suddenly he was holding hands with Yalith and Oholibamah, and the four of them twirled in a joyous dance. Moonlight and starlight bathed them. Dennys, leaping in the night, felt more alive than he had ever felt before.

Sandy and Higgaion sat up, startled, as they heard a roar from the tent. At first it seemed to be a roar of anger. Then laughter. Then there was absolute silence. Sandy could feel his heart beating faster. Higgaion's ears were lifted in alarm. He raised his trunk.

"They wouldn't hurt each other, would they—" Sandy spoke aloud. Higgaion stared at him out of bright, beady eyes.

Then the tent flap was shoved aside, and Lamech and Noah pushed through with difficulty, because they had their arms about each other, and tears were streaming down their cheeks.

Lamech's voice was so choked with emotion that the words were muffled. "This my son was dead and is alive again, was lost and is found."

Noah hugged the old man roughly. "This is my father, my stubborn old father. We are two peas in a pod for stubbornness." He looked at Sandy. "As you and the Den are two peas in a pod."

"Hey," Sandy said, "I'm glad you two have made up."

"It was the Den," Noah said. "He just kept at me and at me."

Sandy looked surprised. At home, at school, Dennys seldom talked first. He followed Sandy's lead, but seldom initiated anything. "Well. That's good."

"He is nearly healed now, too. Soon he will be able to come to you. My father—" He paused. "I would be happy to have the Den stay, but my tent is crowded, and noisy. And my father has invited you to stay with him."

"That's terrific," Sandy said. "Thanks, Grandfather, thanks a lot. And Dennys can help me with the garden."

"So we should celebrate," Noah said, and handed his

father a small wineskin. "There is not much of this, but it is my very best."

"A little will suffice." The old man held the wineskin to his lips, then smacked them in appreciation. "Indeed, your very best." He handed the skin to Sandy, who took a small sip, barely managed to swallow it without making a face.

"El has talked with you, too?" Lamech asked his son.

"He has. When El spoke, I used to understand what was being said. Now it is all confusion. What does El say to you?"

Grandfather Lamech put his arm about his son's shoulders. "El tells me these are end days."

"End of what?" Noah asked.

"Of all that we know, I think," the old man said. "It is not just a question of moving our tents to where there is more water and better pasture for your beasts. Sometimes I, too, feel that the words are all confusion. El talks of many waters, but there is no water anywhere around, except in the wells."

Sandy, sitting next to the old man, with the mammoth lying nearby, shuddered. Grandfather Lamech, if he did not die first, and Noah and his family, and a good many animals, would be the only ones to escape drowning in the great flood.

—I already know the story, he thought, and was glad that the night hid his deep flush of embarrassment. It did not seem right that he should know something that Grandfather Lamech and Noah did not know.

But what did he know? Vague memories of Sunday school. God, angry at the wickedness of the world, and sending a flood, but telling Noah to build an ark and bring the animals on. And then there were terrible rains, and finally a dove brought Noah a sprig of green, and the ark landed on Mount Ararat. Not much of a story unless you were part of it.

Was Grandfather Lamech in the story? He did not remember. Grandfather patted Sandy gently, his usual way of expressing affection, and went on talking. In his concern about the flood, Sandy lost track of the conversation. He heard Grandfather Lamech saying, "My grandfather, Enoch, was three hundred and sixty-five years, and then he was not."

Sandy's ears pricked up. "What do you mean, he was not?"

Grandfather Lamech said, "He walked with El. He was a man of warm heart. And El took him."

It was a weird story. "El took him? How?"

"I was only a boy," Grandfather Lamech said. "He—my Grandfather Enoch was walking through the lemon grove —the same lemon grove I will show you tomorrow—he was walking through the lemon grove with El, and then they were not there."

If this was part of the story of Noah and the flood, Sandy did not remember it. "Is it customary," he asked, "for someone just to be not?"

Grandfather Lamech laughed. "Oh, dear, not at all customary. But my Grandfather Enoch was not an ordinary man. He went away from us to be with El at a very young age. He was only three hundred and sixty-five years old."

"That's exactly a solar year," Sandy said.

"A what?"

"A solar year. For starters, it takes our planet three hundred and sixty-five days to go around the sun."

"Nonsense," Noah said. "We don't go around the sun. It goes around us."

"Oh," Sandy said. "Well. Never mind."

Grandfather Lamech patted his knee. "It is all right. Things may be different where you come from. Do you know El?"

"Well, yes, sort of, though we say God."

Grandfather Lamech appeared not to have heard. "My Grandfather Enoch—how I do miss him. El talks with me, and sometimes I am able to understand, but I have never been able to walk with El in the cool of the evening, like two friends."

"What do you think happened to him, then, to Grandfather Enoch?"

Lamech nodded and nodded, as though answering. Finally he said, "El took him, and that is all I need to know."

"Father," Noah said, "you talk with El more than anyone I know."

"Because my years are long, my son. It was not always so. I am glad indeed that you have come to me before I die."

"You're not going to die for a long time yet!" Noah cried. "You will live as long as our forefather Methuselah."

"No, my son." Grandfather Lamech's arm about Noah's shoulders tightened again. "My time is near."

"Perhaps El will take you, as he took Grandfather Enoch."

Grandfather Lamech laughed again. "Oh, my son, I am

full of years, and now that you have come to me, I am ready to die. El does not need to take me in the same way he took Grandfather Enoch."

Sandy looked at the two small men, hugging and laughing and crying all at the same time. It seemed likely that Grandfather Lamech would die before the flood. How soon? And how soon was the flood? He had come to love Grandfather Lamech, who, with Higgaion, had nursed him so tenderly.

—And what about Yalith? he wondered suddenly. He did not remember her name in the story.

—And what about us, Sandy and Dennys? What would happen to us if there was a flood?

7 ❧ The seraphim

Sandy slept that night as usual on Adnarel's cloak. He wondered if Adnarel knew about the coming flood and the destruction of almost all life on earth. His arms tightened about Higgaion, with whom he slept much as, when he was a small boy, he had slept with his arms around a small brown plush triceratops. His fingers moved through Higgaion's shaggy hair, stroked a great fan of an ear. Felt something hard. The scarab beetle.

It gave him a feeling of comfort, although he found it difficult to associate the bronze beetle with the great seraph. Well. Thinking about this could wait till morning. Dennys was the thinker, Sandy the doer. The gentle tip of Higgaion's trunk stroked the back of Sandy's neck, and he relaxed into sleep.

Adnarel came in the morning, in his seraphic form.

Sandy said, "I've been thinking." After all, not only Dennys could think.

Adnarel smiled. "Sometimes that is a good idea. Sometimes not."

"Dennys and I are in the middle of the story of Noah and the flood, aren't we?"

Adnarel's azure eyes regarded him. "So it would seem."

"How are we going to get home?"

Adnarel shrugged his golden wings. "The way you arrived, perhaps?"

"Somehow, I don't think that's going to be possible. In the meanwhile, Dennys is in one of Noah's tents, halfway across the oasis."

"That is true. But he is nearly ready to come to you."

"It's a long way. Is he strong enough to walk it?"

"Possibly."

"I was thinking maybe you could call a unicorn for him."

"Certainly. That is a possibility."

"But then I thought"—Sandy's forehead wrinkled anxiously—"when we were riding the unicorns to the oasis, he went out with the unicorn."

"That is no problem," Adnarel reassured him. "If we should call a unicorn to bring him from Noah's tents to Lamech's, and if, for some reason, they were both to go out, then we would recall the unicorn to Grandfather Lamech's tent, and Dennys would be here, too."

Sandy asked curiously, "If Dennys fell off the unicorn right away, and if the unicorn went out of being with him, could you call them to Grandfather Lamech's tent faster than it would take them in, sort of, the ordinary way."

"Oh, certainly. Fear not."

"Wow. Wait till I tell our father. That's what he's working on, traveling without the restrictions of time. Tessering."

Adnarel nodded. "That is indeed one way of thinking about it. Your father is on the right track."

Sandy wrinkled his brow in concentration. "Okay, then. If Dennys and the unicorn went out, and then you called them back into being, and they appeared here, that would be a quantum leap, wouldn't it?"

"Tell me what you mean." Adnarel's azure eyes probed Sandy.

"Well, it's like, oh, in particle physics—well, you can measure a quantum where it is, but not on its journey from there to here. At least—you can't measure a quantum in both its speed and its place in space, not at the same time. A quantum can be measured where it is, and then it can be measured where it's got to. So—" He paused for breath.

"So?" Adnarel asked, smiling.

"Oh, I wish Dennys was here. He could explain it better than I can. But . . . when you call a unicorn into being, you can see it, maybe measure it. But you can't measure it when it's gone out. Not until you call it back into being. So maybe that's what space and time travel is going to have to be like. A quantum leap. Or what my father would call a tesseract."

"You are an intelligent young man," Adnarel said. "This is not easy to understand."

Sandy realized that he had closed his eyes, almost stopped breathing, in order better to concentrate. He opened his eyes, took in a deep gulp of air. "Can *you* do it?"

"Do what?"

"Tesser. Take a quantum leap."

Adnarel smiled again. "When I am in the scarab beetle,

as I have told you, I am limited by what limits the beetle. When I am in my seraphic form, I have fewer limits."

"Can you get off this planet if you want to?" Sandy asked. "I mean, can you travel to other solar systems or other galaxies?"

"Oh, certainly. We are here because there is need. Our brothers, the nephilim, cannot leave this planet. They have lost some of their freedoms."

"Why?" Sandy asked.

But Adnarel was examining Sandy's healed skin. "You are beginning to get a nice protective tan. When your twin comes, each of you must spend a little time, and then a little more, in the sun, until your skin can bear the rays without burning. You must always remember to stay in the tent during the noon hours. Even in the shade, you can burn from the sun's reflection."

"I've been sunburned before," Sandy said. "Once when our Scout troop went to the beach for the day, and we all got burned. But it was nothing like this."

"I think you come from a more northerly part of the planet," Adnarel said, "and this sun is younger than it is in your time."

"And not so much pollution now between earth and sun. Does anybody here ever have allergies?"

Adnarel smiled. "Allergies do not come until later."

"Hey," Sandy said. "Grandfather Lamech's grand-daughter Yalith, the one with hair the color of you when you're in the scarab beetle—why has she never come back with the night-light? Why is it always somebody else?"

"Yalith has been busy, taking care of your brother."

For a moment Sandy was washed over with a sick wave of jealousy. He shook himself. If he and Dennys were not interested in mythical beasts, neither were they interested in girls. They went to the regional school dances, but usually stuck with the other members of the hockey and basketball teams. There was going to be plenty of time for girls later. Sometime after they had their driver's licenses and weren't dependent on parents to drive them. Sometime when they met girls who were not silly and giggly and showing off.

But Yalith was not silly or giggly and she did not show off and she was not at all like any of the girls at school. Even though he had been dizzy with fever that first night in Grandfather Lamech's tent, his memory of Yalith was as vivid as though she had come with the stone lamp the night before. Her bronze hair had held sunlight even in the dark shadows of the tent. Her body was tiny and perfect. Her eyes, like her hair, held sunlight. Trying to keep his voice level and not succeeding, for it cracked immediately, he said, "Well, I wish Yalith would bring the night-light tonight."

Adnarel looked at him, and Sandy blushed. He understood why he was feeling the way he was feeling, and at the same time he did not at all understand the way he was feeling, and this conflicting mixture of emotion confused him. His cheeks were as hot as they had been from fever and sunburn. He wondered how much Adnarel saw. But the seraph looked at him calmly. "Now I have business elsewhere. You worked very hard in the garden this morning during the dawn hours. Good work. You may stay out for fifteen more minutes. I will send my griffin friend to tell you when it is time to go inside."

"What's a griffin?"

"Ah, yes, I forget again," Adnarel said. "A griffin is a mythical beast."

"Not like the manticore, I hope." Sandy was not likely to forget the manticore.

"Griffins have a larger vocabulary than the manticore. Some of them can be fierce, but my friend is as gentle as a lamb."

"What does he look like?"

"*She* is half lion, half eagle."

"Which half is which?" Sandy's mind for the moment was off Yalith.

"Her front half is that of an eagle, her rear half that of a lion. She can fly like an eagle, and she has the strength of a lion." Adnarel turned and strode through Grandfather Lamech's grove of royal palms, date palms, coconut palms, scrub palms, all of which blocked the hot wind and provided such a thick shade that Sandy felt comfortably cool. He lay back and looked at the vast expanse of sky, then quickly shut his eyes against the glare.

At home the summer sky was blue, and the blue was made brighter by the white cumulus clouds. Except for an occasional grey day, the sky was constantly in motion, protected by the encircling hills. Here the sky stretched naked from horizon to horizon, licked by volcanic flames, burning in the sun.

A shadow deeper than the shadow of the trees fell across his face. He opened his eyes, expecting to see the griffin.

Instead, a young woman was looking down at him. He caught his breath. She was the most spectacularly beautiful girl he had ever seen. Tiny, like all the people of the oasis. She wore a white goatskin which covered one shoulder. Her hair was a sunburst of red. Her eyes were almond-shaped and as green as the spring grass at home. Her body was perfect, her skin the color of a peach.

"Hello!" she said, looking at him with a radiant smile. "I'm really glad to see you again."

Sandy looked at her in astonishment.

"You haven't forgotten me, have you? I'm really sorry for what happened, when my father and brother . . ."

"I don't know what you're talking about." Sandy could not keep his eyes off her.

"About when you suddenly appeared in our tent, and my father and brother . . ." Again her words trailed off, as though she didn't want to finish the sentence.

"I've never been in your tent." Sandy was confused. "I've only been out of Grandfather Lamech's tent to work in the garden. —Oh. Maybe you mean my brother."

She opened her eyes wide. Her lashes were long and dark and beautiful. "Your brother?"

"My twin brother," Sandy said. "We do look very much alike."

"You haven't been staying in one of Noah's tents?"

"No. That's my brother Dennys."

"Oh. Who are you, then?"

"I'm Sandy."

"Well, then, Sandy, I'm very happy to meet you, and I'm glad you're being nicely cared for."

"What's your name?" Sandy asked.

"I'm Tiglah. I'm Anah's sister."

"Anah?"

"Ham's wife. Noah's daughter-in-law. And I'm Mahlah's friend. Do you know Mahlah?"

"No."

"Mahlah is Noah's daughter, the next-to-the-youngest. Yalith is the youngest. Mahlah is the beauty of that family. We've been giving Yalith and Oholibamah salves to help heal your brother. Oh, dear, this is confusing. I mean, I was really startled to find you here, instead of at Noah's, and then you aren't you at all, I mean you're not the one who appeared in my father's tent that night and who . . . Giants who look alike! And have no wings . . ."

Sandy sighed. "In our time and place we're not anywhere near as tall as giants. We're just tall, and we probably haven't even finished growing."

"You aren't as white of skin as the nephilim, and you don't have wings, but you're as tall as they are. And as handsome, in a different sort of way." She reached out and stroked his face. Then she bent closer, and he was half-fascinated, half-repelled by the strong odor of perspiration mingled with heavy perfume. She had rubbed something red onto her lips and over her cheekbones. It looked like the juice of some kind of berry. She bent closer and brushed her lips against his.

"Hey!" Sandy protested.

"You're sweet, you know," she said. "You're really sweet. You're young, aren't you?"

Sandy said, stiffly, "We're adolescents."

"What's that?"

"Teenagers."

She shook her head. "The nephilim don't have any age at all. They just are. But they've been around. There isn't anything they don't know."

Sandy sighed. "Well, I'm not like the nephilim."

Her lips touched his again, warm and fruit-smelling.

A bird's scream cut across the sky. Above them was the shadow of two dark, flapping wings, then a thud, and a flailing of a long, ropy tail, as the griffin landed. Out of the beak came a negative squawk which was quite evidently "No, no, no." And another squawk which sounded very like "Tiglah."

Tiglah leaned against the trunk of a tall palm, stretching her arm up to reveal her figure to perfection. "Go away, griffin. I like this young giant, and I think he likes me."

The griffin cried an eagle cry, and pushed herself between Tiglah and Sandy. Her beak opened. "Go, go, go."

"No, no, no," Tiglah mimicked. "He's just fine right here with me to tend him. The other one that looks like him has Yalith and all those other women hovering over him. It's only fair that he should have some female care, too, isn't it, Sandy?"

Before he could answer, the griffin had gently but firmly pushed Tiglah toward the path.

"You'd better not hurt me!" she shouted indignantly. "Rofocale is my friend."

From the griffin's beak came a sound very much like a mosquito shrilling. Tiglah kicked at it, hitting just where eagle and lion joined. Her toenails were long and sharp. The lion's tail flicked back and forth in irritation. Then the griffin pushed at Sandy, urging him toward the tent.

"I don't want to go in yet." Sandy looked at Tiglah's smiling green eyes.

Tiglah's voice was cajoling. "Wouldn't you like to come with me to one of the bathhouses?"

"Bathhouses with *water*?" Sandy asked eagerly. Dirt from the garden was deep in his nails, and he could not clean it all off with sand.

"Water? Whatever for?" she asked.

"To bathe in."

"Goodness no!" She sounded shocked. "What an unhealthy idea! We bathe by being rubbed with oil, and we have lovely perfumes that cover all the bad smells." She giggled. "Whoever heard of bathing with water?"

Sandy felt himself being propelled toward the tent by the griffin. He was not sure how he felt about bathhouses with no water, and where perfume covered the bad smells, any more than he was sure about Tiglah. There was nobody remotely like her in school or in the village. She gave him a pleasurable prickly feeling. And, as she had pointed out, Dennys was being tended by Yalith.

The griffin pushed him into the tent.

Grandfather Lamech was waiting for him with a bowl of soup. He looked smaller than ever, and incredibly ancient. His hand, holding the bowl, shook slightly. Sandy looked at him anxiously.

He said, "Sand dear, you're late."

"Sorry, Grandfather Lamech. I was talking to a girl."

Grandfather Lamech asked, suspiciously, "What girl?"

"Her name is Tiglah, and she's the sister of one of Noah's daughters-in-law."

"Anah's sister," the old man said. "Be careful, Sand."

"She's beautiful," Sandy said. "I mean, she is absolutely gorgeous."

"That may be," Grandfather Lamech said. "But it is not enough."

Sandy thought the subject had better be changed. "I'm thirsty. The soup was great, Grandfather, but is there anything cool to drink? Water?"

The old man shook his head. "I can give you some fruit juice. Water is too precious to waste it in drinking. You do not have wells where you come from?"

"Sure we do," Sandy said. "There isn't any town water where we live, and we have an artesian well."

"And your water just keeps on coming?"

"Well, in the autumn when it hasn't rained for a while, we aren't allowed to take long showers, and our parents warn us not to flush the toilet every time we use it—"

"The what?"

"Sorry," Sandy apologized. "I keep forgetting." Grandfather Lamech was tidier about his body's needs than many of the people on the pathways near his compound. Sandy had been requested courteously to go to a small grove which drained onto the desert, whenever he needed. But many people used no special place at all. When Sandy had wandered away from Grandfather Lamech's, and onto the public path, he had seen that the streets were full of human dung as well as camel dung, goat dung, cow dung.

Perhaps the fierceness of the sun burned away things that would cause disease. He'd have to ask Dennys. Dennys knew more about sanitation and viruses and germs than Sandy did. Although, if he went into environmental law when he grew up, he'd have to learn about such things.

Grandfather Lamech gave him a bowl of still-unfermented grape juice, and Sandy drank it thirstily. He sniffed at the pot sitting in the banked embers of the fire. Grandfather Lamech cooked in the cool of the night, then set the pot in the ashes, where it kept comfortably warm.

"Smells good, Grandfather Lamech. What is it?"

"Pottage," the old man said.

"What's that?"

"Lentils, onions, and rice, well seasoned."

"Hey, I'm going to have to tell my mother how to make that when I get home." A brief wave of homesickness enveloped him as his mind's eye saw the lab, and a casserole of pottage cooking over the Bunsen burner.

Higgaion, too, sniffed. He had his own bowl, and he ate the same food as Sandy and the old man.

Grandfather Lamech seemed daily more tottery. If Dennys came to the tent, would it be too much for him?

But now that Noah and Lamech were reconciled, Noah not only came to Lamech's tent to talk, he brought great kettles of food, skins of wine, bunches of grapes. And the two men laughed and cried, and Noah hugged his father. "Oh, my father, you must live forever!"

And Lamech did not answer.

In the end, Dennys was to cross the oasis on a camel, a white camel with a long, supercilious nose, sneering rubbery lips, and extraordinary gentian eyes, shaded by long lashes.

Noah had cut his foot on a sharp stone, and Matred forbade him to accompany Dennys. "Now that you and your father are reconciled, do you want to spoil everything with an infected foot? It is healing well, but the public paths are full of filth. You are not to leave the tent until it has healed."

"Women," Noah grunted. But he obeyed Matred.

"Our Den will be all right," she reassured him. "If he is in the care of the seraphim, he will reach Grandfather Lamech safely."

Alarid, the seraph whose host was the pelican, and who brought water to the tent for Dennys; Alarid, who had warned him not to change anything, came with another seraph. This one had wings of pale blue, and eyes like moonstones, a deeper, brighter blue.

"So," Alarid said to Dennys, not quite accusingly, "you have already made changes."

"But I haven't!" Dennys expostulated.

"You persuaded Noah to go to his father, when he would listen to no one else."

"I didn't really say all that much," Dennys said. "I sort of just listened to the stars. So I wasn't really the one—"

"I am not here to accuse you," Alarid said. "We are full of joy that Lamech and Noah are speaking again, and it may well be that it was necessary for your brother to prepare the old man for reconciliation." He indicated the other seraph, who had been standing quietly listening. "This is Admael."

The seraph did not extend his hand. Seraphim evidently

did not shake hands. Admael bowed, and Dennys returned the bow.

Together, the two seraphim carefully examined Dennys. "Yalith and Oholibamah have taken excellent care of you," Alarid said.

Admael nodded in quiet approval.

"They've been marvelous," Dennys agreed. "I think I'd be dead if they hadn't." The scabs were long gone from his skin. He could run across the desert without tiring. He knew that it was time.

He looked at Alarid. "And you, too. Thank you." He bowed to the seraph.

"Admael will carry you to Grandfather Lamech's tent," Alarid said.

Admael's moonstone eyes beamed toward Dennys. "I will wait outside." With a grave look, the seraph left.

"I should thank everybody." Dennys hesitated. He was eager to be with Sandy again, yes, and yet he was not at all eager to leave Yalith. And, of course, Oholibamah and Japheth. If he went to Grandfather Lamech's tent, would he ever see Yalith again? Would her delicate fingers slide confidingly into his hand the way they did when she took him out at night to listen to the stars, or when they danced under the desert sky?

"Fear not," Alarid said. "I have thanked them for you, all of them, Noah and Matred, Shem and Elisheba, Ham and Anah, Japheth and Oholibamah, and oh, yes, Yalith, too. In any event, you will be seeing them frequently. Now that Grandfather Lamech and Noah are reconciled, there will be much coming and going between the two tents. Are you ready?"

"Ready." He would see Yalith again. Surely she would come to Grandfather Lamech's tent to visit him. Surely he would feel the touch of her delicate fingers.

He followed Alarid out of the tent. Night had fallen, and the sky was crusted with stars. He was getting used to the pattern of early rising, the long afternoon nap, and going late to sleep when the fiery sands had cooled down and the very air had lost its burning quality.

He looked for Admael, but there was no seraph. Instead, a white camel stood in the dim shadow of the tent.

Noah was waiting for him, standing by the camel, leaning on a stick, his foot bound in a clean skin. "This is not goodbye, my son. We are all eager to see you and the Sand together. Then maybe we will believe that you really are two. The seraphim has looked at my foot and says that I will be able to walk on it safely in a couple of days." He held out his hand, palm up. "Put your foot there, and I will help you up onto the camel's back. Even for a young giant like you, a camel's back is a long way up."

The camel had no real saddle, but heavy skins were spread on its back. Dennys was not at all sure how easy it was going to be for him to stay seated. There was nothing for him to hold on to, no reins, no pommel. But Admael in his camel form seemed to be a real flesh-and-blood camel, not nebulous, like the virtual unicorns. He did not think the camel would lose its tendency to life.

Matred came hurrying out of the tent, carrying a bundle, tears streaming down her cheeks. "Here are your clothes. Perhaps, sometime, you will need them. Goodbye, our dear twin. We will miss you."

And suddenly he was surrounded by the entire family,

weeping, laughing, reaching up to the camel's flanks to hug Dennys's feet, which was as close to him as they could reach, even on tiptoe.

Japheth had his arm around Oholibamah, and Yalith was standing with them. They blew him kisses, which he blew back, and then, without warning, the camel took off, and everybody called after them, "Goodbye, twin Den, goodbye, and we'll see you soon!"

"Goodbye!" he called in return, trying to wave at them without falling off.

The camel turned off the oasis onto the desert as the calls faded into the distance. Dennys clutched the bundle of clothes Matred had given him—what remained of his clothes after he had thrown away the ones fouled in the garbage pit. He could not imagine ever needing winter clothes again. He could not imagine going farther than Lamech's tent, where he and Sandy would be reunited.

He remembered reading somewhere that to ride a camel was like being on a small ship rolling in rough seas, and that seemed to him to be a very good description. He bent over and clutched the white hair on the camel's neck, trying to let his body swing with the camel's odd rhythm. A soft night breeze only faintly gritty with sand touched his cheeks. Above them, the desert stars gave out a cooling light. In the distance the mountain smoked, and the horizon burned red. Dennys was glad the oasis was as far away as it was from the still active volcano.

The camel lurched swiftly across the desert. Dennys found that the more he leaned into the animal's syncopated rhythm the less tendency he had to slither off. The camel was going with such speed that it would be halfway across the desert before it realized that Dennys had fallen, so he'd better hang on.

He tried to breathe in time with the arhythmic ride. He would be incredibly sore in the morning. This was far harder on the muscles than riding a horse. He noticed a shift in pace, a quickening of rhythm. He clutched at the camel's neck, barely managing to hold on. Barely. He began to slip to one side, with the skins under him sliding with him.

The white camel was racing across the desert. Suddenly Dennys realized that the sound of camel's hooves on sand, on stone under sand, was echoed by another sound.

A voice from close behind them roared, *"Hungry!"* and Dennys felt a breath so hot that it seared. He felt himself slipping farther and farther off the camel, until he was clinging to the side, and then he realized that the camel had turned, so that it was between Dennys and whatever it was that was roaring. He found himself sliding so that he was head down, peering under the camel's belly.

Something was peering at him from the other side of the camel. A face. Whiskers. A bulbous nose. Bleary eyes. Horns which curved down, with sharp, wicked points. Dennys looked for the body that belonged to the face and saw, instead, a lion's body. Looked along the lion's body to where the tail should be and saw, instead, a scorpion's tail, its sting rattling. He had never seen anything like it before. He did not want to see it now. Clutching the camel's white hair, he tried to struggle up onto its back again.

The camel whickered, and continued to race across the desert.

"*Hungry!*" the creature roared.

Dennys felt very small. Very young. Very afraid. "Is it going to eat me?"

The camel glanced back at Dennys, the gentian eyes enigmatic.

"Hey!" he protested. "Aren't you going to stop *it*?"

The huge face loomed over the camel's back. "*Hungry!*" it roared again. The enormous lips opened, to reveal a double set of ugly, stumpy teeth, which looked as though they had been worn down from gnawing. The purplish lips opened.

Dennys pulled at the camel's hair. "Hey. Help." The ugly creature's breath came closer. The bloodshot eyes were looking directly at Dennys's grey ones. He tried to stare it down. The tongue, thick but long as a snake's, flicked toward him. He drew back, shielding himself with the camel, but the man/lion/scorpion bounded over the camel's back, landing on the sand beside Dennys.

"Camel!" he shouted. "Please be Admael!" He sidestepped away from the monster.

Again the camel agilely placed itself between Dennys and the creature. Gave Dennys a glance. Dennys remembered that seraphim did not like to interfere or change things.

"Hey!" he shouted. "If he eats me, won't that change the course of things?"

With a flash of lightning almost like the unicorn's, the camel stretched its whiteness up to the sky, seeming to brush against the stars, to catch blue fire, and then Admael stood beside Dennys. "Go, manticore, go quickly. And don't go to any of the tents. And don't even think of eating any of the mammoths. Do your hunting in the desert."

Tears began to trickle down the manticore's cheeks, dampening its scraggly beard.

"And don't try to make me feel sorry for you." Admael paused. "Though I am sorry for you. You appear to be one of nature's more peculiar efforts."

The manticore turned, head drooping, and with its lion's body it padded across the desert, scorpion sting clacking as it went.

"Wow!" Dennys said. "That was a close call."

"Not really. Manticore's courage is as skimpy as its vocabulary." Admael picked up the skins which had served as saddle. "Let's go." Dennys looked at him questioningly. "It isn't far. I've been running parallel to the oasis. Can you walk a little?"

"Sure." He'd just as soon walk as be bounced around on the camel's back. But he asked, curiously, "You're not going to be a camel?"

Admael had slung the skins over one shoulder. "Not now. It takes considerable energy to transfer. We do not like to waste power when it is not necessary. The manticore is basically a coward, but there may be other dangers in the night desert. It's best that we keep moving."

Admael glanced upward, and when Dennys looked skyward, he saw the dark wings of a vulture blotting out the stars in swift circles.

The circle of the nephilim was dark against the desert, a dark shot with flames brighter than those from the mountain as they flickered in and out of their animal hosts in a show of power. They spoke from their nephil forms in bursts of primal energy, reverting in negative lightning to their animal hosts, and bursting with bright wings again in order to speak.

The crocodile opened its enormous jaws, then lifted green wings as it stretched skyward. "What are they doing here?"

"What *are* they?" Pewter wings faded like smoke and a rat's tail swished back and forth over the sand.

There was a sulfurous smell as the nephilim flickered in and out, charging the air. "Not true giants." Red wings and hair flamed in the hot wind and then a mosquito whined shrilly.

"Not one of us." Purple wings misted and the dragon/ lizard stretched its useless wings.

"Though they speak the ancient tongue."

"They burn in the sun."

"They can't change form."

"Young. Infants."

"Almost men, though."

"They don't belong here."

"What to do with them?" Bronze wings dissolved and shrank with a tearing sound as the cockroach lifted its armored wings.

"Do we let them live?" Great garnet wings dimmed the clouds, dropped with a sharp crack, and the red ant's small body cast a dark shadow in the starlight.

Flicker. Flame. Shadow. In and out in prideful bursts of energy.

"Ummm," moaned the nephil who was the cobra. "Maybe we promise them that they will live."

"Ummm, kkk." The vulture appeared briefly and clicked its beak. Then dark wings shadowed the stars. "Power. Put them in our power."

Yellow wings puffed into sulfur and the flea leapt from the dragon/lizard to the vulture, then raised wings high. "Power. That's right."

"Temptation," the dragon/lizard nephil suggested.

"Temptation. Good." And the mosquito droned.

"Lust," suggested the cobra, and the nephil's face was whiter than the sand.

"Ummm. Lust," agreed the vulture. "Kkk. Lust."

"We'll sleep tomorrow in the heat of the day." The re-united Sandy and Dennys sat outside Grandfather Lamech's tent as the stars wheeled across the sky. The old man had gone in, after having sat outside with them to eat a fresh mess of pottage, and to prepare bowls of fig juice.

Higgaion was curled in the star shade of the tree, his flanks heaving in and out as he slept, occasionally twitching in dreams.

"Noah and Matred have a mammoth called Selah," Dennys said. "Usually she sleeps by Yalith's sleeping skins, but sometimes she came into my tent and slept with me. It was weird being without you." Dennys wriggled his bare toes in the sand.

"Yeah," Sandy agreed. "It was weird for me, too. Higgy and Grandfather Lamech have been very good to me." He wanted to ask about Yalith. But something stayed his tongue. He said, instead, "I love Grandfather Lamech. You will, too."

"He seems okay," Dennys agreed. "I'm glad Japheth was the first person we saw. Otherwise, I'd suspect everybody of being like those awful people who threw me out of their tent into the town dump."

"It sounds rough."

"Well, everybody in Noah's tenthold was wonderful to me."

"Dennys." Sandy was suddenly somber. "Do you remember the story? The story of Noah and the ark?"

Dennys shifted uncomfortably. "The story we got blown into. At first I thought we were in some way-out solar system."

"It might be easier if we were," Sandy said. "Grandfather Lamech sent me into town today to trade fruit for lentils. I passed a lot of people. They're all going to be drowned."

Dennys looked at the glow of the volcano on the horizon. "I know. Everybody except Noah and Matred, Shem and Elisheba, Ham and Anah, Japheth and Oholibamah."

Now Sandy's voice cracked. "What about Yalith?"

Dennys managed to keep his voice from soaring. "I don't know. But I don't think Oholibamah, Elisheba, or Anah are called by name in the story. Matred isn't, either." His voice jumped an octave. "Nor Yalith. At least as far as I can remember. I wish we had a Bible."

"It was a very patriarchal society," Sandy said. "I do remember that."

"Meg would call it chauvinistic," Dennys said. "Whoever wrote the Bible was a man. Men."

"I thought it was supposed to be God. Wasn't that what we were taught in Sunday school?"

"When we were little maybe. The thing is, the Bible was set down by lots of people over lots of years. Centuries. It's supposed to be the Word of God, not written by God."

"Okay," Sandy said, "but nobody ever mentioned that there were twins named Sandy and Dennys Murry with Noah and his family."

"Do you have any idea," Dennys ventured, "when the rains are supposed to start?"

Sandy shook his head. "No, I don't. And I don't know how we're going to get out of here and go home. Do you?"

"I thought you might have thought of something to do," Dennys said.

"I don't have a clue. You pay more attention than I do when everybody goes on at the dinner table about tessering and red shifts and mitochondria and farandolae and stuff."

"Mitochondria." Dennys looked at his twin. "Do you remember when something was wrong with Charles Wallace's mitochondria, and we thought he was going to die?"

"We went out to the vegetable garden," Sandy said.

"Because we had to *do* something."

"Even though we knew it didn't have anything to do with helping Charles Wallace get well."

"But it was something to do."

They were silent for a dark space. Then Sandy said, "Well, we can do it again, work in a garden. Grandfather Lamech has this huge vegetable garden—I mean, you've never seen such gigantic plants. And weeds. I've pulled up a mountain of weeds, wait and see, and I've hardly made a dent. And then there are his groves to prune and water. There's plenty to do. Whether it helps anything or not."

Under them the ground trembled slightly, but by now they were both so used to the shifting and sliding of the young planet that they hardly noticed. "Well. That's good. The garden, I mean. As long as we don't get sunstroke again."

"Oh, we work only in the early morning and the evening. Grandfather Lamech is very careful about that."

"Good, then."

"Yes, but none of that gets us home. What do we do now?" Sandy was asking himself, rather than his twin.

"I think," Dennys spoke slowly, "that we don't do anything. I mean, this is way outside our experience."

"Outside anybody's experience," Sandy added. "I think you're right. We wait. With our eyes and ears open." He looked over to where Higgaion was sleeping. The scarab was not in its usual place on Higgaion's ear. Therefore, he thought, Adnarel must be somewhere else. Doing what?

"We wait," Adnarel said. "To do anything is to make changes, to cause a paradox."

"Does not their very being here in itself constitute a paradox?" Alarid, who was sometimes a pelican, asked.

Admael, who had carried Dennys across the desert, said, "They have already made changes. The boy, Dennys, caused Noah to reconcile with his father, when it seemed that nothing would ever make that come about."

Adnachiel, his wings as sunny as the hide of his giraffe host, said, "Perhaps the boy Sandy played a part."

Aalbiel, with wings as white as those of a snow goose, asked, "Could they have been sent for this?"

Aariel, tawny as a lion, said softly, "We do not know. Perhaps they are part of the pattern."

Abdiel, sometimes a golden bat, spoke equally softly. "There are many things that even the angels in heaven do not know. And we have chosen—"

"Been chosen," Abasdarhon, whose host was the golden snake, corrected.

"Accepted being chosen," Akatriel, whose eyes were as round and wise and fierce as an owl's, corrected further.

"—to stay with the children of humankind," Abdiel continued. "Therefore, we have relinquished some of our powers and there is much that we do not know."

Abuzohar, who was sometimes a white leopard, inclined his head, his face luminous as the moon. "As long as the One knows, there is no need for us to know."

Achsah, with wings and hair the soft grey velvet of his mouse host, nodded. "They are innocent boys, for the children of men. Likable. And they speak the Old Language."

Adabiel, orange wings vivid as the tiger, agreed. "Good in their hearts. And they brought out Noah's goodness. Could that be part of the plan?"

Admael said, "We still have no real idea why they are here, or how they are to be returned to wherever it is they come from."

Adnachiel, sometimes a giraffe, looked up at the stars. "We willingly gave up some of our powers when we chose to stay on this planet."

"We do not *have* to stay." Abdiel's seraphim wings were as bright a gold as his bat ones. "We are free to leave at any time and to resume our full powers."

Adnarel threw off light like the sun flashing against the scarab beetle. "It was our free choice. And now—I would not leave while they—the twins—are still here."

"We may not be able to save them," Alarid warned.

"Then I will stay with them," Admael said, for a fraction of a second looking more like a white camel than like a seraphim.

Eleven luminous heads slowly nodded in agreement with Admael.

8 ❧ Oholibamah, Japheth's wife

Mahlah and Tiglah were waiting near Grandfather Lamech's ancient fig tree. Mahlah's belly was softly rounded.
Tiglah was round by nature, all soft curves and delicate
plumpness that had not yet run to softness, as Anah's was
doing.

The twins came from the garden, where they had weeded
two long rows of plants which might have been forebears
of tomatoes, and pulled off the suckers. Higgaion was in
the tent with Grandfather Lamech. The twins did not see
Mahlah and Tiglah until the two girls came to meet them.
Tiglah walked slowly toward Sandy. She tossed her head
so that her red hair flew about her face. She lowered the
heavy fringes of her lashes. "I'm sorry my father and
brother didn't treat you better when you appeared in our
tent that time." She paused, and added virtuously, "They
have to be very careful that strange men don't take advantage of me." Then she stopped. "Am I speaking to the
right one?"

"No," Dennys said.

Mahlah fluttered her small hands like birds. Her dark

hair concealed her swollen belly. "But which one of you was guest in my father's tent?"

Sandy stepped forward. "My brother Dennys. You're Yalith's sister?"

"Yes. Mahlah. But I am Ugiel's bride and no longer live in the home tent."

Sandy looked at her, thinking that although Mahlah was beautiful, it was in an obvious way; she had none of the subtle loveliness he associated with Yalith. Tiglah's flashy beauty was almost an assault. He still didn't know what to make of her. "Tiglah?"

She giggled, so that dimples came and went on either side of her reddened lips. "Don't you remember me?"

"You were talking to me the other day, before the griffin came."

"Yes, and the silly griffin interrupted us. I think she was jealous. But she's not here now. Would you like to come with us?" She turned from Sandy, to include Dennys in the invitation.

"Where?" Dennys asked suspiciously. His first encounter with Tiglah's family had made him far more cautious than Sandy had cause to be. He did not trust her, nor, indeed, any of the small people who did not come from Noah's tenthold.

Mahlah, unlike Tiglah, was not a giggler. She smiled. "We'd like to get to know you better. My father thinks the world of you. So let's go for a little walk."

Dennys looked at the sky, which was already beginning to shimmer with heat. "It's too hot. Thank you, anyhow."

Tiglah pushed her fingers through her curls, so that they glinted with gold in the sunlight. She, too, looked at the sky. "It's not going to be really hot until the sun is above the palm trees." She turned her dimpled smile toward Sandy. "We'd really love to show you around a little. You haven't seen much of the oasis."

Sandy stepped forward. He had not enjoyed his brief excursions onto the public path, but if Tiglah and Mahlah were there to show them where to go, it might be fun. It was time to go farther than Grandfather Lamech's compound and the nearby shops. "Well—"

"You go, if you like." Dennys was firm. "I nearly died of sunstroke, and I'm keeping out of the sun."

Sandy looked at his brother, noticing the still pinkly mottled skin. "I'm sorry. My skin's all healed. I forgot—"

"You go, if you like," Dennys repeated.

Sandy shook his head. "No. Grandfather Lamech wanted us to bring him some onions for his stew, and we were too busy weeding. We'd better go pull them before the sun gets too high."

A great whirring of wings shook the sky above them, and the griffin landed between the two boys and Mahlah and Tiglah.

"Go away, spoilsport." Tiglah kicked at the griffin, and her green eyes sparked with resentment.

Dennys backed away in fear. The griffin looked to him as fierce as the manticore.

"It's all right," Sandy reassured him. "It's a griffin, and she's a friend."

The griffin spread her eagle wings so that the two girls were screened. Opened her bill and squawked something like "On-yons."

"Okay, okay," Sandy said. "We won't forget."

The griffin folded her wings. Her lion's tail swished back and forth. Tiglah walked cautiously around her, and put her small hand on Sandy's arm. "Later, then? You would like to come for a walk, wouldn't you?"

Would he? Tiglah made Sandy feel very peculiar. She was both alluring and unsettling. And she was very different from Yalith, of the bronze hair and eyes and luminous smile. He would go anywhere with Yalith. But Tiglah? "I don't know," he said cautiously. "Dennys and I have a lot to talk about."

Mahlah, too, skirted the griffin, asking, "Are you sure you are two separate people? My husband, Ugiel, can take different forms, yet it is always he."

"We are twins," Dennys stated. "Aren't there any twins around here?"

Tiglah moved her fingers slowly up and down Sandy's arm, and it prickled, so that the freckles he had acquired in the sun seemed to stand up. "Two look-exactly-alikes? No. Of course, we can tell you apart right now, because *your* skin"—her fingers caressed Sandy's forearm—"is strong, and you are getting quite tanned, and you both have freckles across your nose. Whereas *his*"—she indicated Dennys—"still looks raw and uncooked."

"But handsome," Mahlah purred. "We don't have any men on the oasis who are as tall and like gods as you are."

The griffin cried again, "On-yons."

Sandy had already turned in the direction of the vegetable garden when he noticed Dennys looking past the clump of trees to the public path. Yalith and Oholibamah were coming toward them, carrying a large kettle between them.

Mahlah drew her lips up in what was more a grimace than a smile. "Well, sisters dear, are you pursuing the twin giants?"

Oholibamah's low voice was pleasant. "Good morning. Matred sent us with a meal. Grandfather Lamech is too old to cook for so many."

Unheeding, Yalith looked at the twins, from Dennys to Sandy, and back to Dennys. "It is not just the difference in your skins that tells you apart." She looked troubled.

"Let's put the kettle on the fire," Oholibamah suggested.

"You don't have to go with them." Tiglah wrinkled her nose in distaste as Yalith and Oholibamah started into the tent.

"Stay and talk with us," Mahlah wheedled.

But the twins had turned their backs on the two girls and were looking after Yalith as she disappeared into the tent.

The griffin shrieked with pleasure and flew off, spiraling higher and higher into the sky.

Dennys had picked half a basketful of onions before he began to recount for Sandy, in detail this time, his experience in Tiglah's tent.

"But it was her father and brother who threw you out, wasn't it?"

"She was there."

"But it wasn't really her fault."

"She didn't even try to stop them," Dennys said. "And even if it wasn't her fault, I wouldn't trust anybody who came from that tent."

"Well." Sandy picked up his basket of onions and hefted

it to one shoulder. "I can't say I blame you for feeling the way you do." He did not add that, nevertheless, Tiglah was still the most absolutely gorgeous girl he had ever seen. Except Yalith. Who wasn't gorgeous at all. Whatever Yalith had, it was better than gorgeousness.

And were Yalith and Mahlah and Tiglah going to be drowned?

Dennys, picking up at least part of Sandy's thoughts, said, "Still—I wouldn't want Tiglah to be drowned. And I guess she's going to be."

Sandy felt a chill move over his skin, despite the sun, which was rising higher and hotter. "And Yalith?"

Dennys picked up his basket. "Oholibamah is Japheth's wife. Ham, Shem, and Japheth, with their wives, go on the ark. That's the story. Oholibamah loves Yalith. I mean, they're really friends. I don't think Oholibamah would let Yalith drown."

"If she doesn't have any say about who goes on the ark, can she prevent it?"

Dennys said, "Hey, we're talking as if that old ark story is true. But Noah doesn't seem to have any inkling of it, and he talks with this El of theirs."

"God." Sandy shifted his basket of onions from one shoulder to the other. "Isn't there some kind of flood story in all cultures?"

"I think so," Dennys replied. "I mean, even in our day the planet is still shifting its plates and causing earthquakes. We've had an awful lot of weird weather, volcanoes erupting all over the planet, and tornadoes and hurricanes."

"Well, about those flood stories," Sandy continued. "There must have been some kind of major weather cataclysm."

"Yeah, but there've been wild weather patterns all through history. Ice ages. Whatever it was that finished off the dinosaurs, a comet, or that Nemesis star. Or the earth shifting slightly on its axis and altering climate and seasons. So a big flood isn't all that impossible."

Sandy said in a flat voice, "Maybe we'll get drowned, too. Maybe it would be better than being nuked."

"More inevitable than nuking. Nothing that hasn't happened yet has to happen." Dennys pushed into the tent and wearily set his basket of onions down near Grandfather Lamech's cooking stones. Sandy followed suit. They looked over to where the old man lay napping on his pile of skins, eyes closed, breathing shallowly. Higgaion was curled at his feet, and little bubbling sounds came rhythmically from his trunk.

Sandy said, thoughtfully, "If we get nuked, it will be because of people. Power and greed and corruption. It wouldn't be a natural disaster. But a flood is a natural disaster."

Dennys nodded. "Nuking would be something completely different. Not natural."

"Yeah, but remember, Dad says it doesn't have to happen. People *can* restrain themselves. We've had the power for half a century, and we've refrained. But if the plates of the earth slide, that can't be stopped. If a comet should hit us, we couldn't stop it. And storms and blizzards. Those are inevitable."

"When we had the hurricane, and the big oak was ripped out by the roots, nobody could have stopped that. It *is* different—things that can be stopped and things that can't, like tornadoes and earthquakes and—"

"And floods," Sandy said flatly.

Grandfather Lamech startled them with a loud snore.

"It doesn't do any good to talk about it," Dennys said. "Any of it. If there's going to be a flood, we can't do anything about it. But we *can* work in Grandfather Lamech's garden."

The old man snored again.

"Right now, we'd better nap, too," Sandy suggested.

Dennys dropped onto the clean sleeping skins which had been provided for him. "Hey, it's good to be back with you again."

But he missed Yalith's gentle fingers against his burned skin.

Every day, someone from Noah's tenthold came to Grandfather Lamech's tent with the main meal. When Yalith and Oholibamah came, they often stayed to eat with the old man and the twins. Yalith was equally gracious with each of them, but sometimes she sat looking at them in bemusement, letting Oholibamah do the work. The twins, in their turn, looked at Yalith and did not look at each other.

Occasionally, one of the men brought the meal. Japheth, like his wife and Yalith, would stay to eat, to talk.

Shem, who was the hunter, was cordial, but not chatty. He would stand, leaning on his spear, until he was certain that Grandfather Lamech had everything he needed. Then he would leave.

Japheth had told the twins that when Shem went hunting, he would always stop to thank the animal he had killed, thank it for giving them the food necessary for life.

"Do all the hunters give thanks?" Sandy asked.

"Not anymore. I think they used to, long ago. But now most of the hunters just kill, and often more than they need. Some kill just for the sake of killing."

Dennys said, "That is true in our time, too. At home, our land is posted against hunters and trappers, but that doesn't stop the jacklighters."

"The what?" Japheth asked.

Dennys tried to explain. "Hunters who shine a bright light into the eyes of the deer. It blinds them and they freeze and can't move, and then the hunters shoot. Jacklighting is illegal, but that doesn't stop a lot of people."

"A lot?" Japheth asked.

Dennys stated, "A few can seem like a lot."

Sandy nodded. The twins liked what Japheth had told them about Shem.

One morning Anah and Elisheba came with the food for the day. Anah, Ham's wife, was obviously Tiglah's sister, but her hair did not have the brilliance of Tiglah's, and her eyes were not as rich a green. She was becoming flabby, with dimples all over, in her cheeks, her chin, her elbows, her knees. She was softer than Tiglah.

Elisheba was like Shem, solid, muscled, kind. At home, in the twins' part of the world, she would have looked comfortable in a flowered housedress, and she would scrub her kitchen floor every day, and shift all the furniture to sweep under it. There was something more familiar about Elisheba than about many of the other women, who had an Oriental strangeness. Anah's and Tiglah's eyes were almond-shaped, their cheekbones high.

After the pot had been set on the stones, Anah put her hands on her rounded hips, looking in open admiration at Sandy and Dennys. "Another hundred years and you'll be the most handsome men on the desert."

Dennys looked at Grandfather Lamech's wrinkled face and trembling hands, thinking that the old man, at any rate, was not going to live for another hundred years. And even if the flood held off, he and Sandy did not have the life span of these tiny desert people. But he said nothing. He did not like Anah; Anah was Tiglah's sister.

Elisheba picked up the empty pot from the day before, which the twins had scoured clean with sand. "I wonder if they'll grow wings?" She tended to speak of Sandy and Dennys as though they could not hear.

"I think they're a new breed," Anah said, "not seraph or nephil, but a completely different kind of giant." Her gaze slid from one twin to the other, then back to Elisheba. "What," she suggested, "would you think of having two husbands?"

Elisheba laughed. "One is all I can manage."

"Thank you for the dinner." Sandy turned away from Anah's gaze, which was uncomfortably reminiscent of Tiglah's. "It smells good."

"And please thank Matred for us."

Anah put her fingers lightly against Sandy's wrist. "You're welcome to come eat in Noah's tent at any time, you know that."

Sandy was glad when she was gone.

The big tent was dark and quiet. Matred poked her elbow against Noah's ribs. "What about Mahlah?"

"Humph?" Noah mumbled sleepily.

"Husband. It cannot have escaped your notice that Mahlah is with child."

Noah rolled over. "I have been very busy."

"*Noah.*"

"It is time Mahlah brought her young man to our tent," Noah said. "We will prepare a feast."

"It is not a young man," Matred said. "At least, it is not one of our young men, and I don't think they're young, I think they are old, far older than any of us, even Grandfather Methuselah."

"Woman, what—or who—are you talking about?"

"Mahlah," Matred said impatiently, "and her nephil."

Noah sat up. "What are you trying to tell me?"

"I am telling you"—Matred kept her voice low—"that Mahlah is with child by a nephil, and that she has had some kind of nephil wedding." Quickly she put her hand over Noah's mouth to stifle his roar of outrage.

"This is not how things are done." He pushed her hand away, but kept his voice under control. "There has been no wedding feast. No nephil has come to our tent."

"The nephilim do not do things the way we do. Their customs are not our customs."

"This is Mahlah's will? She loves this nephil?"

"So it would seem. She sends messages by Yalith. She does not want to tell us these things herself."

Noah growled. "It is the way of things to lose a daughter to another man's tent, but not without the proper formalities."

"When Mahlah does speak to me"—Matred's voice was heavy—"she keeps reminding me that times have changed."

Noah sighed. "It is not what we would have chosen for our daughter, but after all, Oholibamah—"

Matred leaned against her husband, and he put his arm around her. "I would rather have it one of our young giants. At least they are truly young, and I think they are good."

"They fit in with us," Noah agreed, "and the nephilim do not. It seems now as though our twins have been with us always."

"The moons have slipped by," Matred said. "Seven or eight of them, at least."

"They have worked wonders in my father's gardens and groves. It is hard work, and yet they never complain."

"Perhaps Yalith—" Matred started, then said, "It is time we asked them to take another evening off and come to our tent. I wish Mahlah had not been lured by the nephilim. They glitter, but I do not think they are loving."

"I will speak to Mahlah." Noah pulled Matred down onto the sleeping skins.

"If she will speak with you," Matred said.

.   .   .

The twins enjoyed their visits to the big tent, the noise and singing and laughter. Once, at the time of the full moon, Noah's married daughters were there with their husbands and children, and there was dancing and music and loud quarreling and reconciling.

"I wish Mahlah were here," Matred said.

Less than a moon later, Anah and Elisheba, bringing a big pot of vegetable stew to Grandfather Lamech's tent, again invited the twins to the big tent. "But you should feel free to come more often," Anah said. "You don't have to wait for an invitation."

Sandy felt her eyes inviting him. He turned away. "We don't like to leave Grandfather Lamech too often."

Higgaion, lying stretched out by the embers, swished his stringy little tail, raised his head, and put it back down with a thump.

Again Anah lavished her smile on Sandy. "You're getting nearly as brown as one of us, and you have freckles all across your nose."

"The Den, too." Elisheba's smile was friendly. "I never believed he'd make it. Matred thought he was going to die. But Oholibamah is a healer. And Yalith was marvelous with him."

Sandy felt a sharp twinge of jealousy. When Yalith came with the night-light or with the evening meal, she was careful, overcareful, he thought, to smile no more at one twin than at the other. "All that was a long time ago." He was surprised at how cross his voice sounded. "We've both been well for months now."

"For what?"

"Oh. Many moons." *Moon* and *month* did come from the same root, after all, but the people of the oasis thought of time in moons and crops and the movement of the stars.

"Yalith will be looking for a husband one of these years." Anah's voice was suggestive.

Elisheba was brusque. "Yalith will make a good wife. But not yet."

Anah's eyes strayed from twin to twin. "Hmm." She pursed her lips.

Elisheba jiggled Anah's arm. "We'd better be getting back, or Matred will be after us."

"She doesn't scare me," Anah said.

"Who said anything about being scared? There's a lot of work to do, and she's getting too old to do it all herself."

"Too fat," Anah muttered.

"Who's talking?"

Still bickering, the two women left, taking the empty pot with them.

The twins went out to the vegetable garden, putting on Matred's straw-woven hats. The sun was not yet high, the shadows still long. "We'll stay just a little while," Sandy said.

They worked hard. The weeds, it seemed, grew up as fast as they could clear them. Weeding was a never-ending job. They did not mention Yalith. They had more than enough to do to keep them busy.

Grandfather Lamech no longer came out to the garden with them, but spent most of the day in the tent, drowsing. After the long afternoon sleep he would sometimes accompany them to the well, where they drew water, filling large clay jars, one for use in the tent. The others were for the garden, which Higgaion helped them water, spraying with his trunk, which was almost as good as a hose.

"It's good to be working in a garden," Sandy said, "even if it's not the garden at home."

"Who do you suppose is tending to the garden at home?" Dennys asked. "It's got to be at least harvest time by now. That is, if time there is passing like time here."

"Everything is different here," Sandy said. "People living longer, for instance."

"So maybe time is different, too. At home we had alarm clocks and those electronic bells at school, and here time just slides by and I hardly even notice it."

"I don't want to think about it, about time," Sandy said. He looked at his twin. "We're browner than we ever got at home. Anah's right about that."

"And our hair is bleached. At least, if mine is like yours, it is."

Sandy looked at his twin. "Well, your hair is lots lighter than it used to be."

"I wonder what it would feel like to wear clothes again?" They were used to wearing loincloths. They were even used to no showers, no water for bathing. The smells of the tent were hardly noticeable.

With a strong green vine, Sandy was tying up tall, green-leafed bushes, giant versions of the basil they planted between the tomatoes in the garden at home. Grandfather Lamech often chopped up the leaves to season his stews. "I'm not homesick anymore. At least, I'm not home*sick*."

"I try not to think about it too often," Dennys said,

"except to remind myself that since I didn't die of sun-stroke, then somehow or other we ought to be able to get home."

"We won't be the same," Sandy said.

Sandy made a face. "Hey, I don't like the way Tiglah keeps coming around. I don't think I'm ready for Tiglah."

"Tiglah," Dennys said, "is what the kids at school would call an easy lay."

"Except," Sandy said, "there isn't *any*body remotely like Tiglah at school."

"She's older." Still, neither of them mentioned Yalith.

"Yeah," Sandy said.

"The thing is—" Dennys paused. "Something's happened. We're not just kids anymore."

"I know." Sandy bent over one of the plants.

Dennys pulled up a resisting weed with such force that he sat down. "We haven't seen Adnarel lately. Or any of the other seraphim."

Sandy finished tying the plant to a bamboo stalk. Images of scarab beetle and pelican, camel and lion, flashed before him. He always felt better if Adnarel was with them. When the seraph was in his scarab-beetle form, he was usually near Grandfather Lamech's sleeping skins, or on Higgaion's ear. He gave Sandy a sense of security. "I think the seraphim like us."

"But the others don't," Dennys said. "I mean, the other ones, the nephilim. I've seen them looking at us when they thought we weren't noticing. And a mosquito kept buzzing around me the other day after Tiglah had been around. I don't think it was just a mosquito."

"Rofocale," Sandy said. "I heard her call one of the nephilim Rofocale."

"They don't like us," Dennys said.

When supplies were needed, the twins left Grandfather Lamech's and went to the nearby shops, carrying figs, dates, and the produce of their garden to barter for rice or lentils. On the dusty paths they passed many of the people of the oasis, who always paused to look up at Sandy and Dennys, surreptitiously if not openly.

When they passed nephilim, with whom they could look eye-to-eye, brilliant wings quivered, but the nephilim did not acknowledge their presence, except in sudden reversion to the animal host, so that a tall, bright-winged man would vanish, and there would be a skink scuttling across the path, or a red ant, or a slug leaving its slimy trail.

The women, at least the young ones, let Sandy and Dennys know that they were admired. Small hands reached up to touch them. They were bathed in lavish smiles. Tiglah seemed to know when they needed rice or beans or lentils, and would be waiting at whichever stall they were headed for.

The men and the older women were different. Sometimes the twins were cursed at, spat at. They did not tell Grandfather Lamech, who would have been distressed. They learned to go to the few venders who treated them kindly and did not try to cheat.

Dennys said, one day, "Hey, Sand. If you want to go for a walk with Tiglah, don't let me stop you."

"I don't want to." Sandy turned his gaze from the side

of the path, where a vulture was picking the flesh from a small carcass.

"I mean, just because it was her father and brother who threw me into the garbage pit—I mean, I'm not stopping you, or anything."

"No problem," Sandy agreed.

They were careful with each other as they had never been careful before.

And still they did not mention Yalith.

Yalith and Oholibamah were helping Matred to clean the big tent when they were disturbed by the flap being pushed open, and a lavender-winged nephil came in. He spoke without greeting. "It is nearly Mahlah's time. She will need you to help with the birthing of the baby."

Matred held the broken palm branch which she was using as a broom. "Do you not have one of your own kind to help?"

Ugiel looked at Oholibamah with hooded eyes. Flicked a long finger in her direction. "She will be of use. And Mahlah will need her mother and sister."

Oholibamah took a step away from the nephil. "How will we know when to come?"

"Tonight. At the time of the moonrise. I, Ugiel of the nephilim, tell you so."

"We will come," Matred pronounced. "I will not have my daughter labor alone."

"Good. I will expect you."

"We will come," Matred repeated, "but you will wait outside."

Ugiel shrugged. "Have it your own way. It is a woman's job to see to all the blood and mess of a birth." He started out, then turned his burning gaze on Yalith.

She did not drop her eyes. Biting her lower lip, she met his stare.

"You cannot have them both, you know," Ugiel said.

Then he was gone.

Yalith and Oholibamah spread skins over some low scrub palms. Some skins they would discard, if they were too soiled. Others they would scrape and beat clean.

"What did he mean?" Oholibamah asked.

"Who?"

"Ugiel."

"About what?"

"About not having them both."

Yalith picked up a skin foul with spills and put it in the dump pile. "Who ever knows what a nephil means?"

"You do, and I do," Oholibamah said. "He meant our young twins."

Yalith picked up another skin, appearing to examine it closely. "The Sand was the first one I met. The Den is the one we saved from the sun death."

"And they are two people, not one," Oholibamah reminded her.

"I know. Oh, yes, Oholi, I know that. They are very different when you get to know them."

"And you do not love one more than the other?"

Yalith shook her head. "Anyhow, they are too young."

"Are they that young in their own time?"

"We don't know anything about their own time."

Oholibamah sat on a stump, a pile of cleaned skins across her knees. "I love my Japheth. I am very happy with him. I want you to be happy, too."

Yalith shivered. "Mahlah seems to be happy, married to a nephil."

"Our twins are not nephilim."

"But they are different. They are not like us."

"And you love them."

"Yes."

"You love them both."

Yalith picked up a pile of skins to be discarded. "I'm going to throw these away. Then we'd better stop. The sun's getting high and it's too hot for this kind of work."

Matred said to Elisheba, "You have not been to the women's tent for two moons."

Elisheba nodded, put her hands to flushed cheeks in an unwontedly girlish gesture.

Matred embraced her. "Is it true?"

"Yes. You will have yet another grandchild." Hugging each other, they danced with joy.

Eblis the dragon/lizard was waiting for Yalith when she went to the well for water. He was not in his animal host, but was leaning against the trunk of a royal palm, purple wings wrapped around him, so that he was almost lost in shadows.

When he stepped forward, Yalith was so startled that she almost dropped the clay pitcher which she carried on one shoulder.

Eblis rescued the pitcher and put it down. "Every day you grow lovelier." He touched her gently on one cheek.

Yalith blushed and reached for the pitcher.

"Let me help you," Eblis said. When the pitcher was full, he touched her again, tracing her brows with one pale finger. "Ugiel is right, you know."

"I don't know what you're talking about."

"Oh, yes, you do, my sweet one, yes, you do. And I am the only answer to your problem."

She looked at him questioningly.

"I want you, lovely little one. You know that I want you. I can give you all that Ugiel gives your sister Mahlah, and you know how happy she is."

"I know . . ."

"Those stupid young giants who dazzle you with their youth can give you nothing except grief. You cannot choose between them, and if you should choose one, what would happen to the other?"

"They have not asked me—" She faltered.

"But I have. I do. I want you."

He bent toward her, and suddenly she felt nothing but fear. It was as he said: he wanted her. He did not love her. She picked up the water pitcher and fled, heedless of the water splashing on the ground.

9 ᵥ Mahlah's time, Lamech's time

The afternoon was the hottest the twins had ever experienced. Sandy woke from unpleasant dreams of erupting volcanoes, to see Dennys sitting up on his sleeping skins, shiny with sweat.

Higgaion spent the midday sleeping hours with Lamech. At night he dutifully took turns with the twins, but Sandy suspected that the past few nights had been spent at Grandfather Lamech's feet. The old man's extremities tended to get cold from lack of circulation.

"Is anything wrong?" Sandy asked.

"It's terribly hot."

Thunder rumbled in the distance.

"That might mean rain," Sandy said. For the moment he had forgotten that rain might mean flood.

So had Dennys. "Oh, good, for the orchards and the garden. Even with all our watering—"

The thunder came again, with a crackling, electrical sound.

Higgaion padded over to them, whimpering, looking across the tent to Grandfather Lamech.

The two boys hurried to the old man. The flap had been pegged open to let in as much breeze as possible, and the air outside was sulfurous, the sky a greenish-yellow.

Sandy squatted at one side of Grandfather Lamech, Dennys at the other. The old man was propped high on folded skins. Dennys took one of his hands and was shocked at how cold it was. He began to massage it, trying to get some circulation into the withered fingers.

Lamech opened his eyes and smiled, first at one twin, then the other. When he spoke, his voice was so faint that they had to strain to hear. "In your time and place—over the mountain—is it better?"

Sandy and Dennys looked at each other.

Sandy said, "It's very different."

"How?" the voice whispered.

"Well. People are taller. And we don't live as long."

"How long?"

Dennys answered in words which seemed to him an echo of something long lost. "Threescore years and ten."

"Sometimes fourscore," Dennys amended.

Dennys looked at Sandy, at his tan, healthy skin, muscled arms and legs, clear eyes. "We have big hospitals—places to take care of sick people. But I'm not sure I'd have had any better care for my sunstroke there than I got from Yalith and Oholibamah."

Sandy said, "We have showers and washing machines. And radios and rockets and television. And jet planes."

Dennys smiled. "But I came to your tent on a white camel. Almost all the way."

Lamech whispered, and both boys bent down to hear. "People's hearts—are they kinder?"

Sandy thought of the first vender who had tried to give him half the amount of lentils Grandfather Lamech had requested, and who had snarled and cursed when Sandy protested.

Dennys wondered how much real difference there was between terrorists who hijacked a plane and Tiglah's father and brother, who had thrown him into the garbage pit.

"People are people—" Sandy started.

Simultaneously, Dennys said, "I guess human nature is human nature."

Lamech reached out a trembling hand to each boy. "But you have been to me as my own."

Dennys gently squeezed the cold hand.

Sandy mumbled, "We love you, Grandfather Lamech."

"And I you, my sons."

"El's words are strange words. I don't understand," Lamech said. "I don't understand the thoughts of El."

Neither did the twins.

Lightning and thunder came simultaneously. Light splashed through the roof hole and the open tent flap. The walls of the tent shook from the violence of the thunder and a long earth tremor.

But no rain fell.

The twins sat on the root bench to watch the stars come out. Higgaion stayed in the tent with Grandfather Lamech. The sky still had a yellow tinge, though there was no further lightning or thunder. Tongues of flame licked up from the volcano. High in the trees, the baboons chittered nervously.

Sandy curled his toes on the soft moss under the tree root. "We've never been to a deathbed."

"No."

"I thought *that* was going to be one, this afternoon with Grandfather Lamech."

Dennys shook his head. "I think he wanted to ask us those questions."

"Does he know there's going to be a great flood?"

"I think his El that he talks to has told him."

Sandy picked up a fallen frond of palm and looked at it in the last light. "But the flood was a natural phenomenon."

Dennys shook his head slightly. "Primitive peoples have always tended to believe that what we call natural disasters are sent by an angry god. Or gods."

"What do you think?" Sandy asked.

Again Dennys shook his head. "I don't know. I know a lot less than I did before we came to the oasis."

"Anyhow"—Sandy's voice was flat—"it didn't work."

"What didn't work?"

"The flood. Wiping out all those people, and then starting all over again. People are taller, and we do even worse things to one another because we know more."

Dennys took the palm frond out of Sandy's hand. "I wouldn't choose Ham and Anah to repopulate the world, if I were doing the choosing."

"Oh, they're not that bad," Sandy said. "And Shem and

Elisheba are all right. Not terribly exciting. But solid. And Japheth and Oholibamah are terrific."

"Well. What you said. It didn't work."

"Maybe nobody should've been saved." Sandy's voice was hoarse.

Yet again, Dennys shook his head. "Human beings— people have done terrible things, but we're not all that bad, not all of us."

"Like who?"

"There've been people like—oh, Euclid and Pasteur and Tycho Brahe."

Sandy nodded. His voice came out more normally. "I like the way Tycho Brahe was so in awe of the maker of the heavens that he put on his court robes before going to his telescope."

"Who told you that?"

"Meg."

"I like that, I really do. Hey, and I think Meg would like us to mention Maria Mitchell. Wasn't she the first famous woman astronomer?"

"I miss Meg. And Charles Wallace. And our parents."

But Dennys was still involved in his list. "And the wise men who followed the star. They were astronomers. Hey!"

"What?"

"If the flood had drowned everybody, if the earth hadn't been repopulated, then Jesus would never have been born."

Sandy, his nostrils assailed by a now familiar but still disturbing odor, hardly heard. "Shh."

"What?"

"Look."

A small, shadowy form left the public path and came toward them. "Tiglah."

"She doesn't give up," Dennys mumbled.

Tiglah had learned that Dennys was not to be touched, not by her fingers, at any rate. She approached the twins demurely, eyes cast down, giving her eyelashes the full benefit of their lustrous length. She reached out and put her hand lightly against Sandy, as though to steady herself. "It's a fine evening, after all," she said.

Dennys pulled back from the mingled odor of sweat and perfume.

"It's okay." Sandy looked dubiously at the yellow light pulsing on the horizon.

Tiglah said, "I thought you might like to know that Mahlah is going to have her baby tonight."

"How do you know?" Dennys demanded.

"Rofocale told me."

"How does *he* know?" Sandy asked.

"He and Ugiel are friends. Yalith and Oholibamah are going to help."

The twins had seen kittens and puppies being born, and once a calf, and they had played with baby lambs and piglets on a neighboring farm. They looked at each other. "I'll bet Oholibamah's a good midwife," Dennys said.

Tiglah continued, "They tell me that Oholibamah's mother had a hard time birthing her. Nephil babies tend to be large." She sounded anxious.

Dennys looked at her sharply. "Does that worry you?"

"It might, one day. I hope it won't be too hard on Mahlah. She's such a little thing. Like me."

"Well," Dennys said. "Thanks for telling us." His tone was dismissive.

"It's going to be a beautiful night." Tiglah's fingers strayed toward Sandy's arm.

Dennys turned his face away and looked toward the tent. The flap was still pegged open. Higgaion was sitting in the opening, waving his trunk slightly, as though to catch the breeze.

Sandy looked at Tiglah, hesitated.

Swiftly, Tiglah coaxed. "It's such a nice night for a walk. After Mahlah's baby is born, Yalith and Oholibamah will be walking home and we might meet them . . ."

Sandy rose to the bait. "Well . . . but not far . . . or for long . . ."

"Of course not," Tiglah reassured. "Just a little walk."

Sandy became aware of Dennys carefully not looking at him. "Are you coming?"

"No."

"Do you mind if I go?"

"Of course not."

"I won't be long."

"Feel free."

They were not communicating. Sandy did not like the feeling. But he stood. Tiglah reached up and put her small hand in his much larger one. When they reached the public path, he looked back. Higgaion had left the tent and was standing by Dennys.

The night was heavier than usual. The stars looked blurred, and almost close enough to touch. The rainless storm had increased rather than decreased the heat. The mountain smoked.

"Let's go by the desert," Tiglah suggested, "and watch the moonrise."

To step off the oasis onto the desert was like stepping off a ship onto the sea. The desert sand felt cool to Sandy's feet, which were now accustomed to the hot sands by day, to walking on stones, on sharp, dry grasses.

Tiglah led the way to a ledge of rock. "Let's sit."

Moonrise over this early desert was very different from moonrise at home. At home, as the moon lifted above the horizon, it was a deep yellow, sometimes almost red. Here, in a time when the sea of air above the planet was still clear and clean, the moon rose with a great blaze of diamonds.

Sandy's eyes were focused on the brilliant light of the rising moon, and he was not prepared to have the light suddenly darkened by Tiglah's face as she pressed her lips against his. She was up on her knees in order to reach him, and her lips smelled of berries. Then he was surrounded by her particular odor of scented oils and her own unwashed body.

He knew what she wanted, and he wanted it, too; he was ready, but not, despite her gorgeousness, with Tiglah. Tiglah was not worth losing his ability to touch a unicorn.

But Yalith—

He knew that he and Dennys should do nothing to change the story, to alter history. Even with Yalith . . .

He was getting ahead of himself. Yalith was not Tiglah. Yalith smiled on both of them with equal loveliness.

Tiglah's red hair, turned silver-gold in the moonlight, tumbled about his face, drowning him in its scent. She massaged the back of his head, his neck. Her breathing mingled with his. He knew that if he did not break this off, he would not be able to. With a deep inward sigh, he pulled away. Stood.

Tiglah scrambled to her feet, stared up at him reproachfully. "Don't you like it? Don't you like what I was doing?"

"Yes, I like it." His voice was hoarse. "I like it too much."

"Too much? How can anything be too much? What is there in life except pleasure, and the more the better! How can you talk of too much?"

"You're too much." He tried to laugh. "I think I'd better go now. Grandfather Lamech isn't well."

"He's dying," Tiglah said bluntly. "Rofocale told me."

"Rofocale doesn't know everything."

"He knows more than we do, more than any mortal."

Sandy stood still. He thought he heard the shrill whine of a mosquito. Then silence. He turned and started walking back to the oasis. Tiglah slid down from the rock, ran to catch up with him, and reached for his hand.

"You, too," she said. "You must be of the same breed as Rofocale, so tall, so strong. You could pick me up, and throw me over your shoulder. Where do you come from?"

He was tired of answering the old questions. "Another part of the planet. Another time."

"Why have you come?"

"It was a mistake," he said shortly.

"But why was it a mistake to come? It's wonderful that you're here! How long are you going to stay?"

"I don't know."

"But you do have plans? What are you going to do?"

"Take care of Grandfather Lamech's garden and groves."

"Is that all? You didn't come all this way just for that! You must have come for some reason."

"No," he said. He removed his arm from her hand.

"No," Tiglah said. "I didn't find out anything. I asked him all the questions you told me to, but he didn't tell me anything."

Rofocale towered over her, his wings flaming like the sun even in the moonlight. "He must have said something."

"He said he came from far away, and that it was a mistake to come."

"Mistake?" Rofocale queried. The garnet pool of his eyes looked opaque. "Could El have made another mistake?"

"You think your El sent them?"

"Who else? They are certainly not native. They may be as much of a threat to us as the seraphim. At least the seraphim are careful not to manipulate or change things."

"You think the young giants will?"

"Who knows? And you couldn't get anything out of him?"

The dimple in Tiglah's chin deepened. "At least he came with me this time."

"So he did. And did you kiss him?"

She nodded. "He tasted so young. Young as the morning."

"Did he like it?"

"He liked it. But just as I thought he was ready to go further, he pulled back. But give me time, Rofocale. This is, after all, the first time he's been willing to go with me."

Rofocale in a movement of swift grace knelt so that their eyes were level. "You must work fast, my little Tiglah."

"Why? What's the hurry?"

Rofocale rubbed the back of his hand against his forehead. "Some of our powers have been weakened. We can no longer tell—but Noah knows something. His sons married abnormally young, and hurriedly. Noah still speaks with the One on whom I have turned my back. There may not be another hundred years."

"But why do you want me to—to seduce him?"

"Wouldn't that put him in your—and my—power?" He drew her to him. "What you do with the naked giant will not make you any less mine, little lovely one. I like my women to be experienced in the ways of lust."

"Will I make a baby for you?"

He spread his wings so that she was wrapped in a cloud of flame. "Soon."

"Soon," Oholibamah said. "Soon. Press down, Mahlah, press down. Hard."

"Soon," Yalith echoed reassuringly. "It will come soon."

Matred said nothing.

Mahlah, lying on her back on a pile of skins, screamed. Her hands groped frantically, and Matred took them in a firm grasp, while Mahlah clutched.

"It's gone on so long," Yalith whispered. "How much more can she take?"

"Get up," Matred ordered Mahlah.

Mahlah wailed, "I can't. I can't. Oh, let it come, let it come soon—"

"Get up," Matred repeated. "Squat."

"I did, I did, until I was so tired I couldn't—"

"You've rested enough." Matred's voice was rough. "Help her up," she ordered Yalith and Oholibamah.

The two girls had to use all their strength to pull the resisting Mahlah off the skins.

"Squat," Matred said. "Bear down. Now. Now. Push."

"The moon is setting," Yalith said.

Oholibamah looked at Matred. "My mother went through this. She is still alive."

"Yes, my dear," Matred said. "Thank you." It was Oholibamah's first open acknowledgment that she had been sired by one of the nephilim, and Matred pressed her shoulder in gratitude.

The moon set. The sun rose. It was stifling in the small white clay house. The four women streamed sweat. Mahlah's hair was as wet as though it had been dipped in the water jar. Her eyes were wide open in agony. She moaned, screamed, shrieked. Occasionally, between contractions, her mouth would fall open laxly and her lids would droop shut as she dropped into an exhausted sleep, only to be wakened as she was assailed by a fresh pain.

The sun slid low in the sky.

"Squat," Matred ordered. "You must squat again."

Three nights and three days. Squatting, lying, screaming.

—She will die, Yalith thought. —This cannot go on.

"Soon," Oholibamah continued to reassure the tortured Mahlah. "It will come soon. Press down. Harder."

Matred's voice was sharp with anxiety. "Work, Mahlah, work. We cannot have this baby for you. Work. Push."

For the fourth night, the moon rose.

"*Push,*" Matred commanded.

A long, grunting groan came from Mahlah, more terrible than her screams.

"Now. *Now.*"

The groan seemed as though it would tear Mahlah apart.

"*Now.*" And at last Matred reached between Mahlah's legs to help draw the baby out of her body. The baby's head was so large that Yalith could hear Mahlah's flesh rip as the child came out. Matred shook it, patted its buttocks, and the air rushed into its lungs and it howled.

While Sandy was with Tiglah, Dennys went in to Grandfather Lamech, uneasy about him. He walked to where the old man was lying.

"Son?"

"It's Dennys, Grandfather."

An old hand groped for his. Dennys held it, and it was cold, deathly cold. "Can I do something for you, Grandfather?"

A serene smile wreathed the old man's face. "El has spoken."

Dennys waited.

The old man seemed to be trying to suck in enough air

to speak. Finally he said, "All will not be lost. Oh, my son, Den, El has repented. While you were in the garden, El spoke to me here in the tent. I have never heard him here before. Oh, my son, Den, my son, my son, Noah will be spared. Noah and his family. El has spoken."

"From what, Grandfather Lamech?"

"Eh?"

"From what will they be spared?"

The old fingers trembled in Dennys's hand. "El spoke of many waters. This I do not understand. But no matter. What is of concern is that my son will be spared." The fingers pressed against Dennys's. "But you, my son? What will happen to you? I do not know."

"I don't know either, Grandfather." Dennys massaged the withered old hand until a little warmth returned.

Ugiel stood looking down at the baby lying between Mahlah's breasts. The young mother looked pale and exhausted, but radiant.

The three women who had shared her labor were nearly as exhausted as Mahlah. Oholibamah had deep circles under her eyes, and her cheeks were ashen. It was she who had somehow or other stanched the blood that poured out, nearly taking Mahlah's life with it; she who had brought the afterbirth out safely. Her hands and arms were stained red from holding Mahlah's torn flesh together until the rush of blood slowed to a trickle and the danger of hemorrhaging was over.

Ugiel paid no attention to the others. He gazed at his baby. It had a full head of hair, black, like Mahlah's. He flipped it over and fingered the soft down outlining the shoulder blades. "I am pleased," he said.

Matred was sharp. "And well you might be. It almost killed her. Without Oholibamah, it would have." She turned away from Ugiel and fed Mahlah some of the strengthening broth Elisheba had sent over.

"Go home," she said to Yalith and Oholibamah. "Go and get something to eat, and rest. I will stay with Mahlah. Elisheba will be by later."

Oholibamah, also ignoring Ugiel, looked at mother and child. "She will need much care for the next several days. Be sure to call me if the bleeding starts again."

"I will," Matred promised.

Ugiel bent over Mahlah and with one long finger touched the baby on its eyelids, its nose. "I am pleased," Ugiel said again.

Oholibamah sat in the big tent, letting Elisheba feed them lentil soup.

Oholibamah said, "He didn't care whether she lived or not, as long as she had the baby."

Yalith paused in the act of raising her bowl to her lips. "Do you really think that?"

"You heard him, didn't you? 'Why doesn't she get on with it?' he said. 'Why is it taking so long?' And then he would go away and not come back for hours and hours."

"Mother said she didn't want him around—" Then Yalith stopped. Matred had been with her older daughters when they gave birth, shooing their husbands away but giving a running account of the delivery. Nor had the husbands gone far away. They had, in fact, been maddeningly underfoot. They had not simply vanished, like Ugiel, leaving everything to the women. She finished her soup in silence.

Oholibamah, too, drank. Her dark brows drew together. Her raven-black hair had come loose from its thong and fallen about her shoulders.

"Oholibamah—" Yalith said softly.

"What is it?"

"The nephilim marry our women, give them babies. But the seraphim—"

"They do not marry. Or give babies."

"But in many ways they are like the nephilim."

Oholibamah pushed her dark hair back in a weary gesture. "No. I think that once the nephilim were like the seraphim."

"What happened to change them?"

"I don't know."

Yalith thought of Aariel, with the bright amber eyes and leonine grace, and then of Eblis, and she was glad she had run from the purple-winged nephil. She wanted nothing to do with Eblis, if he was like Ugiel, who did not care whether his wife lived or died. Could Ugiel once have been like Aariel? Could Eblis?

Oholibamah said, "I think that the seraphim are free to leave us for the stars at any time if they want to. I don't think the nephilim can. Not anymore. They stay with us, not because they have chosen to, but because they have to."

Noah and Japheth came into the tent, their arms and hands as stained with grape juice as Oholibamah's had been with blood. Japheth embraced his wife. Yalith ran to her father. "Mahlah has had her baby! It is all right!"

Noah put his arms around his youngest child, but he seemed strangely disinterested.

"Did you hear, Father?" Yalith demanded. "Mahlah's long travail is over at last!"

"That is good to hear," Noah said heavily. "We were worried."

"What is it?" Oholibamah asked. "Is something wrong?"

Japheth's arm tightened about his wife.

Noah drew Yalith close. "El has spoken. Strange words."

"Good words?" Yalith asked.

Oholibamah looked at Japheth questioningly, but he shook his head.

"Strange words," Noah repeated. "I do not know what to make of them."

"Be happy for Mahlah, Father," Yalith said. "It was such a hard birth, so long. If it had not been for Oholi—"

"Mahlah will be all right," Oholibamah said. "She is young and strong and will heal quickly."

"It is a big baby, Father," Yalith continued. "It is the biggest baby I have ever seen, with dark hair, like Mahlah's, and a button of a nose."

"At least it is a baby." Noah's voice was bitter.

"You are upset," Oholibamah said.

"Yes, I suppose I am upset. El has asked me to do strange things. I do not understand. Great changes are coming. Terrible changes."

"Japheth—" Oholibamah whispered.

"Hush. Later."

Within the comfort of her father's arms, Yalith shivered. "But now we can rejoice, Father, because Mahlah has had a safe delivery."

Noah continued to hold his daughter, pressing his lips against her bright hair. "We did not have a wedding feast for Mahlah. That hurt Matred. I had hoped that we could have a wedding feast for you."

"Oh, but I hope you will!" Yalith exclaimed. She thought of Mahlah's strange wedding, and she did not want one like that, isolated from her family and friends. Then she thought of the twins. In their own way, they were as alien as the nephilim and the seraphim, and yet they were human, totally human. And she loved them. She pressed her cheek against her father's chest, so that she did not see the expression on his face.

Oholibamah did, but before she could speak, Japheth had pulled her to him again in a loving embrace.

A soft whimpering woke the twins. Higgaion had come over to their sleeping skins to summon them.

Sandy opened his eyes. "Higgy, what's the matter?"

Dennys sat up, abruptly wide awake. "Is it Grandfather Lamech?" He looked at Higgaion, asking, "Should we get Noah?"

"Is Grandfather—" Sandy could not finish the sentence.

The two boys scrambled across the tent to the old man's sleeping skins. Grandfather Lamech was breathing in strange, shallow pants. Dennys reached to touch him, and saw the scarab beetle. He felt a surge of relief. Spoke urgently. "Adnarel, we need Admael. If he could be his camel self, he could carry one of us to Noah's tent far more quickly than either Sandy or I could run." Dennys gently touched the bronze armor of the scarab beetle, which thinned out and disappeared under his finger, so that he was touching only a corner of the old man's sleeping skin. Adnarel stood by them, a golden glimmer in the gloom of the tent. "I will get Admael. Wait with Grandfather Lamech." With one of his swift, graceful gestures, he bowed and went out.

Sandy and Dennys each took one of Grandfather Lamech's hands, which felt as cold and lifeless as marble. Sandy said, "Adnarel is calling Admael for us. We'll get Noah for you, as quickly as we can."

The old man breathed softly. "My good boys."

Dennys watched Grandfather Lamech's straining effort to breathe. Gently he put his arm under the small, frail body, easing it into a sitting position. The old man leaned against the boy, and his breathing lightened. "I'll stay with you, Grandfather." Dennys looked at Sandy and nodded.

Sandy nodded back.

"I can wait," the old man whispered, "until the last star goes out."

Adnarel returned. He knelt by Grandfather Lamech, examining him gently. He turned to the twins. "Admael is waiting outside. You don't need to rush, Sand. There will be time."

Grandfather Lamech gasped. "Until the baboons—"

Adnarel smiled. "Until the baboons clap their hands and shout for joy to welcome the dawn."

Dennys said, "I'll stay with Grandfather."

Adnarel nodded, touching Dennys's shoulder lightly. "Good. I will be here if you need me." His bright form misted, swirled softly like fog, and the scarab beetle shone against Higgaion's ear.

When Dennys had ridden the white camel across the desert, coming from Noah's tent, he had still been weak from his sunstroke. Sandy was well and strong, and had little difficulty keeping his seat, his body quickly becoming accustomed to the erratically rolling rhythm. They crossed the desert without trouble. On a high outcropping of white rock, a lion stood majestically to watch their progress.

There was no sound around Noah's tenthold beyond contented snores. Sandy pulled back the flap to the big tent, calling, "Noah!"

It was Matred's sleepy voice that answered, "Who is it?"

"It's Sandy. Grandfather Lamech sent me to get Noah."

"El." Noah's voice was deep. "I'll be right out."

Sandy stood outside, listening to the sound of night insects mingling with snores from Ham and Elisheba's tent. He looked up at the sky and the low, blurred stars seemed to be calling him, but he could not understand what they were trying to say.

Noah came out, wearing a fresh loincloth.

"Dennys is with Grandfather," Sandy said, "and Higgaion."

Noah nodded.

"Adnarel said there would be time, but you'll get there faster if you ride the camel alone. I'll walk back."

Again Noah nodded, accepting the offer. The camel's legs

were folded under it so that Noah could climb up easily. He sat astride, his work-gnarled fingers gripping the hair at the camel's neck. The white beast rose slowly, leaned its head on the long, arched neck low enough so that it could nuzzle Sandy softly, then took off, heading for the desert.

Sandy followed slowly. He knew that as soon as Noah reached the tent, Dennys would leave Grandfather Lamech, to allow the old man his last minutes with his son. Dennys would be waiting for him, probably sitting out on the root bench, perhaps with Higgaion to wait with him. But Sandy could not make his feet hurry. He jumped down onto the desert, and sand lapped at his feet. He let it run like water through his toes.

When Grandfather Lamech died, what then? Would it be near time for the flood? Would Sandy and Dennys be allowed to stay in the old man's tent and take care of his garden and groves?

Asking these questions of the silent stars did nothing to ease the lump of sorrow in his throat. He moved slowly over the sand, stubbed his toe on a hidden rock. Said "Ouch" in a loud voice. Walked on.

On his rock, the lion now lay still, watchful, its ears pricking as Sandy plodded by.

The horizon was touched with a faint rose color. The stars were dimming. The birds were waking in the trees. He thought he heard a sleepy jabbering from the baboons. He turned in toward the oasis. He could not delay his return any longer.

His head was down; he was looking at his feet moving

across the sand. He did not notice sounds behind him. Suddenly something noxious was thrown over his head, blinding him. He was picked up roughly, his feet jerked out from under him. Two people were carrying him. The foul-smelling skin over his head was pressed hard against his mouth so that he could not scream. He tried to wriggle out of the clutch of whoever was carrying him, and a fist crashed into his belly, winding him, and something sharp pricked his arm.

10 ~ *The song of the stars*

Yalith left the tent and slipped away, to the desert, to the rock where the great lion lay. He jumped down from the rock as she approached, and she ran to him, flinging her arms around his great ruffed neck, and sobbing, so that her words were barely coherent. "Grandfather Lamech is dying." Her tears spotted his fur. When her weeping was spent, the great cat's tongue gently licked her tears away, and then they sat, Yalith between the front paws, in silent communion.

The stars moved in their slow dance, dimmed. Neither lion nor girl moved. But Yalith, leaning against the great tawny chest, hearing the thudding of the lion's heart in time with the soft singing of the stars, moved into peace.

Outside Grandfather Lamech's tent, Dennys sat on the old root of the fig tree, Higgaion at his feet. Neither moved. Above them, the stars were quiet.

Within the tent, Noah held his father up so that the old man could breathe.

"My son," Lamech whispered. "You have been a blessing to me and to the land . . ."

Noah's tears rolled quietly down his cheeks, into his beard. "I have been stubborn and stupid—"

A faint laugh came from his father. "I did not say that you are not human. But you listen to El?"

"I try, Father. I try."

"El has told me that through you shall blessing . . ." The old man's breath failed.

"Hush, Father. Don't try to talk."

"It is . . . it is our last . . ."

"I listen, Father. To you. To El."

"You will do what—"

"Yes, Father. I will do what El tells me."

"No matter . . ."

"No matter how strange it seems."

"Yalith—"

Noah's tears flowed more freely. "Oh, Father, I don't know."

"Never fear." For a moment Lamech's voice was strong, and he sounded almost like one of the seraphim. Then the strength faded, and he spoke in a thin whisper. "El will take care of . . ."

"Father. Father. Don't go."

"Don't hold me back, my son . . . my son . . ."

Noah's tears fell like rain.

"Our dear twins—"

"What, Father?"

The old man gasped, and then smiled a surprised smile

of joy, so radiant that it seemed to light the darkened tent. Had lightning flashed to make the smile visible?

"Father!" Noah cried. And then, "Father!" And then his sobs broke like waves across the dry sands of the desert.

The stars did not sing. The sky was silent. Higgaion sat up, ears alert. Dennys raised his head, and it seemed that the stars were holding their light.

And suddenly the bright presence of a seraphim stood before him, and the starlight again fell onto his upturned face.

Japheth and Oholibamah held vigil for Grandfather Lamech in their own way. They went to the desert, to their particular resting rock, and sat quietly, holding hands.

At last Japheth spoke: "Thank El that my father and grandfather are reconciled. It would be much harder to bear this if—"

Oholibamah smiled. "Two stubborn old men. Yes, it is better this way. We have the Den to thank for this."

"It was a happy day when I first found them in the desert, our young giants. They have taken good care of Grandfather."

Oholibamah sighed. "We are going to miss him. Yalith, especially; she was the closest to him of us all."

"True." Japheth cradled her dark head with his hand. "But Father says it is best that death has come to get him now. He is too old and frail to stand the trip."

"What trip?" Oholibamah asked.

Japheth's eyes were darkly unhappy. "Oh, my dear one,

it is what I promised to tell you. Father says that El has told him strange things. And that he has been given very specific instructions."

"What instructions?"

Japheth sounded uncomfortable. "Oh, my wife, it is very strange indeed. El has told my father to build a boat, an ark."

Oholibamah, who had been leaning against her husband, sat up abruptly. "An ark? In the middle of the desert?"

"I said it was strange."

"Could he have made a mistake?"

"El?"

"Not El. Your father. Could he have misunderstood what El was telling him?"

Japheth shook his head. "He sounded very certain. He said that El had also told Grandfather Lamech the things which are to come."

"An ark." Oholibamah's dark brows drew together. "An ark, in a desert land. It makes no sense. Has your father told the others?"

"Not yet." Japheth pulled Oholibamah back against him. "He says they will laugh."

"They will," Oholibamah agreed. But she did not laugh.

"I have never seen him more serious," Japheth said.

"What's the ark to be built of?" Oholibamah asked.

"Gopher wood. At least we have plenty of that. And then he is to put pitch inside and outside to make it watertight."

"From what water?" Japheth was silent. She turned so that she could look at him. "This does not sound like your father."

Japheth spoke in a low voice. "Nor does it sound like El."

Oholibamah stroked his face. "We do not know what El does or does not sound like. El is a great mystery."

Japheth laughed. "So is a big boat in the desert."

"How big?" Oholibamah asked.

Japheth flung out his hands. "Three hundred cubits long, fifty cubits wide, and thirty cubits high."

Oholibamah asked curiously, "El gave these precise measurements?"

"According to Father."

"I don't understand," Oholibamah said. "I wish you'd had a chance to talk to Grandfather."

Japheth shook his head, wiping the tears from his eyes.

"And our twins," Oholibamah said. "What will happen to our twins now?"

"It is possible they might go on taking care of Grandfather's garden and groves. But I'm not sure. Grandfather's death is the beginning of a big change."

Oholibamah nodded. "There are dissonances in the song of the stars."

"Have you heard it?" Japheth asked.

Oholibamah nodded. "The song has changed. Yes, I have heard it. But why should Grandfather Lamech's death be the beginning of change? He is a very old man."

Japheth agreed. "It is not at all strange that he should die."

Oholibamah mused, "Perhaps it is strange that Grandfather Lamech should die just as El gives extraordinary commands to Lamech's son."

"Oh, my beloved," Japheth said. "You are wise. Sometimes I wish you were not quite so wise."

They twined their arms about each other. Japheth put his lips against hers, and they took comfort in their love.

When it became apparent that Sandy had not returned to Lamech's tent, nor had he stayed in Noah's, there was great consternation.

Noah's sons and their wives had come with Matred across the desert, and stood sadly outside Grandfather Lamech's tent.

"We haven't seen him," Japheth said anxiously to his father. "We thought he was following you."

Yalith reached for her brother. "We were so busy with our grief, we didn't even think . . ."

Noah pulled at his beard. "He said he would follow me."

Ham said, not unkindly, "Whatever's happened, we can't look for him now, not with the morning sun rising."

Shem explained to Dennys, "In our country, in this heat, the dead must be buried quickly."

Dennys tried to hide his panic at Sandy's inexplicable absence. Sandy was reliable. If there was a reason for his not having followed Noah to Grandfather Lamech's tent, he would somehow or other send word.

How? There were no telephones. But wouldn't he have tried to find one of the seraphim? He wouldn't just have gone off somewhere, without telling anybody.

Matred put a motherly arm about Dennys. "Now we must anoint Grandfather Lamech's body and prepare it for burial at sundown. Then we will leave our grief and look for the Sand. There is some reasonable explanation for his absence, I'm sure."

Anah suggested, "Perhaps he's somewhere with my sister. I think they're very taken with each other."

Dennys shook his head. He did not believe it. Sandy would not go off with Tiglah, knowing that Grandfather Lamech was dying.

Yalith slipped her hand into his and squeezed it comfortingly. She kissed him lightly on the cheek, like a butterfly, and then went with her mother and the other women into the tent. The men stayed outside while Lamech's body was rubbed with oil and spices and wrapped in clean white skins.

The sun rose high in the sky, beat down on them with the fierceness of a brass gong.

Japheth said, "Do not even think of going off to look for him in this heat, Den. The sun would strike you down, and that would not help your brother."

Had it not been for Japheth, Dennys would have put on one of Matred's woven hats and gone to look for Sandy. But Dennys knew that Japheth was right.

"Surely he's somewhere in the shade," Shem said. The palm grove where they were sitting shielded them with its dense shade. "Don't worry, Den. The Sand is a sensible lad."

"Yes, but—" Dennys started. And stopped himself. The people of Noah's tenthold were grieving for Lamech. Higgaion was in the tent with the women and the old men, and Dennys knew that it was irrational of him to feel abandoned by the mammoth. He was, after all, Lamech's mammoth.

The tent flap was pushed open slightly and Higgaion trudged out, and toward Dennys, raising his trunk in sorrowful greeting and asking to be picked up, much as a small child will raise its arms to be lifted.

Dennys gathered up the little creature and held it against him, letting his tears drop onto the mammoth's shaggy head.

At sunset, Noah and his sons carried Grandfather Lamech's body to a shallow cave not far across the desert. The women followed. Dennys stood between Yalith and Oholibamah, as Noah and Shem, Ham and Japheth dug a grave in the sand just inside the cave. Dennys had offered to help with the difficult digging, not only out of love for the old man, but also to take his mind off his near-terror over Sandy.

Noah told him, gently, that it was the custom that only the sons should do this final act of love, but that Dennys should stay with the women and the sons-in-law, because he had become a child of the family.

The sun slid below the horizon. The sky was a deep crimson. As the sun vanished, there was a faint glow on the far horizon, and the young moon began to peer over the edge of the planet. The moon's diamond crescent seemed strangely subdued as it rose, and Dennys, standing to one side, thought that he could hear a soft and mournful dirge. A star trembled into being, then another, and another. They joined the singing of the moon, singing for Lamech, whose years had been long, whose life had been full, and who, at the end, had been reconciled with his son.

Noah and Matred's older daughters, Seerah and Hoglah,

and their husbands and children, stood in a cluster, wailing loudly. Mahlah stood to one side with her baby. Ugiel, she apologized, was not able to come. She looked curiously at Dennys.

Sandy, Noah told Mahlah in the same words she had used of Ugiel, was not able to come.

"Why?" Mahlah asked. No one answered.

Oholibamah spoke in a low voice, for Japheth, Dennys, and Yalith alone. "Mahlah will ask Ugiel about Sandy when she goes back."

Yalith whispered, "Will he know?"

Oholibamah shook her head. "If he does, he won't tell. I suspect the nephilim have something to do with this."

Japheth frowned. "I hope you aren't right about that."

Dennys looked at them with fresh fear.

The grave was dug.

As the son and grandsons picked the old man up to place him in the grave, Dennys sensed, rather than heard, presences behind them, and turned to see the golden bodies of seraphim standing in a half circle. Once again, he could hear clearly the singing of the moon and the stars.

Aariel called, "Yalith!"

Startled, she let out a small cry.

Aariel raised arms and wings skyward, and the song increased in intensity. "Sing for Grandfather Lamech."

Obediently, Yalith raised her head and sang, a wordless melody, achingly lovely. Above her, the stars and the moon sang with her, and behind her the seraphim joined in great organ tones of harmony.

Japheth took Oholibamah's hands and drew her out onto

the clear sands, and they began to dance in rhythm with the song. They were joined by Ham and Anah, and the four of them wove patterns under the stars, touching hands, moving apart, twirling, touching, leaping. Shem and Elisheba joined in, then Noah and Matred and the older daughters and their husbands, and then Yalith took Dennys's hands and drew him into the kaleidoscope of moving bodies, an alleluia of joy and grief and wonder, until Dennys forgot Sandy, forgot that Grandfather Lamech would never be in his tent again, forgot his longing to go home. The crimson flush at the horizon turned a soft ashrose, then mauve, then blue, as more and more stars brightened, and the harmony of the spheres and the dance of the galaxies interwove in radiance. Slowly the dancers moved apart, stopped. Dennys closed his eyes in a combination of joy and fierce grief, opening them only when the requiem was over. The sky was brilliant with the light of the moon and the stars. The seraphim were gone. Yalith stood beside him, tears streaming down her cheeks.

Noah and his sons tamped down the earth over Grandfather Lamech's grave.

Sandy opened his eyes and could see nothing. His limbs felt numb. Whatever had pricked him had temporarily paralyzed him. There was a strange tingling in his limbs as feeling began to return. He knew about the tiny darts that Japheth and Yalith and some of the others in Noah's tenthold used, and guessed that something similar had been used on him.

Why?

He smelled goat, urine, sweat. As his eyes adjusted to the darkness, he could see that he was in a small tent. The smoke hole was covered, so that very little light came through. It was a much smaller tent than Noah's or Grandfather Lamech's. He tried to move his arms and found that his hands were tied, bound firmly with thong. So were his feet.

As sensation returned to him, he wriggled around and finally managed to sit up, his back against the rough skins of the tent, his bound hands in front of him. He raised them and tried to bite at the thongs. The taste made him gag. The thongs had been wound about his wrists so many times that it was futile to try to chew through them, nor could he find a knot to try to bite.

He stopped his useless reflexive efforts and tried to think.

He had been kidnapped on his way from Noah's tent to Lamech's. Why? When terrorists hijacked a plane, they wanted something. What use would he be to anybody as a hostage? This was a world still without money, without political prisoners. As far as he knew, nobody held anything against Lamech or Noah.

So, why?

His stomach growled. How long had the poisoned dart kept him asleep? What time was it? He could not see even a line of light to indicate where the tent flap was. The light from the covered smoke hole was so faint that it might even have come from stars.

There had to be a tent flap. He wriggled around so that his feet touched the tent wall, and kept wriggling, feeling with his toes. Wriggled until he was exhausted and had found no way out. Rested. Wriggled again. Again. At last his feet felt a line of roughness. He pushed, and the flap moved slightly, enough so that he could tell that it was indeed night outside. Stars. A single palm tree silhouetted against them. He had no idea where he was, or even if he was still on his own oasis.

Worn out from his efforts, he fell asleep, his head just out of the tent. Sunlight blazing against his lids woke him, and he managed to slither back into the tent and sat leaning against the taut skins by the entrance. His stomach made loud, hungry noises. What wouldn't he give for a mess of Grandfather Lamech's pottage.

Grandfather.

When he got out of this tent and back where he belonged, there would no longer be the tiny, shriveled old man tending the hearth fire.

Come on, Sandy. He's *old*. Seven hundred seventy-seven years. And Noah was pushing six hundred years old. It didn't make any sense. Except, he believed them. And after the flood people weren't going to live that long. At least, he thought that was how it was going to be.

"Twin!"

It was a girl's soft voice. His heart leaped. Yalith.

Then smell followed sound. Not Yalith. Tiglah.

"Twin?" she repeated.

"Hello, Tiglah." He did not sound welcoming. He remembered what Dennys had told him about the people in Tiglah's tent. So it was they who were the terrorists. Terrorism was not just a twentieth-century phenomenon. It was evidently part of human nature, and it didn't get wiped out by the flood. There seemed less and less point to the flood.

"You recognized my voice!" she chortled.

—No, your smell, you slut, he wanted to say.

She pushed in through the flap and pegged it back to let in the light. She had taken unusual pains with her hair, so that it glistened brightly. Her loincloth was of white goatskin. "Dennys?" She was tentative.

"Sandy."

"Oh, I'm so glad it's you! Dennys doesn't seem to like me, and I think you do, don't you?"

"Why would I like anybody who's kidnapped me and tied me up and starved me?"

"But *I* didn't do that!"

"You obviously knew about it."

"But I didn't do it! My father and brother did. I wouldn't hurt you for anything!"

"But you don't mind if your father or brother hurt me?"

"Oh, beloved Sand, I can't stop them! I've come to bring you food and comfort."

He sniffed. There was a nourishing smell of stew beyond the odor of the tent, as well of Tiglah's perfumed and unwashed body. If they'd already used some kind of poisoned dart on him, was it safe to eat the stew?

Tiglah said, "I made it myself, so I know it's all right, and it's good, too."

"I can't eat with my hands tied up."

She paused. Appeared to be thinking. "I'll feed you!" Her dimples came and went with her lavish smile.

"No. I'm not a baby. Untie my hands." He did not say please. How could he ever have been attracted by this girl?

She paused again. "All right. I'll untie your hands and stay with you while you eat."

"My feet, too," Sandy ordered. "I need to go to the bathroom."

"What?"

"I need to urinate."

"Oh, for auk's sakes. Can't you just do it in the tent?"

"No. You can come with me if you want. I don't care, but I need to go."

She knelt by him and began working at the thongs, first on his wrists, then his ankles. When he was freed, he stood up, feeling very wobbly. This tent was not nearly as high as Grandfather Lamech's or Noah's, and he bumped his head on the roof skins.

She took his hands and rubbed his wrists where the thongs had chafed them.

"Let's go," he said.

"Where?"

"I told you. I need to relieve myself."

"Come along, then." She pulled him out of the tent and to a small, grassy hummock a few feet away. There was no grove to provide privacy or a modicum of sanitation. "Go ahead."

"Turn around."

"You'll run away."

He looked about. He did not recognize the part of the oasis where this solitary tent was. A few yards away were some palms, and a rocky field dotted with black-and-white goats grazing under the high brassy sky. He had no idea in which direction to go. "I won't run. Turn around."

"Promise?"

"I promise." He suspected that his promise meant more than would Tiglah's. When he was through, he said, "All right."

She whirled around and caught his hand again. "Now come and have some of my good goat-meat stew."

They ducked back into the tent, and she brought him a wooden bowl full of meat and vegetables. He had learned to eat with his fingers, if not as delicately as Yalith, at least tidily enough so that he did not slop food on himself. Tiglah's concoction was not bad. The goat meat was a little strong, but she had cooked it until it was tender. When he finished, cleaning the bowl with his fingers, he felt better.

"I'll have to tie you up again," Tiglah apologized. "They won't like it that I let you loose at all."

"Who're *they*?"

"Oh, the men of my father's tent."

"What's it all about?"

"What?"

"Kidnapping me. Keeping me tied in this stinking tent."

She shrugged and giggled. "How would I know? They're always up to things."

"And you're not?"

"I'm only a girl." She was full of righteous indignation. "I like you! Why would I want to tie you up?"

"Then don't."

She had the thongs in her hands. "But I have to."

"Why?"

"They'd be furious. They'd hit me. They might kill me."

Would they? He wasn't sure. But he understood Dennys's refusal to have anything to do with Tiglah. Never again.

"How long are they going to keep me here? What do they think they're going to get out of it?"

"Noah's vineyards," she said.

"What!"

"Noah's vineyards. They're the best on any oasis."

"That's idiotic. Noah wouldn't give up his vineyards. They're his livelihood."

"He'd better give them up," Tiglah said, "or they'll kill you."

Sandy stood up, outraged, hitting his head against the roof skins. "Do they know Grandfather Lamech is dying— is dead?"

"Of course."

"They're monstrous."

"They're clever. They knew everybody would be paying attention to silly old Lamech and wouldn't miss you. They're *very* clever."

"Oh, no, they're not," Sandy said. "No one gives in to terrorists. Noah won't give anybody his vineyards."

"Then they'll kill you."

"And what good will that do? They still won't have the vineyards, and they'll have murder on their hands."

"Oh, Sand. Sit down. This tent wasn't made for giants. I hate to tie you up again, but I have to. Unless—"

"Unless what?"

"Come with me."

"What would your family think of that?"

"They'd hate it. But I care more about you than I do about them."

Sandy did not believe her. There was a trap here. This

had something to do with the nephilim, with that mosquito Rofocale. What, he did not know. Tiglah did not love him enough to anger her family. She did not love him at all. But she would obey Rofocale.

He felt a sharp sting and slapped, but missed the mosquito, who buzzed out of the tent. Furious, he scratched at the bite. "Tie me up and go away."

She pressed her face close to his. "You won't come with me?"

"No."

"You'll risk being killed?"

His mouth twisted into a half grin. "There are fates worse than death," and he laughed, because Tiglah did not have the faintest idea what he was talking about.

"I haven't bound you yet . . ." she whispered.

"No."

"You're a giant. You could grab me and run off with me, and you could tell them you'll kill me if they try to capture you again."

It was tempting. He shook his head, and a great wave of sadness washed over him. Tiglah had never heard of the great heroes of lance and spear, of longbow and sword. But this was what she was tempting him to be. What he could be if he wanted to be.

What in him was urging him to reject this attractive role? What was telling him to say no? It was more than his suspicion that all this was some kind of nephil trap.

The sadness washed over him again. Violence was no longer an option. The splitting of the atom had put an end to that, though the world was slow to realize it.

Yes, he could overcome Tiglah with ease. She was inviting him. But even if there was no trick in it, he would not
do it. Violence met with violence produced only more violence. His stomach knotted.

"Are you sure?" Tiglah's voice had a little whine in it.

"Of what?"

"That you won't come with me."

He smiled without mirth. There was poison in Tiglah's
offer, of that he was certain. "No, Tiglah, I won't come
with you. Yes, to you I'm a giant. I'm young and strong.
But then what? I couldn't survive in the desert. I've seen
bones there, and not all of them are animal."

She pouted. "I thought you liked me."

"You're a delicious dish, Tiglah. Now please bind me
again, but perhaps you don't need to do it as tightly as
before."

She was offended. She tied the thongs as tightly as she
could, with vicious little jerks, but Sandy used enough
strength so that she did not succeed. Then she flounced out,
slapping the tent flap closed behind her.

He didn't mind the darkness. Enough light came in
through the edges of the closed roof hole. He needed to
think. He was extremely confused at his own reactions. He
and Dennys had had their fair share of fistfights when they
were younger, though perhaps not as many as their sister,
Meg. They played mostly team games and did not go in for
boxing or wrestling. Was he being a coward? He knew that
Tiglah's father and brother would not hesitate to use bow
and arrow, stone knives, or spears. He knew they were quite
capable of killing him, just as much if he ran away as if he

stayed. In fact, he thought he had more chance of surviving if he stayed and figured out some way and route of escape than if he rushed out to the desert, unthinking. He was not so much afraid as outraged. He did not think he was a coward.

So. What to do? Violence was not going to work. Violence was what these little men turned to, and he did not want to be like them.

He wondered if they had gone to Noah with their wild demand for his vineyards. He did not know Noah as well as Dennys did, but he did not think Noah would give in. Sandy's rejection of violence had nothing to do with giving in. Anything but.

After Grandfather Lamech was buried in the grave in the small cave, and the singing had died out, and the seraphim were gone, Noah and his family walked slowly toward the big tent. Wherever there was an outcropping or rock or a cave, Japheth, holding his tiny bow and darts, would hurry to look, Dennys on his heels.

"I do not like this," Noah said.

Dennys and Japheth returned from peering into the deep shadows of a little cave. The starlight was so bright that the shadows seemed to increase in darkness. "Is Sandy lost in the desert?" Dennys's voice cracked more than usual in his anxiety.

In the distance they heard a howl: *"Hungry!"*

Yalith reached for Dennys's hand and squeezed it.

Shem said, "If the manticore is hungry, then he hasn't found anything to eat."

Oholibamah said, "Don't worry about the manticore. Sandy scared it away from Grandfather Lamech's tent."

Could Sandy scare the manticore again, if they met out on the desert? Dennys was not certain, not after his own encounter with the ugly creature.

Elisheba said, "Sandy would never have just wandered off on his own."

Yalith nodded. "He was following you to Grandfather Lamech's tent."

Noah rubbed his beard. "Yes, yes, that's what we thought. But when he didn't come, then we thought he must have stayed in the big tent."

Anah said, "Well, he didn't, and that's that. I think he's off with my sister, Tiglah, that's what I think."

Nobody replied. The stars moved slowly across the sky. Dennys tried to listen for their singing, but he could hear nothing. After the glorious requiem for Grandfather Lamech, they were silent.

The moon was dipping behind the horizon when they reached Noah's tents, tired, sorrowful, anxious.

"Now, before anything else, all of us must eat," Matred said.

Noah said, "She is right. Come, Den."

Dennys accepted the bowl of broth Matred gave him. He knew that he needed all his strength for whatever lay ahead.

With his strong teeth, Shem pulled the meat off a mutton bone. Elisheba handed him a bowl of broth. "Will you go look for the Sand?" Shem, the hunter, was the one who knew the oasis and the desert best. Japheth and Ham worked in the vineyards, close to home. Shem was the one who should go, and Dennys flashed Elisheba a glance of gratitude. Absently, he patted Selah, who was leaning against him, putting her trunk on his knee.

Shem saw that Dennys had finished his broth, and nodded. He reached for one of the tall spears leaning against the inner wall of the tent. Hefted it. Offered it to Dennys. Dennys took it, though he had never used a spear. Shem checked his small quiver of blow darts, then reached for a second spear, and nodded at Dennys, not speaking. The boy followed the short, stocky man out of the tent, feeling a little hope. There was something about Shem that gave him confidence.

Noah said, "Japheth and I will search the paths of the oasis."

Ham said, "Anah and I will go to the marketplaces."

Matred spoke too cheerfully. "If the Sand returns to the tent, which seems likely, we will let everybody know."

Shem and Dennys pushed out of the tent flap. The stars were dimming. Light tinged the eastern horizon. Heat was already beginning to shimmer in watery mirages on the desert. Dennys had on one of Matred's woven hats and hoped it would be adequate once day broke.

Shem looked at him. "Once the sun is high, you must go back to the tent."

Dennys nodded. Shem, like Japheth, was right about that. Already his skin was prickling from heat as well as anxiety. He tried to keep himself from imagining what might have happened to his twin. He followed Shem. Followed. The heat bore down. The futile searching seemed interminable. After what must have been several hours he asked, "Where's Higgaion?"

Shem said, "He will spend the day mourning at Grand-father Lamech's grave. Then he will come to us. Selah will help lighten his grief."

"Higgaion scents for water," Dennys said with sudden hope. "Do you think he could scent for Sandy?"

Shem leaned on his spear, thinking. "Mammoths are strange creatures. They can do strange things. Let us try."

Shem strode off. He walked at a rapid pace, but Dennys, with his much longer legs, could easily have outstripped him and had to hold himself back. Grandfather Lamech's burial cave was about halfway between his tent and Noah's, and the sun was rising by the time they reached it. Higgaion was stretched out on the sand. His fan-like ears lifted at the approaching footsteps.

Dennys hurried to him. "Higgy, do you think you could scent for Sandy, the way you scent for water?"

The mammoth's little eyes had been shadowed with grief. Now they brightened. Shem dropped to his knees by Higgaion, bending down toward him in intimate communication, speaking softly.

The mammoth raised his trunk in a small, hopeful trumpet.

Dennys's eyes, too, were hopeful. "Oh, Shem, what could have happened to him?"

Shem's voice was heavy. "Some people are wicked, and the imagination of their hearts is only to do evil."

"What about Grandfather?" Dennys asked.

Shem stroked his beard in a gesture much like Noah's. "Grandfather knew. There is much wickedness. It, too, smells. You do not smell wicked, Den, nor does the Sand. Grandfather said that there is a great warmth in your hearts, and that is a pleasing smell." It was the longest speech Shem had ever made.

"Thank you," Dennys said. Then: "Let's go."

Shem shook his head, glancing up at the sun. "I thought we would have found him by now."

"Come *on*," Dennys urged.

"Den, I have hunting to do if we are to eat tonight."

"But—"

"My sisters and their families ate hugely, did you notice?"

—Funeral baked meats, Dennys thought angrily.

"Den, we must eat if we are to have strength for whatever—"

Dennys turned to Higgaion. "Come on, Higgy."

"Den. I hunt best alone. But I will continue to search for the Sand. Find Japheth."

"But he's—"

"He and Father will be searching near the tent. Do not go off with Higgaion alone. It is not safe."

Dennys looked at Shem's anxious face. Not safe. Not safe, because whatever had happened to Sandy might happen to Dennys . . .

"We will not stop until we find him," Shem said. "Go find Japheth. You and Higgaion."

Noah sat in the big tent, cross-legged, his elbows on his knees, his head bent down to his hands. Matred came and sat beside him.

"I don't know where he is," Noah said. "Where he could be."

"Rest, husband," Matred urged. "He will be found."

Noah nodded. "My heart is heavy. I grieve for my father."

"He was an old man, full of years," Matred consoled him.

"The Sand is not."

"You think something has happened to him?"

"Why else would he not have joined me at my father's tent? He is not like the young men of the oasis, thinking of nobody but themselves."

"He and the Den are not like anybody else," Matred said. "We do not know that something terrible has happened."

Noah did not reply, nor did he look at her. "And I must begin to build the ark."

Matred said, "El has never before asked you to do anything wild."

"Is it so wild? If the rains cover the earth, as he says they will, it will not be a wild thing to have an ark."

"The rains had better not cover the earth for a while," Matred said. "You have to build the ark, find all the animals."

"I will begin right away."

"And you will be laughed at. You will be the big joke of the oasis."

"I do not find it amusing," Noah said. "My father is dead. The Sand is El knows where."

"Why don't you ask El?"

"I have. El says only that I must begin to build the ark. El says nothing about the Sand."

"Or the Den?"

Noah grunted in agreement.

"Will you bring them onto the ark?"

"Of people, only you, and our sons, and their wives. No more."

"Yalith—" Matred started, but stopped as two men came, unannounced, through the open tent flap.

Tiglah's father and brother.

11 ✒ *Many waters cannot quench love*

Yalith went out into the desert. She was anxious, and anything but sleepy. She wanted to fling herself into Matred's lap and sob, as though she were still a little girl. She wanted to cry herself to sleep.

But she was no longer a little girl, and her eyes felt dry and burning. She was not used to being out at this time of day. She was not sure what drew her to the desert, because there was no hope that she might see Aariel. He would be in his cave, sleeping.

Nevertheless, she walked in that direction, and as she approached she was amazed to see him lying in the shadows at the mouth of the cave. Although she was certain it was Aariel, she was cautious. She had been certain that it was Aariel when the lion turned into the dragon/lizard Eblis.

She whispered, "Aariel—"

The lion rose, stretched, yawned, then paced toward her.

"Oh, Aariel!" She flung her arms about the tawny neck, though her tears were spent. "We don't know where the Sand is! Grandfather Lamech sent him to get my father. The Sand knew that Grandfather was dying, so he gave the

camel to my father so that he could get back to Grandfather Lamech in time, and the Sand said that he would
walk back. And Grandfather died, and everybody was
thinking about him, and we didn't even notice, at first, that
the Sand was not with any of us, and then we had to bury
Grandfather, and—oh, oh, Aariel, we don't know what has
happened—"

Aariel let her talk. When her voice faded and she
pressed her face once again into his fur, he transformed
slowly, gently, until she was enfolded in his wings. "Higgaion has gone to scent for him."

"He left Grandfather's grave?"

"For the living, yes. The Den and Japheth will go with
him."

"Oh, that's good, I'm glad, I'm glad! Higgaion will be
sure to find him, and Japheth will know what to do, and
the Den, too."

Aariel drew her into the shade of the entrance to his cave.

"Aariel—my father is going to build a boat, an enormous boat."

"That is wise," Aariel said gravely.

"For my brothers and their wives. For animals of every
kind."

"Yes, to preserve the species."

"But not for my sisters, Seerah and Hoglah, and their
husbands and children. Not for Mahlah and her nephil
baby. Not for—not for me."

Aariel drew her close. "Many waters cannot quench love,
neither can the floods drown it." His voice was calm, gentle.

"What about the twins?" Again her eyes filled.

The seraph's arm was strong as it held her. "I do not know."

"But you know that El told my father to build an ark?"

"Yes. That I know."

"But you don't know about the twins?"

"We do not have to know everything."

"But you could ask—"

"We have asked."

"Are the stars silent, too?"

"The stars are silent."

"Aariel, I'm afraid."

"Fear not. I will hold you," he promised.

"I am more afraid for the Sand and the Den than I am for myself. I love them."

"And they love you."

"I don't want them to die. Will they die?"

Aariel folded his wings about her. He did not look at her. "I do not know."

Sandy slept. He still did not understand his reaction to Tiglah and her proposals for escape, but after a while he stopped questioning himself. When the time came for him to do something, he would know what to do.

Daylight was not a good time for escape. Perhaps in the cover of the night . . .

"Twin!"

It was Tiglah's voice, Tiglah's smell.

She pegged open the flap. "You have a visitor," she said.

He sat up, instantly alert. So her father and brother had come to kill him.

But it was Rofocale who came into the tent, bowing low to enter, so that his flaming wings dragged in the dust. Like Sandy, he was too tall to stand upright in this small tent. With swift grace he sat, facing Sandy, staring at him with garnet eyes. His bright hair was tied back, his cheeks white as snow.

He thrust out one hand and touched Sandy on the knee. The touch was that cold which is so cold that it burns. Sandy flinched, but did not cry out. "Why are you still here?" Rofocale demanded.

Sandy replied in his calmest voice. "I have been kidnapped and am being held hostage. If I escape and leave this tent, I will be easily seen. There is no way I can lose myself in a crowd. I am as tall as you are. I'd make an easy target."

"Why have you come?"

"Come? I didn't come. Tiglah's father and brother kidnapped me, and I suspect you put them up to it."

Rofocale said, "I am not asking why you are here, in this tent. I am asking why you and your brother chose to come to this oasis."

"It was a mistake," Sandy said, as he had said to Tiglah.

Rofocale again stretched out his hand, again touched Sandy on the knee. Sandy had had frostbite one winter, and this was how it had felt. "If it was a mistake for you to come, why do you not leave?"

Sandy said, slowly, deliberately, "We will leave when it is time to leave."

"And how, then, do you plan to leave?"

How, indeed? "We will know that when the time comes."

"You do not belong here."

"No. I belong with Noah and his family."

Rofocale made a noise like a mosquito shrill. "You do not belong here on this oasis. There are no giants like you in this time and place. Why do you not have wings?"

"We fly in planes and spaceships."

"What?"

The nephilim did not know everything. Sandy said, "We have machines that fly."

"Can you leave the planet?"

"We have gone to the moon. We fly among the stars."

"You?"

"I am too young," Sandy said. "My father has made several space flights."

"Did El send you to torment us?"

"What do you think?" Sandy asked.

"You are not of us, the nephilim. Neither are you, I think, of the seraphim."

"No. We are human beings."

"Mortals?"

"Yes."

"Then why have you come?"

"It was a mistake," Sandy said again.

"Would you like me to take you out of this place, this little tent?"

"No."

"They will come and kill you."

"Perhaps."

"Noah is unwilling to give up his vineyards."

"He is quite right. One does not give in to terrorists."

"You are foolish. I could give him a message, if you like. If you ask him, I think he will give up the vineyards."

"I wouldn't ask him."

"Then you will die."

"You'd like that, wouldn't you?" Sandy asked. "Perhaps you'd like to kill me yourself?"

"I will leave you. You are insolent."

"Why don't you like us, my brother and me?"

"You do not belong to our world. You will cause trouble. I think you have been sent to cause trouble to the nephilim." Rofocale rose. Energy crackled in the air, so that Sandy's skin prickled, and a mosquito flew away.

In a few minutes, Tiglah came in. "Did he tell you?" She was giggling. In the light slanting from outside, the dimple in her chin seemed a cleft.

"That your father and brother plan to kill me, yes, he told me."

"Not that." She was consumed with laughter.

He saw nothing funny. "What, then?"

"About Noah."

"He said that Noah is unwilling to give up his vineyards."

"No, no, not that, either."

"What, then?" He was irritated at her giggles.

"Noah is building a boat. A boat!" Her laughter peeled out.

Sandy sat up. Asked, carefully, "Why is he building a boat?"

"An ark, he says." Her laughter was derisive. "The nearest sea or river is moons away."

"Then why is he doing it?" Sandy asked.

"Who knows."

"Is he building it by himself?"

"Oh, no, it's a very big boat. I mean, hugely big. His sons are helping him. He says it is going to rain!" Her laughter jarred against Sandy's ears. "We have rain only in the spring, and then not much. He is the laughingstock of the oasis."

Sandy sat, alert, watching her.

"Rofocale thinks he may be building it to get rid of you. A boat where there is no water is silly."

"I'm hungry," Sandy said.

"Oh, I've brought you more food."

"Then just leave it with me."

She pouted. "You don't want me to sit and talk with you while you eat? I'll unbind your hands and feet."

"I'll manage." Sandy flexed his muscles so that the thongs looked tight. "I need to think."

"About the silly ark?"

"About a lot of things."

"Well . . . all right." She left the tent, returned with a bowl of stew. "You're sure you don't want me to stay?"

Sandy was firm. "Quite sure. Give up, Tiglah. Go."

Pouting, she went.

He sniffed at the stew. Ugh. It was spoiling. He pushed it aside, worked his hands out of the thongs, unbound his feet. If Noah was already building the ark, there was no time to wait. Dangerous or not, as soon as it got dark, Sandy would leave the tent, head for the desert, try to find out where on the oasis he was being held, and head for whichever was nearer, Grandfather Lamech's tent or Noah's.

Then he lay down to rest and wait for nightfall.

"They have gone too far," Noah said, "taking our Sand."

The family was gathered back in the tent, retreating from the heat of the sun.

Ham said, "You're certainly not going to give them the vineyards!"

Noah shook his head. "I told them that I would not. But now—I have already turned one of the older vineyards that needed replanting into a lumberyard. What difference will the vineyards make if they are all covered with water?"

Ham said, "We are helping you with this idiocy, Father, because you have asked us to. But surely you don't believe that there will be that much rain?"

"That is what I have been told."

Shem had returned from hunting, and was sitting on a pile of skins with Selah next to him. "You're sure it was the voice of El?"

"I am sure."

Elisheba suggested, "It couldn't, maybe, have been the voice of a nephil?"

"I know the voice of El from that of a nephil."

"They mimic very cleverly."

"El is El. If one of the nephilim tried to sound like El, then El would tell me that."

Matred looked up from her stewpot. "When will the rain start?"

"When the ark is ready."

Shem said, "What about our sisters and their husbands and their children?"

Noah wiped his hands across his beard. "I am to make a window in the ark, and set a door in the side, with lower, second, and third stories. El told me that I am to bring in animals of every kind, and my wife, my sons, and their wives."

Oholibamah's voice was sharp. "What about Yalith?"

Noah shook his head sorrowfully.

Shem protested, "But it's going to be a big boat, Father! Surely there's room for more than just the eight of us."

"Animals," Noah repeated, "of every kind, so that, when the flood waters abate, there will be both animal and human beings to repopulate the earth."

"I don't believe any of this," Ham said. "But if it should come to pass, I will give my place on the ark to Yalith."

Oholibamah looked at him in grateful surprise.

"Nonsense," Anah said. "When you build this ark, and nothing happens, how are you going to face everybody?"

Noah stroked his beard. "I obey El."

"And our twins?" Oholibamah asked. "What about them?"

"And where is the Sand?" Elisheba asked.

"Japheth and the Den will surely find him," Noah said. Selah raised her trunk and bugled. "And if they do not return with the Sand by sunrise, I will change my mind. I will give them the vineyards. When the flood waters abate, I will plant new vines."

Ham said, wonderingly, "You really believe that there is going to be a flood! We don't have enough rain, even in the spring, to be any use. If it weren't for our wells, there would be no oasis."

Shem asked, "Has our father ever made a fool of himself before?"

"No," Anah replied. "But there's always a first time."

Admael the white camel crossed the length of the oasis to where Sandy was imprisoned. It was at the farthest end of the oasis, as far from Noah's tent in one direction as was Grandfather Lamech's in the other. Admael did not go up to the tent, but folded himself down on the ground a few yards away, to wait.

Adnachiel the giraffe grazed on some tender leaves, stretching his long, golden neck. High up in the tree, sleeping during the daylight hours, sat Akatriel the owl, his head hunched into his feathers.

Together they waited.

Japheth and Dennys followed Higgaion, who trotted, zigzagging back and forth, from the outlying edges of the oasis to the desert, scenting, shaking his head so that the heightening sun glinted against his curved tusks, scenting. Back and forth. Into the oasis. Onto the desert.

"The sun is high," Japheth said. "You must find shade, Den."

Dennys shook his head, stubbornly. His body gleamed with sweat.

Japheth looked at him with concern. "We're not far from Grandfather Lamech's tent. Perhaps we'll find Adnarel there, and we could ask him for help."

Relieved, Dennys panted, "Fine." Higgaion was staggering with exhaustion. There had been no sign of Sandy.

Higgaion led the way back to the oasis, his energy renewed now that they had a destination. Japheth was untired, jogging along, breathing easily. Dennys was grateful for his own long legs; without them, he would not have been able to keep up.

As they approached Grandfather Lamech's groves and could see the dark shadow of his tent, Higgaion trumpeted and quickened his pace, so that Japheth was running. When they reached the tent, the heat seemed to intensify, and their shadows were dark and squat. Higgaion paused, pointing with his trunk to light flashing off something half buried in the sand by the tent flap.

"Adnarel!" Dennys cried. "Oh, Adnarel!"

Japheth bent down and lifted the scarab beetle out of the sand, stroked it gently with one finger, and it seemed to burst from his hand, and Adnarel stood before them, blazing gold.

"Oh, Adnarel," Dennys cried, "Sandy never came home after he gave Noah the camel! We don't know what's happened to him!"

Adnarel bowed gravely, listening, saying nothing.

Japheth said, "I worry that he may not have gone wherever it is of his own free will."

Adnarel turned to Japheth. "Explain what you are thinking."

"Since he didn't follow my father to Grandfather's tent as he said he would do, then I am afraid that perhaps someone . . ." His voice trailed off.

Adnarel's wings glittered. "You are thinking of Tiglah?"

"It was Anah's suggestion . . ."

"No," Dennys contradicted.

"We know she's a seductress," Japheth said.

"No," Dennys repeated. "Sandy would never have gone off with Tiglah, with Grandfather dying. Never."

Adnarel nodded. "Of course. He would not have disappeared of his own volition."

"Then where is he?" Dennys demanded.

Adnarel raised his wings, slowly lowered them. "What are you doing to try to find him?"

Japheth did not know of the visit of Tiglah's father and brother to Noah's tenthold. "We are all searching, but we have found no trace anywhere."

Adnarel looked at the two young men, eye to eye with Dennys, down for Japheth, small and lean and strong.

Japheth continued: "Sandy cares about Grandfather Lamech. He cares about his brother. It is not in his character to go off at such a time."

"Nephilim," Adnarel said softly.

A ripple of concern rolled across Higgaion's flanks. Japheth said, "That's what we were afraid of. But even they couldn't make him vanish completely, could they?"

"They are masters of illusion," Adnarel said. "They can make any part of the oasis look like someplace else. They can disguise odors. That is why Higgaion's scenting was to no avail."

"But where do you think he is?" Dennys's voice soared with anxiety.

"I think the nephilim have used human greed. I suspect

that some of the less pleasant people of the oasis, perhaps the men of Tiglah's tent, have taken him and put him in some little-used tent and are asking some kind of ransom for him. They are acquisitive, but they don't like to work for what they get, and they would be easy to tempt into doing whatever the nephilim want."

Dennys raised his head as he heard the strong beating of wings, and a pelican plummeted out of the sky, and then Alarid stood beside them. "The nephilim are afraid of the twins." His wings shook silver.

"But why?" Japheth asked. "The twins are good."

Adnarel and Alarid touched wing tips. Adnarel said, "The nephilim fear what they do not understand. Did Higgaion go all the way across the oasis with his scenting?"

Japheth nodded.

"To the far end?" Alarid asked.

"Yes."

"Try once more. This time, go straight across the length of the oasis and concentrate at the farthest point. They will have taken him as far away from Noah's tents as possible."

"And they're not likely to have gone in the direction of Grandfather Lamech's tent," Alarid added.

Higgaion's stringy little tail flicked.

Japheth said, "The sun is high. The Den cannot cross the oasis at full noon without getting the sun sickness again."

Both seraphim looked at Dennys, already red and sweating. "You are right. The Den will stay here, in Grandfather Lamech's tent, for the afternoon rest. One of us will stay with him, in case . . ." Adnarel did not finish.

Alarid said, "And we will see to it that he gets to Noah's tenthold before sundown. Whether you find the Sand or not, you must be home by then."

Higgaion raised his trunk in an impatient trumpet.

"We'll go," Japheth said. He looked up at the seraphim, asking in a low voice, "Are you worried?"

Gravely they acknowledged the question.

In the dark heat of the prison tent, Sandy slept fitfully, dreaming a confusion of meaningless dreams. Tiglah was tying his thongs tightly and shoving a bowl of spoiled meat at him. His nostrils twitched.

It was not Tiglah's smell. It was not even the smell of rancid goat meat. He opened his eyes and saw only a small dark shadow, felt something soft nudging him. He reached out his hand and touched something firm and curved. Moved his hand along whatever it was, until his fingers felt a roughness. It was a tusk, broken off at the point. His eyes adjusted to the dim light and he saw that he was touching a mammoth, not Higgaion or Selah, both of whom were sleek and well fed, with polished tusks, but an underfed mammoth with stringy hair, and one tusk broken off just at the point, the other slightly farther up. It was nudging him with the tip of its trunk.

What the mammoth wanted of him he was not sure. But it was apparent that it meant him no harm, and that its overtures were friendly. Sandy began to stroke the shaggy head, then ran his fingers over the ivory tusks. This little beast had obviously been abused, so it was likely that it came from Tiglah's tent. He was grateful for the company. Perhaps a mammoth, even a mangy mammoth, would be helpful when night came, not so much helpful in the actual escape as in finding Noah's tenthold.

"Now," he said to the mammoth, fondling the fan-shaped ears, "if I only had a unicorn, then I could get out of here." He stopped. Then: "Hey. I didn't think of a unicorn before, because basically I still don't believe in unicorns."

Dennys, he remembered, had summoned a unicorn after Tiglah's father and brother had nearly killed him, dumping him into the garbage pit. It wasn't easy for Dennys to believe in unicorns either, but when he had to, he did.

If Sandy could believe something as outrageous as that he and Dennys had actually landed in the pre-flood desert, and that they had become so close to Noah's tenthold, especially Yalith, that they were like family, and if he could believe that he was now petting a mammoth, why should it be hard to believe in a unicorn, even if it was what Dennys called a virtual unicorn? His mother believed in virtual particles, and his mother was a scientist who had won the Nobel Prize for discovering particles so small they were scarcely conceivable even with a wild leap of the imagination.

"What'll I do?" he asked the mammoth, who responded by cuddling closer to him.

If Sandy left the tent on his own, they would be lying in wait for him—Rofocale, if not Tiglah's father and brother—and they would not hesitate to kill him. Even night would not provide enough cover, with the brilliance of the stars illuminating the oasis.

"The problem is," he said to the mammoth, "that I always have to see things to believe in them. But, after all, I have seen unicorns, two of them. I have seen them, therefore I can believe in them."

The mammoth reached with its trunk to touch, softly, the boy's cheek. In his mind's ear Sandy seemed to hear, "Some things have to be believed to be seen."

"Unicorn!" he whispered, and the mammoth slipped its trunk into the palm of his hand. "Unicorn, please tend to life. Please tend to be."

Against the darkness of the tent came a starburst of light, and a unicorn stood, trembling, beside him.

"Oh, you *are!*" Sandy cried. "Oh, thank you!" He held out his hand. The unicorn came to him with silver steps, folded its delicate legs, and lay down, putting its head in Sandy's lap, so that the light of the horn flowed over the scraggly little mammoth, who lifted its head gratefully. Sandy fondled the silvery mane, soft as moonbeams. "Now what?" he asked the two disparate creatures.

The light of the horn glittered, but neither unicorn nor mammoth answered him.

"If I could fall asleep," Sandy mused, "or stop believing in unicorns, then you would lose your tendency to life and go out, and take me with you, the way you took Dennys. The problem is that now I believe in you. And as long as I believe in you, you'll continue to be, won't you?"

The unicorn nuzzled him, as affectionate as the mammoth.

"As long as I stay with you," Sandy whispered, "I think I'm safe, because I'm absolutely certain that Tiglah couldn't come near you, or her father or brother. But if they try to, and you go out of being, will you take the mammoth and me out of being with you? If we don't take the mammoth, they'll hurt him again. So will you take us?"

It was a rather intimidating thought. He had asked Dennys how it had felt the two times he had gone out with the unicorn, and Dennys had answered that it hadn't felt at all. But perhaps, Sandy thought, that might have been because Dennys had sunstroke and a high fever. Then he remembered Grandfather Lamech—or was it Japheth?— telling him that unicorns never lost anybody.

He put one arm about the unicorn, the other about the mammoth, and waited. This was a far better plan than going with Tiglah, or trying to cross the desert alone.

"You see," he said to the two creatures, who pressed confidingly against him. "When the time came for me to do something, I knew what to do, and I did it."

He held unicorn and mammoth close.

The nephilim gathered. Proud. Arrogant. Flickering in and out of their hosts as they spoke.

Rofocale the mosquito said, "I have put an illusion around the tent. It is on the edge of the desert at the farthest end of the oasis, but the illusion makes it look as though it is surrounded by flocks and groves."

Eblis the dragon/lizard asked, "Are giant twins worth this much trouble?"

Rofocale answered, "I think they know something we do not know. When I questioned the one that Tiglah caught for me, he gave evasive answers."

Ugiel the cobra said, "There is danger in the air. The stars are drawing back. I am concerned for my baby."

Naamah the vulture went "Kkk. We chose to be silent with El. We chose never to hear the Voice again, never to speak with the Presence."

Ertrael the rat said, "We could ask the seraphim."

"Never," said Estael the cockroach.

"But they still speak with El," Ertrael said. "The stars still talk with them."

"I do not care to listen to the stars," Eisheth the crocodile pronounced.

"They might tell us," said Rumjal the red ant, "whether or not we are in danger."

"How can we be in danger?" Eblis asked. "We are immortal."

"And the one we caught," said Rofocale, "told me that he is mortal. If he is to be believed."

Naamah the vulture clacked his beak. "I smell that there will soon be much for us to eat."

"How?" Rofocale demanded. "What is going to happen?"

Eblis the dragon/lizard asked, "Will someone tell me what Noah is building?"

"A good question," said Rumael the slug.

Rofocale gave his screeching laugh. "A boat! That is what my Tiglah tells me. He is building a boat!"

"A boat?" Eisheth the crocodile demanded. "Why on earth would he build a boat?"

Rugziel the worm asked, "Could the twin giants have told him something that we do not know?"

Rofocale said, "We need to get rid of the twin giants. Everything has been different since they came."

"Noah reconciled with his father. Kkk," said Naamah the vulture.

"And Lamech has died," Estael the cockroach agreed.

"My lovely Yalith prefers the young giants to me," Eblis said. "They must have some strange power, to make her turn from me to such soft-skinned, wingless creatures."

"And Noah is building a boat," Rofocale added.

"And Matred weeps," said Rumjal the red ant.

"We should find out," Ugiel suggested, "whether or not they—the young giants—are truly mortal or not."

Rofocale screeched again. "Tiglah's father and brother will find that out for us."

Higgaion finally found the tent where Sandy was imprisoned, because the unicorn was there. Rofocale's power of illusion had indeed made the tent seem to be in the middle of the oasis, had indeed altered Sandy's scent. But the unicorn had come to the tent after the illusion was set. Higgaion sniffed. He smelled silver, and he smelled light. He nudged Japheth excitedly.

Tentatively, Japheth pushed open the tent flap. Enough of the late-afternoon light came through the tent hole so that he could see Sandy and the unicorn, their heads together in affection. The abused mammoth was only a dark shadow under Sandy's arm.

"Sand!"

Sandy opened his eyes. "Jay!"

The young man started to rush forward to embrace him, then stopped short as though held by some invisible barrier. The unicorn's light brightened.

Higgaion followed Japheth into the tent, sitting back on his haunches in surprise as he saw the mammoth who pressed closely against Sandy, blinking fearfully.

Sandy's protective arm tightened. "It's all right. Nobody's going to hurt you." Then: "Jay, how did you find me?"

"Are you all right?" Japheth asked anxiously.

"Oh, I'm fine, but Tiglah's father and brother want to kill me . . ."

"No." Japheth touched his fingers to his tiny bow. "No, Sand."

"And look what they've done to their mammoth," Sandy said indignantly. "They've nearly starved him, and they've broken his tusks."

"All right," Japheth said hurriedly. "We'll take him with us. But we'd better get out of here before they come back."

"I think I'm safe as long as I'm with the unicorn," Sandy said, "because they won't be able to come near."

Japheth smiled. "I can't, either." He stared at boy and unicorn. "Sand. Do you remember when I first met you and the Den in the desert, and we called unicorns, and the Den went out?"

"Of course I remember."

"Can't you go out with the unicorn now?"

Sandy sighed. "The problem is, Jay, that I *believe* in the unicorn."

The mangy mammoth suddenly pricked up its ears and started to whimper. Higgaion pushed himself up onto his feet, and Japheth swung around to see the tent flap open violently. Two small, chunky men came in, carrying spears. Tiglah's father and brother.

"Auk! What have we here?" the older man demanded.

"A *unicorn*," the younger man exclaimed. "And one of Noah's sons. Well, well." He moved toward Sandy and the unicorn, then drew back with a sharp intake of breath. "You, young giant!" he shouted. "Come along! We want you."

"Sorry," Sandy said. "You can't have me." He looked at Japheth and the two men from Tiglah's tent and wondered anew at how small they were. Tiglah's father was made even shorter by his bowed legs. No wonder they had used the poisoned dart on him. In a fair struggle, they would never have captured him.

Japheth's pleasant features were distorted by anger. "You've done enough harm. Get out of here."

The tent was so small that the three little men were close together, with Sandy, his arms still about unicorn and mammoth, near enough to draw back at the odor of the men from Tiglah's tent.

"Auk's nuts to you," Tiglah's brother said.

Japheth glanced swiftly at Sandy, then in a reflex so swift it hardly seemed motion, he drew one of the darts from his quiver and jabbed it into Sandy's arm.

The two men from Tiglah's tent shouted in surprise and anger. Tiglah's father roared, "What happened?"

Where Sandy and the unicorn and mammoth had been there was only a pile of filthy skins.

Japheth replied calmly, "They went out with the unicorn."

Both men roared in frustration. "Call him back," the bowlegged man said.

"Or we'll kill you," the younger man threatened.

"And what good will that do you?" Japheth demanded. "You'll never get the Sand back without me."

Tiglah's brother snarled, deep in his throat, and lunged at Japheth with his spear, but Higgaion jumped between them, tripping the red-bearded man so that he sprawled on the floor of the tent. He snarled up at his father, "Why didn't you stop him?"

"Me? What could I do?"

"You let him go out with the unicorn, and our mammoth, too."

Tiglah's brother scrambled clumsily to his feet, hefting his spear. "Give us your father's vineyards, then."

"No," Japheth said, and reached for his darts.

But the older man swooped on him with the spear, and despite Japheth's quick reflex, the spear cut across his ribs, and a trickle of blood slid down his side.

Higgaion lunged at the man, trumpeting in outrage.

But the two men with their spears were too much for Japheth and the mammoth. Japheth clutched his wounded side as the mammoth lunged again and was viciously kicked by Tiglah's brother.

Suddenly a roar burst over them. *"Hungry!"* And the manticore stuck his hideous face into the tent. *"Hungry!"*

"Go away," Tiglah's father yelled.

In terror, Higgaion backed up, hitting the skins of the tent, which gave slightly. Japheth, trying to reach for the mammoth, saw that the skins were not pegged securely to the ground. Not many people bothered to set up their tents as well as Noah and Grandfather Lamech.

"Run, Hig, run!" Japheth commanded, and Higgaion backed out of the tent.

"*Hungry!*" The manticore's ugly face was followed by his lion's body and scorpion's tail.

Japheth was the farthest of the three men from the tent flap. He reached for a dart and his tiny bow, and let a dart fly, to strike the manticore in the forehead.

"*Hung—*" the manticore started, and fell, unconscious, on Tiglah's father and brother.

Swiftly, Japheth dropped to his knees and pushed out the opening in the rear of the tent through which Higgaion had left.

The mammoth was waiting outside, whimpering in terror but not willing to leave Japheth completely.

"Run!" Japheth shouted as he stood upright; and they ran. Ran without looking behind them. Onto the desert. And then the illusion that Rofocale had set was broken and Japheth knew exactly where they were. They were at the far end of the oasis, the opposite end from Grandfather Lamech's tenthold. He hardly realized that blood was streaming down his side as he hurried toward home.

Admael the camel, Adnachiel the giraffe, and Akatriel the owl left their posts and followed Japheth and the mammoth into the desert.

Japheth, running faster than he had ever run before, suddenly felt dizzy. Everything paled. He slumped slowly onto the sand. Higgaion pushed his feet against rock to slow himself down.

Akatriel flew down to the sand beside the young man, and resumed his seraph form. "He has lost much blood. He is still bleeding."

Adnachiel the giraffe bent his neck to look at Japheth's wound, then lowered himself so that he could reach the torn skin with his tongue. Carefully, thoroughly, he licked the wound.

Admael the camel galloped off.

Higgaion hunkered down beside Japheth and the giraffe, whimpering. Adnachiel continued to lick, cleaning the jagged cut the spear had made.

When it was clean, Admael returned with a furry-looking, cactus-type leaf, which he gently pressed against the wound, holding it until the bleeding slowed and stopped.

Japheth, quivering, opened his eyes, to see the seraphim reaching up out of their hosts and into their seraphic forms.

Akatriel, with eyes as wise as those of the owl he had just left, affirmed, "You are all right. You have lost much blood, and that spearhead cannot have been too clean. But Adnachiel has washed the wound and Admael has stopped the bleeding."

"And you ran much too quickly." Adnachiel nodded.

"Hig—"

Higgaion touched Japheth's hand gently with his trunk tip.

"Sand?"

Adnachiel asked, "What happened?"

"I sent him out with the unicorn," Japheth said, struggling to sit up.

Admael nodded approval. "That was good."

"Should we call the Sand back?" Japheth asked.

"Better," Adnachiel said.

Admael asked courteously of the mammoth, "Will you? Or shall I?"

"Both." Adnachiel was peremptory.

With a light briefly bright as the sun, making them all blink, the unicorn appeared. Sandy's arm slid from around its neck and he slipped onto the sand. A mangy mammoth tumbled beside him.

Japheth explained, "I used one of my darts on him, but it's a very short-lasting—"

Sandy's eyes blinked open, and he sat up.

The three seraphim stood looking at Japheth, Sandy, and the two mammoths.

"Thank you," Sandy gasped. "Oh, Jay, thank you."

Embarrassed, Japheth shrugged.

"What's happened to you?" Sandy demanded. "You're hurt."

"I'll be all right," Japheth reassured him. "The seraphim have cleaned my wound."

"Go home," Admael ordered. "Sandy, you can help Japheth. He is weaker than he realizes."

"But what happened?" Sandy demanded.

Japheth laughed. "I never thought I'd be grateful to a manticore, but I am now. They'd have killed me if a manticore hadn't pushed his way into the tent and stopped them."

The mangy little mammoth pressed against Sandy. "It's all right," Sandy reassured. "We'll never send you back. What happened to them?"

Japheth shrugged.

"Nothing, I suspect," Akatriel said. "I saw the manticore running away, weeping, a dart falling from his forehead, calling out that he was hungry."

Japheth laughed again. "I could almost feel sorry for the manticore."

"Go, now," Admael urged. "Japheth needs food and rest."

"Unicorn?" Sandy asked. "What about you?"

As he looked, the unicorn began to flicker, to fade.

Japheth said, "The unicorn knows we don't need it anymore."

Where the unicorn had been, there was only a shimmer in the air, and the scent of moonbeams and silver.

They were united in the big tent that evening. Japheth, hovered over by Matred, lay on a pile of soft skins, pale but smiling, and sipped at the strengthening broth Matred kept offering him.

The starved mammoth had been fed and lay curled up with Higgaion and Selah.

Sandy and Dennys kept grinning at each other in relief, with Sandy repeating over and over his praise of Japheth and Higgaion. "It was a wonderful idea to have Higgy scent for me. I don't know what would have happened, otherwise."

Anah looked subdued. "I am so ashamed. That my father and my brother—that my sister should have tried—I thought she *liked* the Sand—I don't know what got into any of them! Can you forgive me?"

"It was not your doing, daughter," Noah said gently.

"But to think they tried to force you to give up your vineyards! To threaten to kill the Sand and Japheth—"

"Don't dwell on it," Matred said, rubbing ointment Oholibamah had given her onto the healing wound on Japheth's side.

"Is it over?" Elisheba asked. "Or will they try something else? I don't mean your father and brother, Anah. The nephilim."

Nobody answered.

Sandy held his bowl out for a refill. "It is so much better than what Tiglah cooked for me—I wonder how I could eat the other stuff, even when it was fresh." Then he said, "Rofocale the nephil *used* Tiglah and her father and brother. They are not nice people—sorry, Anah—but I don't think they'd ever have thought of kidnapping me on their own. If the nephilim are after Dennys and me, they'll try something else."

"But why are they after you?" Japheth demanded.

Sandy finished licking his bowl clean. "They know we don't belong here."

Noah's fingers moved against his beard. "But you do. Both of you. The Den made me see that being stubborn was not brave."

Matred added, "And you both made Grandfather Lamech's last moons happy ones."

Noah had tears in his eyes. "You were to him as his own

grandsons. He could not have stayed in his own tent without your help. You have become our beloved twins."

Matred wiped her eyes with the back of her hand. "And yet, husband, you have said that there is no room for them in the ark."

Dennys said quickly, "Don't worry. We know we don't belong on the ark. The nephilim aren't entirely wrong about us."

Sandy said, "But we'll be glad to help you build it. We would like to do at least that much for you, because you've been very kind to us."

Yalith and Oholibamah sat close together, hands clasped. Oholibamah said, "We still have time to be together. It will take at least two moons before the ark is finished and ready to stock. And because we have known each other, we can never be entirely separated."

Japheth said, "As we can never be completely separated from Grandfather Lamech."

Yalith nodded. Pushed back tears. Sandy was safely back with them. Japheth was wounded, but was going to be all right. This was no time for tears.

Dennys looked at Japheth and nodded. "The night that Grandfather Lamech died—how long ago it seems—Higgaion and I sat out under the stars while Noah was in the tent, waiting for Sandy." He hesitated, then plunged on. "At the moment that Grandfather Lamech died, the stars held their breaths. And so I knew. And then, because he understood Higgaion and I needed him, Adnarel was with us, saying *Fear not*, and then he was back in the scarab beetle, on Higgaion's ear, instead of off with the other seraphim, as he's been so often lately."

There was a moment of silence. Then Noah opened a fresh skin of wine. "My love for all of you is too deep for words. Dear twins, we are glad that you have come to us. And now it is time for you to leave, isn't it?"

Sandy said, firmly, "Not until we've helped you build the ark."

Sandy and Dennys stayed in the big tent, having been given sleeping skins and a place to themselves across from Noah and Matred. Higgaion and Selah slept with the little mammoth, whose ribs were beginning to fill out, and whose coat was beginning to shine.

Dennys woke up and the darkness of the tent was heavy. Around him he heard gentle snores, and the night sounds of the desert. He nudged Sandy. "Are you awake?"

"Almost."

"Now what?"

Sandy wriggled into a more comfortable position. "We'll keep on helping Noah with the ark."

"And then?"

Fully awake now, Sandy moved so that he could whisper directly into Dennys's ear. "We'll take a quantum leap."

"And how will we manage that?"

"It came to me when the mammoth and I called the unicorn to *be* in that nasty little tent where I was in prison. The nephilim cannot leave this earth. But the seraphim can."

"More to the point," Dennys asked, "can we? Or, rather, can we leave this time and get back to our own? I wouldn't want to miscalculate and land in the Middle Ages, or the year 3003."

"I'll have to speak to Adnarel about it again."

"You already have?"

"Some. When we first got here. What I think would work for us would be to call unicorns, and ride them, and for Adnarel, or any of the seraphim, to go forward to our time, and then call for the unicorns to come back."

"Wild." Dennys whistled.

"Yes, but it worked when the three seraphim called me back onto the desert sands after Japheth and Higgaion came to rescue me."

"That was space, not time, and a small distance in space, at that," Dennys pointed out.

"True. But experiments with photons, for instance, seem to show that they can communicate with each other instantaneously, and that means faster than the speed of light. And distance doesn't seem to be a problem for them."

"But it's time we have to worry about," Dennys whispered. Noah snored a very loud snore, and they could hear him turn over on his skins. Dennys continued, "If I understand Mother's experiments, an observer is essential in the world of quantum mechanics. I mean, an observer seems to be necessary to make quanta real."

Sandy moved impatiently. "I don't understand it. But Mother seems to, and so do a lot of other particle physicists. That's enough for me. I'll talk to Adnarel."

There was a heavy silence. Then Dennys said, "Anything seems to be possible. I hope this is."

Another silence. Then Sandy asked, "Do you think we could take Yalith with us?"

Dennys did not answer for a while. Then: "No. I don't think so. We're not supposed to change history."

"But she'll drown."

"I know. I love her, too." At last. It had been said.

"But if we love her—"

Dennys's voice was bleak. "I don't think we can take her with us."

Sandy reached for his twin's hand and grasped it. "A lot of people are going to drown. Would you mind changing history if it would save Yalith?"

Dennys said, "I wouldn't mind. I'd be willing to try. To try absolutely anything. But I have a feeling that we can't."

"I hate it!"

"Shh. I hate it, too."

Sandy whispered, "It's going to be dangerous, taking a quantum leap."

"Dad obviously thinks such things are possible. After all, wasn't he programming some kind of quantum leap, or tesser, when we messed around with his experiment?"

"So, if he believes in it, it's not that wild."

"Sure it's that wild. It's got to be that wild in order to work."

Sandy gave a slightly hysterical laugh. "Our father was not programming unicorns into his experiment."

Higgaion jerked in a sleeping dream, whimpered. Selah made little murmuring noises, and Tiglah's mammoth moved closer to the others.

Sandy asked, "What about the mammoths?"

Dennys stretched his arm out so that he could touch, gently, Higgaion's shaggy fur. "I wonder if they can swim?"

"It wouldn't do any good. Not for forty days and forty nights."

Dennys closed his eyes. Listened. Heard the wind high in the sky above the tent, but the words would not come clear. He whispered, "Does—does Yalith know she's not going on the ark?"

"I think so. I think Noah has told her."

"I understand that floods and other disasters happen. But if this flood is really being sent by El—"

Sandy said, "If it's being sent by El, then I don't like El, not if Yalith is going to drown."

The wind murmured. "We aren't sure yet, are we?" Dennys asked. "I mean, it hasn't happened yet. Yalith isn't in the story, so we don't know what happened to her. Grandfather Lamech truly loved his El. So we can't be sure. Grandfather loved Yalith. She was his very favorite."

"Grandfather is dead," Sandy said flatly. "If we're going to be any use building the ark, we'd better sleep now."

The wind wrapped itself about the tent. Sandy slipped quickly into sleep. Dennys lay on his back, listening, listening. The wind's song was gentle, unalarming. Although he could not make out the words, he felt the wind calming him. Slept.

"Stupid. Stupid," Ugiel, husband of Mahlah, hissed.

Rofocale's contempt came out with a mosquito shrill. "The idiots almost let the manticore get them."

"Tiglah would have done better by herself," said Eblis, who wanted Yalith.

Ertrael, sometimes a rat, demanded, "What do we do now?"

The nephilim were gathered in the darkness of the desert, for once conserving their energies. Naamah, still sounding like a vulture, went, "Kkk. Tiglah did not, in fact, do better than her father or her brother. She got no answers. The young giant did not listen to her."

Elisheth, of the crocodile-green wings, shimmered them in the starlight. "She tried. I would have thought the Sand would find her irresistible. Why did he reject her?"

"Yalith." Eblis's beautiful red lips lifted in a sneer.

Ugiel wove his neck in a rhythmic dance, as much cobra as nephil. "You are right. Because of Yalith."

"But she has no experience," Rofocale shrilled. "She is still a child. Whereas Tiglah—"

"No," Eblis contradicted, purple eyes glittering. "Yalith is not a child any longer." He wrapped purple wings about himself.

"Could we have used her?" Estael, sometimes a cockroach, asked doubtfully.

"If Ugiel hadn't married her, we might have been able to use Mahlah, Yalith's sister," said Ezequen, whose host was the skink.

Ugiel hissed, "We all know she's Yalith's sister. And my wife. And the mother of my child."

Eblis wrapped himself in wings the color of the sunset. "It is time for us to act. Us. Ourselves."

Rugziel agreed. "It is time we stopped using deputies."

Rumjal grimaced. "What do you suggest?"

Naamah stretched his neck, naked as a vulture's, and raised his wings to their full span, standing in whiteness of skin, darkness of wing, his feathers the indigo of the bird who was his host. "The circle of extinction. Whoever we completely surround we control. Kkk. Let us surround the twin giants."

Ugiel hissed in agreement.

Rofocale shrilled in anticipation.

Eblis suggested, "And let us surround Yalith, since she has foiled our plans."

"Kkk," Naamah reproved. "The giants first."

12 ～ Neither can the floods drown it

Yalith slept at the far end of the tent from the twins, but she heard them whispering, and when they stopped, she could hear the mammoths' triple snores. And she was wide awake.

She slipped out of bed and went to the desert. She saw neither lion nor dragon/lizard masquerading as lion, on the great rock. She chose a smaller rock and sat, wrapping her arms about her knees. She raised her face to the stars.

She heard them chiming, and there was no anxiety in their song.

Nevertheless, she shivered. She believed her father, believed that the rains were going to come. She was willing to die, if that was truly what El wanted.

But what about the twins?

What was going to happen?

The crystal chime of stars sang in her ears, "Fear not, Yalith."

The stars never gave false comfort.

She was less afraid.

. . .

They worked on the ark all day, taking time out in the heat to sleep. Then they worked again until it was too dark to see.

Every evening Matred prepared a festive meal. Therefore, Shem was often out hunting, rather than busy with the ark. Sandy and Dennys worked along with Noah, Ham, and Japheth. There were no hammers or nails or any of the modern tools to which they were accustomed. The boards had to be joined and pegged. At night they were tired and hungry, ate well, slept well. They were building an ark, but they did not talk of the rain.

Dennys looked at Elisheba, Anah, and Oholibamah. They were in the story, even if not by name. They would go with Noah and Matred and all the animals onto the ark. He looked at Yalith, her hair amber in the lamplight.

He slipped out of the tent, feeling a little strange. He was the follower, Sandy the leader. And now he was off, without even consulting his twin.

He walked swiftly toward Noah's well. His skin prickled as he saw the vulture, huddled on the tall trunk of a long-dead palm, then looking up as Dennys approached, peering this way and that, stretching its naked neck, staring at Dennys with hooded, suspicious eyes.

At first, Dennys saw only the dark bird. Then his eye caught a glimpse of white, and on a young fig tree near the well sat a pelican, its head tucked under its wing, so that it seemed no more than a bundle of white. Dennys heaved a sigh of relief. He had left the big tent to find one of the seraphim, and it didn't really matter which one, but he was more familiar with Alarid than with many of the others. He went up to the sleeping bird. "Hsst."

The pelican did not move.

"Alarid!" Dennys shouted. "I need to talk to you!"

The feathers quivered as the bird shoved its head farther under its wing.

"Alarid!"

The feathers ruffled, hunched, indicating, "Go away. I have nothing to say."

"But I have to speak to you. About Yalith."

At last the head emerged from the fluff of feathers, and the dark bead of eye blinked.

"Please." Dennys indicated the vulture. "Please, Alarid."

The white bird hopped down from its perch, clumsy and cumbersome.

The vulture was an ink blob of immobile darkness.

"Please," Dennys pleaded.

The pelican stretched its wings up, up, until the seraph appeared. Without speaking, Alarid turned from the well and walked toward the desert. Dennys followed. When they had left the oasis far enough behind so that the vulture was no longer visible, Alarid turned to the boy. "What is it?"

"You can't let Yalith drown in the flood."

"Why not?"

"Yalith is good. I mean, she is really *good*."

Alarid bowed his head. "Goodness has never been a guarantee of safety."

"But you can't let her drown."

"I have nothing to say in the matter."

"I should have spoken to Aariel," Dennys said in frustration. "Aariel loves her."

"He has no more say than I." The seraph turned his head away.

Dennys realized that he had hurt Alarid, but he plunged ahead. "You're seraphim. You have powers."

"True. But, as I told you, it is dangerous to change things. We do not meddle with the pattern."

"But Yalith isn't *in* the pattern." Dennys's voice rose and cracked. "There's no Yalith in the story. Only Noah and his wife and his sons and their wives."

Alarid's wings quivered slightly.

"So, since she isn't in the story, it won't change anything if you prevent her from being drowned in the flood."

"What do you want me to do?" Alarid asked.

"You aren't going to be drowned, are you?" Dennys demanded. "You, and the other seraphim?"

"No."

"Then take her wherever it is you're going to escape the flood."

"We cannot do that," Alarid said sadly.

"Why not?"

"We cannot." Again, the seraph turned his face away.

"Where are you going, then?"

Alarid turned back to Dennys and smiled, but not in amusement. "We go to the sun."

No. Yalith could not go to the sun. Nor to the moon, which Dennys had been about to suggest. Yalith could not live where there was no atmosphere. But surely there was something to be done! He made a strangled noise of outrage. "We're not in the story, either, Sandy and I. But we're here. And Yalith is here."

"That is so."

"And if we drown, that is, if Sandy and I drown, that's going to change the story, isn't it? I mean, we're not going to be born in our own time if we get drowned now, and even if that makes only a tiny difference, it will make a difference to our family. If Sandy and I don't get born, maybe Charles Wallace won't get born. Maybe Meg will be an only child."

"Who?"

"Our older sister and our little brother. I mean, the story would be *changed.*"

Alarid said, "You must go back to your own time."

"That's easier said than done. Anyhow, what I wanted to talk to you about is Yalith. Listen, it's a stupid story. Only the males have names. It's a chauvinist story. I mean, Matred has a name. She's a mother. And Elisheba and Anah and Oholibamah. They're real people, with names."

"That is true," Alarid agreed.

"The nephilim," Dennys went on. "They're like whoever wrote the silly ark story, seeing things only from their own point of view, *using* people. They don't give a hoot for Tiglah or Mahlah, for instance. They're just women, so they don't matter. They don't care if Yalith gets drowned. But you ought to care!"

Alarid asked gently, "Do you think I don't care?"

Dennys sighed. "Okay. I know you care. But are you just going to stand by and do nothing and then fly off to the sun?"

Again Alarid's wings quivered. "Part of doing something

is listening. We are listening. To the sun. To the stars. To the wind."

Dennys felt chastened. He had not paused to listen, not for days. "They don't tell you anything?"

"To continue to listen."

The breeze lifted, washed over Dennys in a wave of sadness. "I don't like this story," he said. "I don't like it at all."

He left Alarid. Before he reached the oasis he paused, sat on a small rock. Tried to quiet himself so that he could listen. To the wind. How could he unscramble the words of the wind which came to him in overlapping wavelets?

He closed his eyes. Visioned stars exploding into life. Planets being birthed. Yalith had spoken of the violence of Mahlah's baby's birth. The birth of planets was no gentler. Violent swirlings of winds and waters. Land masses as fluid as water. Volcanoes spouting flame so high that it seemed to meet the outward flaming of the sun.

The earth was still in the process of being created. The stability of rock was no more than an illusion. Earthquake, hurricane, volcano, flood, all part of the continuing creation of the cosmos, groaning in travail.

The song of the wind softened, gentled. Behind the violence of the birthing of galaxies and stars and planets came a quiet and tender melody, a gentle love song. All the raging of creation, the continuing hydrogen explosions on the countless suns, the heaving of planetary bodies, all was enfolded in a patient, waiting love.

Dennys opened his eyes as the wind dropped, was silent. He raised his face to the stars, and their light fell against his cheeks like dew. They chimed at him softly. *Do not seek to comprehend. All shall be well. Wait. Patience. Wait. You do not always have to do something. Wait.*

Dennys put his head down on his knees, and a strange quiet flowed through him.

Above his head, the white wings of a pelican beat gently through the flowing streams of stars.

Work on the ark progressed slowly. In the heat of the sun, his body glistening with sweat, Dennys found it hard to remember his vision of understanding and hope. But it was still there, waiting for him, surfacing during the afternoon rest time, or at night when the sun set and the stars blossomed.

Hammer. Peg. Measure for stress.

Noah insisted on following exactly the directions which were given him.

"This El," Sandy said to Dennys, "I don't understand."

"El knows about shipbuilding," Dennys said. "The instructions and measurements are pretty much the basic proportions for modern ships. The ark's not designed for speed, but then, that's not the purpose."

"All those animals—Noah's surely going to have to shovel out a load of manure."

"I bet nobody around here has ever seen a boat this big. Maybe they've never even seen a boat."

Sandy sought out Yalith, feeling a little disloyal to be going to find her without Dennys, but going, nevertheless. Dennys had vetoed it when Sandy had suggested taking Yalith with them.

He waited for her, not far from the tentholds, in the

quiet that precedes dawn. Saw her coming, pale and wraith-like, from the direction of the desert.

"Yalith."

She stopped, startled, head up.

"Yalith, it's Sandy."

"Oh. Twin Sand." Relief was in her voice. "What is it?"

He took her hand. "Yalith, what are you going to do?"

"When?"

"When the floods come."

She spoke in a low voice. "We don't know for sure that the floods are going to come. It is only what my father says."

"Yes, but what do you think? Do you believe your father?"

She was barely audible. "Yes."

"Then what are you going to do?"

"Nothing. This has already given my father and mother much grief. My mother doesn't understand why El has not called me to be in the ark with the others."

"I don't understand it either," Dennys said flatly.

"But the stars have told me not to be afraid."

"And you believe the stars?"

"Yes."

"Well, somebody's wrong, either your father or the stars."

"I trust my father. And I trust the stars."

"Well. Somebody has to *do* something. I mean, we can't just sit back and let you get drowned. Would you consider coming home with us?"

She looked at him, startled. "But where is your home? Is it on the other side of the mountains?"

"On the other side of time," Sandy said.

Her fingers tightened in his. "You and the Den are leaving?" She answered her own question. "Of course. You have to. As soon as the ark is built. As soon as the rains start."

"Will you come with us?"

"With you both?"

"Well—yes." He would love to go off to the end of the world, alone with Yalith. But he knew that he would not try to leave her world without Dennys.

"Is it many days of travel?"

"We got here sort of instantaneously. I have an idea how we might be able to get home, but first I want to know if you'll come with us."

"Oh, twin Sand." She sighed, long and deeply. "Everything is so strange. Ever since you came, nothing has been the same. Grandfather Lamech is dead. The ark is being built. I don't want to drown, but—is it very different, where you come from?"

Sandy acknowledged, "Very different. It isn't nearly as hot, and we have lots of water, so that we can take showers, and drink as much as we want. What I wouldn't give for a long glass of cold water when we're hammering away on the ark! And we wear different kinds of clothes." He looked at Yalith's small and perfect body, barely covered by the loincloth, her breasts delicate and rosy, and had a moment's absurd vision of her in one of the classrooms at the regional high school. But wouldn't anything be better than drowning? "You'll consider it, won't you? Coming with us?"

She was solemn. "Of course. It is very hard for me to

imagine what it would be like without you and the Den.
You are part of me. Both of you."

Sandy slipped back into the tent. Dennys was awake,
waiting for him.

"Where have you been?"

"I asked Yalith to come home with us."

There was a heavy silence. At last Dennys said. "No. No,
Sandy. We can't take her back with us. I mean, even if we
could, we can't."

"Why not?"

"She doesn't have any immunities. Haven't you noticed,
there aren't any diseases here? Don't you remember that
all the natives at the bottom part of South America got
killed by German measles, because they didn't have any
immunities?"

"Couldn't we give her vaccinations?"

"Not for everything. Even if she caught a cold, an ordinary head cold, it would probably kill her. She doesn't
have any protective antibodies. She couldn't adjust to our
climate. It's too cold, too damp. It would be murder to
try to take her back with us."

"Then what's going to happen?"

"I don't know."

"If she stays here, she'll drown. Wouldn't it be worth
the risk to try to take her home with us?"

Dennys shook his head. "How do you think she'd get on
with the kids at school?"

"She wouldn't have to go to school. She's nearly a hundred years old."

"And she doesn't look any older than we do. How would we prove her age to the school authorities? And if she *is* a hundred years old, and we bring her back to our time, what would happen? Would she shrivel all up and be ancient and die of old age?"

"Why are you thinking of all the bad things that could happen?"

"We have to think of them. If we love Yalith."

"Maybe it would be all right."

"And maybe it wouldn't. Maybe what we should do is stay here with Yalith and wait for the flood."

"I'm not willing to give up that easily."

"It's not easily."

"But we have to do something!"

—Maybe, for once, we don't, Dennys thought. "There's time yet," he said. "Maybe something will come to us, but it will have to be something real."

"Hey," Sandy said. "I'm not sure anymore what's real and what isn't. I mean, nephilim and seraphim!"

"I believe in a lot more than I used to," Dennys said. "Even if we're not supposed to change the story, we're changed, you and I."

"We are, oh, we are. And what about Yalith?"

"Wait," Dennys said. He did not tell Sandy about his talk with Alarid. Or what the wind had shown him. Or that the stars had told him to have patience, and wait. Wait.

The new moon was once again a crescent in the sky. Ripened, filled out to a sphere. Dwindled and diminished. Was born again.

Noah sent Japheth and Oholibamah to warn the people of the oasis of the impending flood.

Ham asked, "What's the point? They all know you're building this big boat. They all know you're expecting rain out of season."

Noah was stubborn. "They have a right to be warned. To prepare. And who knows—if they repent, then perhaps El will not send the flood."

"If there's no flood," Ham said, "people will laugh at us even more than they're laughing now."

Anah looked troubled. "I do not think the people of my tent will repent. They are very angry."

Noah said, "They must be given the chance."

When Japheth and Oholibamah returned from their trip about the oasis, they had been laughed at, spat at. Japheth had an ugly bruise on his cheek where an angrily thrown stone had hit him.

Even Noah and Matred's older daughters and their husbands had met them with scorn. They laughed at Japheth's earnest warning, and complained of being made to look like fools because of Noah's folly. Seerah had thrown a bowl of mash at them and screamed at Oholibamah to leave her alone. "And don't you come near my babies, you nephil woman."

Japheth had put his arm protectively about his wife and taken her away.

Hoglah's husband had threatened to strangle them if they kept on spreading stories of flood and doom throughout the oasis. "It reflects on us," he said. "Don't you see

how you're making *us* look with this idiocy? Can't you just
keep quiet about Noah's delusions?"

Japheth and Oholibamah left the oasis, to go home by
the desert. Oholibamah began weeping, strangely, quietly.

Japheth stopped, putting his arms around her. "My wife.
What is it?"

Oholibamah struggled to stifle her silent tears. Said, "If
it is all true, what El has told your father, if there is to be
a great flood, then our baby will be born after—" She
choked on her tears.

Japheth's face lit with delight. "Our—"

Oholibamah leaned her head against his strong shoulder.
"Our baby, Japheth." Suddenly her tears turned to laughter. "Our baby!"

The result of the attempt to warn the people of the oasis
was that now they gathered about the perimeter of Noah's
land.

The desert wind rose hotly. Noah's eyes were fixed on
the ark. He tried to ignore the catcalls and hoots of the
mob.

Grimly, Matred heated wine to the boiling point. "I prefer to use it on manticores, but if they try to hurt my husband, I will make them sorry."

Ham slunk into the tent.

"What are you doing here?" his mother demanded.

"I'm tired of being laughed at."

Matred spoke fiercely. "You go right back out and help
your father."

"He's insane."

"Whatever he is, it's your place to be with him. And with your wife. She's not too proud to work, and carrying your child, too." Matred smiled. There would be three babies coming. She brimmed with joy.

"Can't you stop him, Mother? He's a wild man, his eyes blazing, his beard whipped by the wind, his— Can't you speak to him."

"I have spoken," Matred said. "Go out to him. Now."

Reluctantly, Ham went out into the glaring sunlight, the burning wind. The muttering, jeering crowd was larger, as the people of the oasis gathered to stare.

Noah's hands were black with the pitch with which he was coating the ark.

A stone was thrown. It missed its mark and glanced harmlessly against the dark wood.

Sandy and Dennys left the ark and walked with deliberate steps toward the mob of little people. Dennys did not put down the plank he was sanding. Sandy still held the stone he used for a hammer. Neither boy threatened in any way; nevertheless, the people drew back slightly.

Sandy spoke in a commanding voice. "No stone throwing."

Dennys stood as tall as possible, looming over the small men in the foreground of the crowd. "Go home. Back to your tents. Now." His voice was a deep, man's voice.

There were advantages in being taken for giants. Slowly, the crowd dispersed.

Yalith sat on her favorite starlit rock, huddled over as though for warmth. She was not aware that Oholibamah had joined her until the other woman put her arm about Yalith's shoulders.

Tears sprang to Yalith's eyes. "Twin Sand and twin Den—" Her voice trailed off.

Oholibamah finished for her. "As soon as the ark is built, they will have to leave. To go to wherever it is they came from."

Yalith choked down a sob. "Twin Sand has asked me to go with them."

Oholibamah drew back in surprise. Said, "It is a solution I had not thought of."

"Then—what do you think?"

Oholibamah looked at the sky, intently, listening. Then she shook her head.

Yalith, too, looked heavenward. "The stars have never told me wrong."

Oholibamah spoke thoughtfully. "I do not know why it is not the right solution for you to go with our twins. I know only that I hear the stars, and I agree. There is something here that we do not understand. But do you hear the stars? They are telling you not to be afraid."

A soft wind brushed past their cheeks, murmuring, "Fear not. Fear not. The pattern will be perfected."

"I wish—" Yalith whispered. "I wish Grandfather Lamech was still alive. I wish that El had not told my father to build an ark, or that the rains were going to come."

"And—our twins?"

Tears slid down Yalith's cheeks. "I cannot wish that they had never come to us. Or that I had not become a woman."

Oholibamah held Yalith, rocking her like a child. "I,

too, am afraid, little sister. I am carrying my Japheth's child, and I am afraid for the future. I am afraid of the terrible flood, and all the death and anguish it will bring. Sometimes I am even afraid of Noah, he seems so wild. But I trust Japheth. I trust the stars. I trust El. I trust that all this will be for good."

As the stars slid slowly toward the horizon, the sky paled, flushed with soft colors. A burst of joyous birdsong filled the air around them, and the baboons began to clap their hands.

The ark was nearly finished.

The twins talked at night in the tent, whispering in the dark. During the day they were never alone, and not everybody slept at the same time in the afternoon.

"We haven't seen any of the seraphim," Sandy said. "Not for days."

"Nor the nephilim," Dennys added.

"I'd just as soon not see the nephilim. Particularly Rofocale."

Dennys said, "Every once in a while I think I see one. Or at any rate, when I see an ant, or a worm, I get flickers of color behind my eyes, reds and oranges and blues and purples. But they don't materialize."

"I need to see one of the seraphim," Sandy said. "I need to see Adnarel. I thought maybe the scarab beetle would come with Higgaion, but I haven't seen him."

Dennys said thoughtfully, "I don't think it means that he's stayed at Grandfather Lamech's. The only time I've seen a seraph when there were a lot of people around was

when Grandfather was buried, and they all came. Otherwise, it's been only when there are one or two people. And
what with building the ark, and staying in Noah's tent,
we're always with a gang. Maybe somehow we should slip
away for a little while tomorrow and go out to the desert,
just the two of us."

"Good thinking," Sandy said. "But why wait for tomorrow? We don't want to go in the heat of the day, and we'd
be missed any other time. Noah and Matred are always
checking on us. They're afraid one of us might be kidnapped again. So why not go now?"

"Right now?"

"Why not? We're both awake."

"Let's go."

"Don't wake Higgaion."

"Or Selah."

"Or—"

"Shh."

They slipped out quietly.

But not so quietly that Yalith did not hear them. She
felt a vague disquiet. Rose from her sleeping skins and
followed them.

"Kkk. They come."

"Hsss. This is what we've been waiting for."

"Szzz. At last."

The nephilim slid out of their animal hosts, raising
wings turned dark by night, so that the stars were hidden.

.   .   .

The little mammoth woke with a jerk from a dream of being beaten by Tiglah's brother. Nudged Selah, who nudged Higgaion, who reached toward the twins, and felt only sleeping skins. Snorting in alarm, he padded across the tent toward Yalith's sleeping skins. She, too, was gone. He glanced toward Noah and Matred, both sleeping quietly.

Selah trumpeted, softly, so that only the mammoths heard, and pointed her trunk toward Higgaion's ear. The scarab beetle was there, a small, bright jewel against the grey earflap.

"What should we do?" Higgaion's eyes queried. Cocked his head as though listening. Then he gestured to the other two mammoths with his trunk, and they followed him as he hurried out of the tent and ran toward the desert.

The twins were nearly surrounded before they realized what was happening. The circle of nephilim was closing in on them, slowly, deliberately. The sharp odor of stone and cold filled their nostrils.

Sandy felt as though a hand was pressing hard on his chest. He shouted at Dennys, "Quick!" and flung himself out of the not-quite-closed circle.

Dennys followed, pushing through purple-dark wings that nearly stifled him. "Run!"

The twins' reflexes were swift, but the nephilim were swifter.

Again the circle started to form around them, and it was as though the breath was being squeezed out of them. Sandy ran, head down, like a battering ram, between Rofocale and Ugiel. Dennys rammed Eblis.

But the twins were only two, and the nephilim were many, and sure enough of their powers to proceed with deliberation and without haste. In their rush to get free of the circle, the twins had run in the opposite direction from the oasis. Now they were too far away to think of making a dash back to Noah's tenthold.

The circle of nephilim drew closer.

Yalith saw.

"Aariel!" she screamed. "Aariel!"

The golden lion bounded across the sand, past Yalith, until it was between two of the nephilim, keeping the circle from closing completely.

Came a strange pounding, and then Admael the camel galloped white as moonlight across the desert, inserting himself into the circle. A flutter of wings overhead became visible as a pelican, diving down, broke the circle again.

And three small grey bodies hurtled into the circle, blowing sand and water into the faces of the nephilim, who burst out of their formation in a rush of brilliant wings.

The lion, camel, pelican, with an upward leaping of light, became the radiant beauty of seraphim.

Sandy and Dennys ran to them, ran faster than they had ever run before. Alarid caught Sandy, and Admael held Dennys.

The nephilim sprang angrily into the sky, saw Yalith.

"Her!" Eblis cried. "I want her!"

But Aariel reached her before the nephil. Swift as Eblis was, the seraph was swifter. He enfolded Yalith in gilded wings.

The three mammoths, trumpeting joyfully, bounded around them.

Bronze flashed against Higgaion's ear, and then Adnarel stood before them. "Go!" he commanded the nephilim in a bugling voice.

"Kkk. You have no right to take them from us," Naamah said.

"And you have no right to them whatsoever." Adnarel was fierce. "Go."

From the four corners of the desert the other seraphim came, to stand with Adnarel, Alarid, Admael, and Aariel.

Then Ertrael, whose host was the rat, whined, "Tell us what is about to happen."

"Do you not know?" Alarid asked.

"I assume," Ugiel hissed, "that since Noah is building a boat, he must be planning to find some water."

"Your assumption is correct." Admael had his arm lightly across Dennys's shoulder.

"Kkk. And then what?" Naamah asked.

"Rain," Alarid said. "Much rain." The seraph raised his hand skyward, seeming to touch a bright star. A flash of lightning split the sky, bolted to earth with a great crash of thunder.

"Now," Alarid ordered the nephilim.

As the nephilim slipped, one by one, into their animal hosts, Sandy felt a drop of rain.

The seraphim gravely led the twins and Yalith deeper into the desert, not explaining where they were going.

Sandy started to ask, "Where—" then closed his mouth.

When they reached a single monolith of silvery rock, the seraphim encircled it. Aariel drew Yalith into the center of the circle.

Adnarel took Sandy by the hand, and Admael reached for Dennys, so that they were part of the circle around the monolith, Aariel, and Yalith, who looked at the seraph questioningly but without fear.

Alarid said, "Yalith, child, you did not know your Great-great-grandfather Enoch."

Mutely, she shook her head.

"But you know of him?" Aariel asked.

"I know that he did not die like ordinary men. He walked with El, and then, according to Grandfather Lamech, he was not. That is, he was not with the people of the oasis. He was with El."

With a rush of hope, Sandy remembered his conversation with Noah and Grandfather Lamech and their recounting of this strange happening.

Aariel smiled down on Yalith. "El has told us to bring you, and in the same way."

She shrank back. "I don't understand."

Dennys moved as though to go to her, but Higgaion nudged him to stay still.

Aariel said, "There is no need to understand, little one. I will take you, and it will be all right. Do not fear."

She looked very small, very young. She asked, timidly, "Will it hurt?"

"No, little one. I think you will find it a rapturous experience."

She looked up at him, trustingly.

"Enoch, your forebear, will explain everything you need to know."

Adnarel's fingers held Sandy back. "You will tell Noah and Matred?"

"I will tell them," Sandy said. "I think they will be very happy."

Dennys, who had not heard the extraordinary story of Enoch, looked confused but hopeful. If Aariel was taking Yalith somewhere, she would not be drowned after all. The seraphim were to be trusted. He was certain of that. Aariel would not take Yalith to the sun, or to the moon, or anywhere that was not possible for her with her human limitations.

Aariel said, "It is time."

Yalith remembered the words Aariel had said to her when she had gone out to the desert in the heat of the day. "Many waters cannot quench love," she whispered. "Neither can the floods drown it. Oh, twins, dear twins, I love you."

Sandy and Dennys spoke together, their voices cracking. "Yalith. Oh, Yalith. I love you."

"Will you go back now, to where you came from?"

The twins glanced at each other.

"We will try," Sandy said.

"We think the seraphim will help us," Dennys added.

"If we had been older—" Sandy started.

Dennys laughed. "If we had been older, it would have been very complicated, wouldn't it?"

Yalith, too, laughed. "Oh, I love you both! I love you both!"

Aariel urged, gently, "Come, Yalith."

"I can't say goodbye to my parents? To Japheth and Oholibamah?"

"It is best this way," Aariel said, "without goodbyes, as it was for your forebear Enoch."

Yalith nodded, then reached up to Sandy and kissed him on the lips. Then Dennys. Full, long kisses.

Aariel wrapped her in his creamy wings, glittering with gold at their tips. Then he held her only with his arms, lifted and spread the wings, beat with them softly, and then rose into the air, up, up.

They watched until all they saw was a speck of light in the sky, as though from a new star.

Sandy spoke to Noah, "Do you remember the night when you and Grandfather Lamech were talking and I was there?"

"I remember," Noah said.

"And Grandfather Lamech talked about dying."

"I remember."

"And about his Grandfather Enoch, who walked with El and then he was not, for El took him?"

"I remember that, too. Why?"

"Yalith is not."

"What are you saying?" Noah's eyes widened.

Matred put her hand to her mouth, focusing intently.

Sandy continued, "Aariel, the seraph who loves Yalith, said that she was to be taken up, like her forebear Enoch. And he held her and flew straight up into the sky. We watched."

Dennys nodded.

A light of great joy came into Noah's eyes.

Matred burst into tears.

"I felt a drop of rain," Sandy said.

Noah turned away. "The ark will be finished tomorrow."

That night, the twins sat outside the big tent. The three mammoths curled up together, near them. The rest of the family was within, asleep. Except for Yalith. Yalith's sleeping skins had been folded and put away.

"I didn't have a chance to talk with Adnarel about getting home," Sandy said.

"But Yalith is all right. At the moment, that's all that matters." A drop of rain fell on Dennys's nose.

"The rain is beginning." Sandy reached down to pet Higgaion, who was pressing against his feet. "What was it that she said about many waters?"

"Many waters cannot quench love. I think that's what she said."

Higgaion reached up with his trunk to touch Sandy's arm. "It's time for us to be going home, Higgy. I have to speak to Adnarel."

Higgaion reached with his trunk to touch his ear. The scarab beetle was not there.

Another drop of rain fell. It was a quiet, beginning rain, with occasional droplets. No thunder or lightning.

Sandy asked the sky, "Is God really doing this? Causing a flood to wipe everybody out?"

Dennys raised his face to the sky. The stars were not visible, hidden by thick veils of clouds, but it seemed that he could still hear their chiming, dim but reassuring. "Whenever there's an earthquake, or a terrible fire, or a typhoon, or whatever, everybody gets it. Good people get killed as well as bad."

Sandy was wriggling his toes against Higgaion's shaggy grey flank. "Well. Everybody dies. Sooner or later."

"Even stars die," Dennys added.

"I don't like entropy," Sandy said. "The universe winding down."

"I don't think it is winding down," Dennys contradicted. "I think it's still being birthed. Even the flood is part of the birthing."

"I don't understand." Sandy's voice was flat. "Everybody knows that entropy—"

"Everybody doesn't. And entropy is in question, anyhow. Remember, we had that in science last year. There's no such thing as an unbreakable scientific rule, because, sooner or later, they all seem to get broken. Or to change."

"Grandfather Lamech said that these are last days." The occasional slow drops of rain made Sandy on edge, and argumentative.

Another splash of rain touched Dennys's face, muting the stars. "There have been many times of last days," he said, "and they mark not only endings but beginnings."

"Is there a pattern to it all?" Sandy demanded. "Or is it all chaos and chance?"

"What do you think?" Dennys asked.

Selah had come to lie beside Higgaion, and Sandy reached to scratch her with the toes of his other foot. "Did we come here, to Yalith, to Noah, by chance?"

Dennys wiped his face with the palm of his hand. "No. I don't think so."

Sandy said, "The ark is finished. Yalith is with Grandfather Enoch. And perhaps with Grandfather Lamech. What was it Grandfather said? We know little about such things . . ."

There was a radiance in the air, and Adnarel stood before them.

"Oh, Adnarel." Sandy leapt up. "I need to talk to you about particle physics and quantum leaps."

Adnarel sat beside them, listening.

"So," Sandy concluded, "if you could go to our time and place and call the unicorns to you there, you could tesser us home."

"It does not sound impossible," Adnarel said. "It is consistent with our knowledge of energy and matter. I will talk with the other seraphim." As he turned to go, he said, "Do not stray far from the tent."

"The nephilim," Dennys agreed. Then, in a louder voice, "We will not stray. It is just that somehow we are not sleepy."

Adnarel paused. "Your love for Yalith, and hers for you, *is*, and therefore it always will be." And then he was gone.

They smelled Tiglah before they saw her. Quickly they sprang to their feet and ran to the tent flap, which was half open.

"Oh, don't go, please don't go!" Tiglah cried. "I'm alone, I promise you."

Tiglah's promises meant little. They stood warily by the

tent flap, watching her as she approached. But there was nobody with her, neither father and brother, nor nephilim.

"It's starting to rain," she said. "We never have rain except in the spring. Did Noah really build this big boat because he thinks there's going to be more rain than we've ever seen before?"

Sandy nodded.

"Anah is my sister. Would there be room for me on the ark?"

"There is not room for Sandy and me," Dennys said.

"Then what are you going to do?"

"We're not sure." Sandy was cautious. "We hope to go home."

"I don't like this rain." Tiglah sniffled. "It's cold and wet."

"Rofocale will take care of you," Sandy said.

"Oh, he will, won't he! I'd better go find him. It's very nice to have known you."

"Thanks for nothing," Sandy said rudely.

"Ditto," Dennys echoed.

"You're not blaming *me* for my father and brother, are you?"

"Perhaps not for your father and brother," Sandy said, "but for doing whatever Rofocale tells you, yes."

"So go to him," Dennys urged, although he did not have much faith that the nephilim cared enough about any human being to be willing to help unless it was convenient.

"I still think it's nice to have known you," Tiglah said. "I wish I could have known you better. I mean, really *known* you."

"Sorry, Tiglah," Sandy said. "You are a great deal older and a great deal more experienced than we are."

"I could teach you—"

"No, Tiglah. The timing isn't right."

"Goodbye, then," she said.

"Goodbye," the twins echoed.

Japheth came to them. "I'm worried about you."

Sandy was still looking after Tiglah's retreating form. "Don't worry, Jay. We'll be all right."

"How?" Japheth demanded. "You know we can't take you on the ark."

"We know," Dennys agreed. He looked up at the clouds, which occasionally let a drop of rain fall. Tried to listen for the hidden stars.

"Can you get home?" Japheth asked. "To wherever you came from?" He, too, looked at the sky, shook his head as though baffled by silence.

"We're going to try," Sandy said. "Don't worry about us. You have enough to do, collecting all the animals and food and fodder and grain and everything."

Japheth nodded. "Perhaps—"

"Perhaps what?" Sandy asked.

Japheth rubbed his broad hand across his face, wiping away tears. "Oh, twins—" He rushed at them, and they flung their arms about him and the three of them rocked back and forth, holding one another.

Oholibamah went, just before dawn, to Mahlah's low white dwelling.

Mahlah was alone, nursing the baby. It was indeed a

large baby, drinking greedily, and Mahlah looked pale and fragile, but she crooned over the child while she fed it.

She looked up at Oholibamah and smiled in welcome. "It's good to see you, Oholi. Come in."

Oholibamah stood, looking down at Mahlah and the child. "Is Ugiel good to you?"

"He is very good." There was deep love in Mahlah's shadowed eyes.

"You're happy with him? Truly happy, as I am with Japheth?"

"Truly happy. Though Ugiel is Ugiel and Japheth is Japheth."

"He doesn't ever hurt you?"

"Never."

"He takes care of you?"

"Very good care. And he loves our baby."

"Good," Oholibamah said. "That's all I wanted to know." And she left Mahlah and went back to the tent she shared with Japheth.

The seraphim were gathered together as dawn suffused the desert with a soft pearly light. The clouds were thickening, and in the trees the birds sang more softly than usual, and the baboons' chatter was muted.

"It does look possible, I think," Adnarel said.

Alarid nodded. "We are not bound to this place and time. Two of us should go to the twins' world and call them back."

Admael asked, "Does it really need to be unicorns? I would feel safer if I could carry them."

Adnarel's eyes widened for a moment, then nearly

closed in thought. "I do not think they could take the transition from matter to energy and then back again to matter. Even we find it tiring."

"But what about the unicorns?" Adnachiel, sometimes a giraffe, asked. "What happens when they go out?"

Adnarel said, "They *are* only when they are here. Or when they are there. But not in between. It is not quite the same thing as a transfer of matter and energy."

Alarid nodded. "They have to be observed in order to be."

"Believed in," Adnachiel agreed.

"It is a long distance," Admael said, "both in time and space."

"It is a risk," Adnarel agreed, "but one I think we must take."

"Why are they here at all?" asked Achsah, with wings the same soft gray as his mouse fur.

"Do you think El sent them?" Admael suggested.

Adnarel spoke slowly. "I do not think El sent them. But neither did El prevent their coming."

"Are they part of the pattern?" Admael asked. "Is it right and proper for them to be here?"

Alarid looked up at the veiled sky. "Perhaps Aariel will have word when he returns from taking Yalith to the Presence. But I think, yes, that they are part of the pattern."

"The pattern is not set," Adnarel said. "It is fluid, and constantly changing."

"But it will be worked out in beauty in the end," Admael affirmed.

"Then you agree?" Adnarel asked. "We will try to help them to return to their own time and place in the way in which they have suggested?"

"We agree," affirmed the seraphim.

The air lightened slightly as the hidden sun lifted above the horizon. There was a faint spattering of applause from the baboons, who were confused by the clouds and the occasional drops of rain.

Despite the clouds which obscured the light of the last dim stars, the seraphims' ears were attuned to the song, although it was far away.

"Let us sing with them," Alarid suggested.

And the singing of the seraphim joined with the singing of the hidden stars, and the call of the invisible sun.

Sandy and Dennys slept fitfully. The rain had not really begun in earnest. But there was an occasional patter on the roof skins as a drop fell here, there. The three mammoths were curled into a ball at the foot of the twins' sleeping skins.

The morning songs of the oasis were softer than usual, but both boys roused from sleep and looked at each other. Nodded.

Quietly, they dressed in their clothes from home. Dennys was without the garments he had discarded after the garbage pit, but he pulled on his sweater and his lined jeans, feeling strange and constrained in clothes. The twins had become used to the freedom of being naked except for loincloths. Their winter clothes were hampering as well as hot.

They were careful not to disturb the sleeping mammoths. They looked across the tent to where Noah and Matred were still asleep. To the place which had been Yalith's and which was now empty.

Then they tiptoed out.

Adnarel was waiting for them. "It's best without goodbyes."

Dennys asked, "But you will say goodbye for us? And to Oholibamah and Japheth? And the others?"

"We will say goodbye," Adnarel said, and looked toward a clump of palms and palmettos. Admael and Alarid came out of the shadows and moved toward them, followed by Aariel, who had returned from his journey with Yalith.

"Now," Adnarel said, "we will call the unicorns."

"One more thing." Sandy held back. "You will take care of the mammoths?"

"We will take care of them. Unicorns!"

With a glimmer of silver, two unicorns solidified before them.

"Now," Adnarel said.

The two boys mounted the unicorns, sitting astride the silver backs, bathed in light from the horns.

"We leave you now," Adnarel said, "Admael and I. When we are in your time and place, we will call for the unicorns, and for you."

"You'll recognize it when you get there?" Sandy asked anxiously.

"You have given us very good parameters."

Alarid and Aariel each stood by one of the unicorns. When a drop of rain touched the light of their brilliant horns, it hissed slightly.

The unicorns crossed the oasis and moved onto the desert, Alarid and Aariel running along with them.

When they reached Aariel's great rock, the two seraphim stopped and looked at the unicorns, then at the twins.

"Are you ready?" Alarid asked.

"Ready," Dennys said.

Aariel slapped the two silver rumps, and the unicorns took off across white sand and rock. In his golden voice he cried, "Unicorns! Go home!"

Dennys felt a wave of sleep wash over him, as the rain and the unicorns quickened. Sandy, too, felt his mind softly closing. The rain was a curtain of silver.

"Alar—" Sandy murmured.

"Aar—" Dennys started.

The unicorns and the twins flickered like candles and went out.

Two unicorns in an old stone lab connected to a white clapboard farmhouse were a strange sight. So were two tall, bright-winged seraphim.

The twins looked around. Aside from the unicorns and the seraphim, everything was as usual. Wood still burned brightly in the stove. The smell of stew—of *boeuf bourguignon*—was fragrant over the Bunsen burner. The odd-looking computer was where it had been when they punched into it.

Adnarel was sitting in their mother's reading chair, his golden wings drooping behind it. Admael was peering into one of her complex microscopes, hunching his pale blue wings.

"Do you believe in unicorns?" Adnarel's azure eyes were smiling.

"How was the ride?" Admael, too, smiled, though both seraphim seemed very relieved.

The outside door banged.

Adnarel rose swiftly from the chair. Admael turned from the microscope. The twins stiffened.

Their mother's voice called, "Twins! Are you home?"

"Oh, oh," Sandy said. "We'd better get the unicorns out of here."

"They'll go as soon as they aren't believed in," Adnarel said.

Dennys exclaimed, "But Meg and Charles Wallace believe in unicorns!"

Admael asked, "And in seraphim?"

"And we're not supposed to be in the lab anyhow, with an experiment in progress." Sandy looked anxiously at Adnarel.

"Never fear," the seraph said. "You are all right?"

"Until Mother finds us in here."

Dennys added, "Looking the way we do, all sunburned."

"Compared with some of your other problems—" Admael started.

Their mother's voice called out again. "Twins! Where are you?"

"No farewells," Adnarel said. He glanced at Admael, then put both strong, long hands on Dennys's head. Admael followed suit with Sandy. Both boys felt, rather than a sense of pressure, a sense of the tops of their heads lifting, almost as the animal hosts lifted to become seraphim. And then each twin was staring at a normal winter twin, skins not darkened by the desert sun, hair not bleached almost white.

Sandy glanced briefly at Dennys's still bare feet, started to speak, then stopped as Adnarel held up his hand.

"Many waters—" The seraph reached out and clasped a unicorn horn. The light from the horn flooded back into the seraph's hand, through his body, his wings, until he was streaming with light. Admael, too, was filled with flowing light.

"Cannot quench—" he seemed to be saying. Light blazed fiercely, blinding the twins. Then the brilliance faded.

Unicorns and seraphim were gone.

Brown-haired, winter-skinned twins stared at each other.

Mrs. Murry opened the door to the lab. Behind her, Meg and Charles Wallace peered in, curiously.

"Sandy. Dennys. What are you doing here? Didn't you see the sign on the door?" She sounded extremely displeased.

"We didn't actually see it," Sandy started.

"We just came to get the Dutch cocoa," Sandy explained.

"Look," Meg said, "it's out here on the floor, by the kitchen door. Lucky it didn't spill."

"We were just going to make some," Sandy said. "Shall we make enough for you three?"

"Please," their mother said. "It's turning bitter cold. But, Sandy, Dennys, I beg you, don't go into the lab when you're asked not to. I hope you didn't touch anything you shouldn't have."

Sandy said, slowly, "It all depends. But I don't think we touched anything we shouldn't have, do you, Dennys?"

"Under the circumstances, no," Dennys said.

"Why are your feet bare, Den?" Charles Wallace asked.

"Good heavens!" Mrs. Murry exclaimed. "Put something on your feet this second, Dennys Murry, before you catch cold."

Meg opened the kitchen door, and there was the familiar odor of fresh bread, apples baking in the oven, and warmth, and brightness, and all the reassurance of home.

As they followed the others in, Sandy whispered to Dennys, "I'm very glad the kitchen is all here. But you know what—I'm homesick."

"We probably always will be, a little," Dennys agreed.

"Well." Sandy straightened up. "As soon as we have our birthdays, we can get our driver's licenses."

"And about time," Dennys said. "Now let's make that cocoa."

THE L'ENGLE

THOSE WHO CROSS AND CONNECT
*CHRONOS*** AND *KAIROS**

Canon Tallis
The Arm of the Starfish, The Young Unicorns,
A Circle of Quiet, The Summer of the Great-grandmother,
Dragons in the Waters, The Irrational Season, Walking on Water

Adam Eddington
(Starfish, Light)

Mr. Theotocopoulous
(Unicorns, Dragons)

Katherine Forrester = Justin Michel Vigneras
(A Severed Wasp, The Small Rain, Light)

Felix Bodeway
(Wasp, Rain)

Zachary Gray
(Lotus, Moon, Light)

Virginia Bowen Porcher
(A Winter's Love, Lotus)

Frank Rowan
(Camilla, Lotus)

Emily
(Wasp, Unicorns)

Philippa Hunter
(Wasp, And Both Were Young)

Theron Renier = Stella
(The Other Side of the Sun)

Leonis Phair
(Dragons)

Simon Renier
(Dragons)

**Mimi Renier
Oppenheimer**
(Wasp)

**Queron Renier
"Renny"**
(Lotus)

*Kairos is real time, pure numbers with no measurement.
**Chronos is ordinary, wrist-watch, alarm-clock time.